Blood on
Babywipes

Blood on Babywipes

Prince S. Garrett

To order additional copies of this book, contact:
Xlibris Corporation
1-888-795-4274
www.Xlibris.com
Orders@Xlibris.com
81413

Dedication

This book is dedicated to Donald B. a.k.a. Don Juan, my father, who passed on to the realm of the ancestors on January 26th, 2008. I miss you. I wish you were here to read this. At a time when we were beginning to understand each other you were taken from me. I am sorry for all of the blame I threw on you. You are half of the reason I am who I am . . . You are half of my greatness. I love you. Keep your eye on me!

ACKNOWLEDGEMENTS

First and foremost, I would like to thank my Creator, The All in All, for instilling the idea and desire within me to complete this novel. All things are possible through the Most High. Second I would like to thank my mother, Jacqueline Garrett, for her diligence and patience in raising me, which has served as an example during my trials and tribulation. The most important lesson I have learned in life has come from you, "Fear and trust in no one but the Lord." Next I would like to extend a special thanks to my best friends, Mahdsiah, Karast, Prince, Yashua, and Auset for supporting everything I do. You guys are the greatest children a man can have! You are my foremost inspiration for putting this book out. I love y'all to death!

To my sister, Dawnielle Robinson-Walker, I am ever-grateful to you for your instructions and critiques with regards to my book. Thank you for taking on the job of devouring this work, at a time when life seemed to put a lot on your plate. You gave me the confidence and advice I needed to complete this.

I would be remised if I didn't thank my spiritual and martial art father, Sijo, the man that has guided me for almost a decade and has kept me from harming myself, as well as others. I drink from your fountain of wisdom and strength. Your words have been a shield against all of the negativity I have encountered. You have supported and taken an interest in everything I do. I thank you for giving me and the rest of the world the S.W.A.M. Academy of Martial Arts.

I would like to also extend my appreciation to Elliot Lloyd for pushing me to turn what started off as scribble on the back of commissary sheets into a full fledge novel. Thanks for the hook up on the laptop! Last but not least, I like to thank my two accusers whose lies had me thrown into a cell for a crime I never committed; for it was that cell that gave life to this book. I will pray for you. Thank you!

"Build a nation? What? You talking that back to Africa shit? Look around Ma, the only Black Power is white powder,"—Shaheen Mcfadden

CHAPTER 1

"I wish you were dead!"

Her fiery words exploded from between the sneer of a pair of twisted crimson lips, quivering uncontrollably beneath her red sniffling nose. Undaunted eyes of rage remained fixed on her accused tormentor as she maliciously aimed verbal daggers toward the surface of his ego.

"You bitch ass nigga! I hate you!" With each declaration, she spat venomous blood, from a swollen mouth, that cascaded to the plush ivory carpet covering their living room floor.

The disdain in her voice drowned out her usually feminine tone as it resonated off the cream-colored walls of the two-bedroom apartment, stinging her man's ears.

Shaheen's patience began to dwindle. He struggled with his nature to maintain control over his anger. However, his frustrations were further aggravated by her unfounded accusations, the baby crying, and the clamor coming from the neighbors beneath them banging on their floor with a broom or stick of some sort. To him, it all seemed like a whirlwind of banshees wailing.

He cast a hopeless gaze to his suede Timberland construction boots, then grievously shook his head in disbelief. He scoured his aching brain for an explanation as to how he ended up entangled in this emotional web of finger-pointing and character assassinations. He was astonished he could hear himself think over the bellowing and snarling, which subdued his inner voice of reason. Of all he contemplated during the past few moments, only one thought was clear. He needed to somehow escape the barrage of insults she was hurling at him.

His mouth crept open as he muttered, "If you didn't throw that—"

"Fuck you, muthafucka!" Lola wouldn't allow the tables to be turned on her. "You deserve to get hit, take it like a man!"

His golden bronze hue instantly became red, revealing the exasperation that was consuming him.

"I did take it like a man!" He ceased his complaining to scan the apartment, as if to make certain no eavesdroppers or onlookers were secretly hiding within. He continued, "If someone hit me, they should know to duck. Your moms should've taught you how to keep you hands to yourself and you sh—"

Lola infringed once more, "And that bitch that gave birth to you, should've taught you how to come home at night!"

Shaheen's right eyelid lowered. As he retorted, "You bitch!", his face became a portrait of disgust. He imagined choking her until she recanted her words but never got the chance to bring his vision into fruition.

Whap! Lola's right hand swept across his face while the nails on her other burrowed deeply into the flesh below his right eye. In an attempt to dodge her catlike paws, he fell backward onto the couch. She followed him, landing on top, swinging, scratching, and clawing. Shaheen struggled to clutch her arms, but Lola, in her hysteria, was too nimble for him, so he did what came natural. He captured a fistful of her silky jet-black hair and, with his free paw, gave her an openhanded slap. *Whap!*

She tumbled backward in what would have resulted in a complete somersault if he had used all of his power. Instead she landed on her chest in front of their mahogany coffee table. Placing her palms on the carpet and raising herself from off her belly, she sat propped up against the coffee table like an old unwanted rag doll.

Though she initiated their physical altercation, the purple blackened bruise that bordered her swollen lip would have led one to believe, she suffered all the abuse. That is, was it not for the scarlet gashes leaking from his face. They appeared to be bent on ravaging each other.

Tears flooded Lola's eyes. She began whimpering and frantically wiping her face, as if in an effort to use the wet streams to wash away the discoloring of her flesh. Suddenly, she concluded her bemoaning and just sat motionless.

Shaheen sucked his teeth, tired of the cycle he knew was beginning to repeat itself. He rose to his feet, unaware of his scars, gawked down at her, and made his way toward the bedroom in the back.

"I . . . I . . . I'm sorry, baby . . . ," she murmured, more to herself than to him.

Standing in the middle of the doorway to the master bedroom of their third-floor apartment was their three-year-old son, Shane. Shaheen halted his steps in front of his son, hoisted him up, and tightly embraced him as if he would never see him again, then kissed him on the cheek.

"Sorry, lil man," he said apologetically as he gazed mournfully into his eyes.

Shaheen's pupils glistened from the tears that began to surround them; however, he refused to allow a single drop to escape while he stood face-to-face with his only son.

"Me and mommy just don't get along."

He gently placed Shane back to his feet.

"Love ya, lil man . . ."

Shaheen entered the room and shuffled toward a large light-colored wooden wardrobe closet. Opening the doors, he feverishly inspected its contents. He fetched a small purple and velvet Crown Royal whiskey pouch. After loosening the golden strings on the bag, he reached inside it and seized a fistful of money. He crammed the ball of cash into the pocket of his black denim jeans without bothering to count it and tossed the pouch back into the closet.

He closed the door, then abruptly spun around and faced the mirror that hung above the head of his bed. He surveyed his scars intently. A sneer formed beneath the thin mustache bordering the sides of his lips. His eyes assessed his visage for any other wounds he might have acquired. Seeing none, he turn toward the door and headed past his curious son, who dragged his tiny bare feet behind him. He approached the front of the apartment where Lola was prostrating on the floor. It appeared as if she was praying, but he knew better; she was an atheist. She was seeking sympathy.

"You're gonna stain the new carpet with your blood," he cautioned, lacking any concern in his voice.

Relieved that he acknowledged her, she excitedly popped her head up.

"I'm sorry, baby, it's my fault." She quickly acquiesced.

Again he shook his head in anguish after canvassing the living room. He tried to make sense of what just occurred. Then, stretching out his right hand, with his thumb and index finger, he lifted her chin up. He made an effort to squint his eyes to observe her wounds. The guilt of his actions leaped out at him from the swelling around her mouth. He cursed himself under his breath, then softly placed his lips on her forehead.

"Na, girly girl, it's our fault."

Releasing her chin, he strolled over to the beige Badcock love seat, reached beneath the cushion, and pulled out a shining silver P-89 Rueger pistol.

Lola and Shane's eyes widened, and their mouths shot open, but no words came out. They watched as he pressed the little button located on the handle of the pistol, causing the clip to drop out into his empty palm. He brought it up to his face and examined it curiously, lips moving without making a sound. He silently tallied the bullets with his thumb. Once satisfied he had all he needed, he thrust the clip back in position and cocked the gun, loading one into the chamber.

Lola's face became distraught with worry. "Please, baby, don't . . ."

He shoved the gun into his pants, on the right side of his waist.

Shane glanced at his mother and, in his most innocent tone, asked, "Mommy, why Daddy have gun under sofa?"

Lola, avoiding her son's question, directed her attention back to Shaheen and pleaded, "Baby, not tonight . . . Don't leave . . ."

He ignored her request and calmly snatched his Mark Buchanan butter-soft leather from the loveseat, swung his arms into it, then marched out of the door.

Lola ran after him, stopping at the entrance of the apartment. She started to apologize once more and beg him to stay, but the voices of two teenage boys rolling dice in the hallway dissuaded her.

The two youths ceased their gambling and conversation when they became aware of Shaheen approaching them. Upon noticing his scars, they gaped at him in awe. The boy holding the dice held out his hand to Shaheen.

Shaheen heeded the attempt to give him five but ignored the gesture. The other boy, who was the younger of the two, stuck his chin up and spoke.

"What up, Sha?"

"What up?" Shaheen replied.

The one with dice started tapping his friend's leg. "Ask him," he urged.

Shaheen peered at the boy who addressed him. "Ask me what?"

Lola viewed the interaction from the doorway. She loathed the way some of the people in the neighborhood lauded her man.

The boy with dice spoke up for his friend, "We were wondering if we could work for you. We need doe."

Shaheen snickered. "You need doe! Ha! For what? Video games?"

The boy, who initially spoke to Shaheen, sunk his head in embarrassment. Shaheen detected it.

"I know your grandmoms. I used to run to the store for her. She takes good care of you. You be rockin' all types of fly gear to school. Your name John John, right?" The boy nodded his head. "Whatchoo need to hustle for?"

The older one decided to chime in. "Yo, son, we need doe just like you. I got a seed and a wifey to take care of just like you. I mean, we can handle our own, if that's what you worried 'bout. We gangsta with those burners, fam. Trust!" The boy raised his beige army fatigue jacket up to reveal a .44 Magnum in his waist.

Shaheen was infuriated by the interruption of the loudmouth. His face displayed an expression of abhorrence for the teen.

"How old are you?" he inquired.

"Seventeen!" the loudmouth retorted boldly as he let his jacket down.

Shaheen brought his sight upon the other boy. "And you?"

"Fourteen," John John revealed while still drooping his head to the floor.

Shaheen released a sigh of disappointment. He raised his right eyebrow and studied the young boy. Without taking his eyes off him, he pointed to the seventeen-year-old and flatly asserted, "Man, don't follow behind this cat. You'll be in a pile shit one day if you do. You feel me?"

The loudmouth sucked his teeth. "Son, please, when you long gone, I'll be doing my thang. Before my uncle got locked up, he showed me how to bust guns, cut up work, and all that. I ain't new to this, son. You just been doing it longer than me, so I was trying to get a look out. That's all."

Shaheen contemplated placing his fist in the youth's face. Instead, he restrained himself and allowed a small chuckle to escape the grin he forced to surface from his mouth. Lola stood in the doorway staring at him, hoping the kids wouldn't push him to harm them.

She knew the fourteen-year-old John John. He lived next door. She would talk to his grandmother, Old Lady Wellington, from time to time. She would express how hard it was keeping up with her grandson and his curiosity for trouble ever since his parents died. Lola did not want to see her man hurt him. He seemed to be a nice boy. He reminded her of a younger version of Shaheen, who also lost both of his parents at a young age.

The smirk that masked Shaheen's true feelings gradually left his face. A look of hostility replaced it.

"Nigga, that's the main reason you'd never work for me. You too ignorant!

Nobody care 'bout a gangsta other than these muthafuckas who get paid off the shit you sell!" Shaheen shouted at the boy.

The teen's toughness began to erode. Lola endeavored to intrude. "Shaheen!" she called out.

He raised his index finger in the air toward her. "Hold on."

He continued, "You think you're tough 'cause you bang. Nigga, the people who scared of you now are gonna grow up, go to college, get a job, marry, and have a fam. They will prosper and live life! And probably will run the country and the same streets you thuggin' on one day. But, you!" Shaheen stuck his index finger in the face of the teen. "You only got 'bout seven more years, if that, of your bullshittin', and then you'd be either locked up for a long time, dead, or broke as hell because you ain't got no diploma!"

The teen hid his shame well but not his anger. He grinded his teeth while his jaw repeatedly twitched. He opened his mouth and divulged the first thought that came to his mind. "So I guess you'll be dead or locked up soon then. I mean . . . Nigga, you out there banging and slanging."

The fourteen-year-old sprung in front of his friend and positioned his hands on his chest. "Chill, Ant." He pivoted toward Shaheen. "Yo, he bugging. We respect you and yours. You know? We just wanna be like you, that's all."

Shaheen hurled his most horrid expression at the seventeen-year-old and calmly demanded, "Yeah, Ant, you better chill."

Anthony said nothing. Instead he spun around and continued shaking the dice in his hand.

The younger of the two spoke again, "Everything straight, right, Shaheen?"

Shaheen wasn't sure how to respond if he wanted to. *Shit, that little nigga, Ant may be right,* he thought. Instead, he nodded his head in agreement and walked past the two. He had begun his journey down the staircase when he stopped abruptly and shot his eyes back at the youths. Without looking at Lola, he ordered, "Lock the door!" and then proceeded down the stairs.

Lola obeyed him without hesitation. She wanted to say something but instead glared at the closed door as if it was a gigantic mouth belonging to a hungry and hateful Satan that just engulfed her man.

She earnestly tried to believe that each time he ventured out into the dark cesspool of thieves, drug dealers, crooked cops, murderers, drug fiends, and prostitutes of the night, he was only out there, as he claimed, trying to get money from the weak to make his family strong. However, insecurities pervaded her mind and would not allow his reassuring words to register fully. Was her heart deceiving her? Was there another woman—no, bitch—in his life trying to ruin her family? These thoughts consumed her each time he left the house at night.

Lola remembered ever too clearly the bitter words of her mother. "If your man isn't in your bed by midnight, you better believe he'll be in the shower before sunrise." Sure enough, every morning upon his return, she would hear the water running.

Once, after fixing breakfast, she discovered bloodstains around the drain in the tub. While Shaheen sat at the table eating his plate of bacon and eggs, she assessed his body for any visible marks but found none. She quickly dismissed her curiosity, knowing they had not fought in weeks.

In Lola's nescience, she concluded her man wanted a woman with an attitude, a ghetto girl. His enjoyment of rough sex convinced her she was right in her assumption. She deemed she needed to possess a tougher disposition in order to appeal to him because he was from the mean streets of Brooklyn, New York, more precisely, Tilden housing projects.

She, on the other hand, spent the majority of her life protected and secluded in the wealthy suburban area of Plains, Georgia, the Peanut Capital, and birthplace of Jimmy Carter. Her family enjoyed wealth from land passed down through generations by ancestors who benefited from General Sherman's march on Georgia during the Civil War.

This was one reason her mother detested Shaheen because he did not come from what she esteemed to be the proper background. He was a product of the inner city and only attended, though briefly, a community college. She also could not fathom the idea of her precious Lola spending the rest of her life with a hoodlum born and raised in the north.

She viewed northern blacks as a generation of traitors who, supposing they were more sophisticated than their southern families and heritage, fled the small country to indulge in the sin and crimes of the big city. Lola's mother judged this wretched and impoverished delinquent to be in no way good enough for her daughter, but to Lola, she wasn't acceptable enough for Shaheen.

Though born in a mostly white neighborhood, Lola grew up during a time when hip-hop music influenced and dominated the popular culture in the United States. The ghetto and all its atrocities were now glorified among the youths, both black and white, regardless of gender and class. She held disdain for her comfortable life, wishing to incur the sufferings of those victimized by poverty. She felt, because of their struggle and obstacles, they were in possession of a stronger will than she and her peers. She idolized their lifestyle and fearlessness. This is why she fell in love with Shaheen.

The two met in New York while she was attending New York University for journalism to the vehement disapproval of her family. Her mother found it difficult apprehending why she would leave the south for the north to continue her education, let alone engage in a relationship with a thug from there.

When Shaheen first spoke to Lola on the A-train, she was instantly swept off her feet by the way he articulated his words so passionately with an accent boldly flowing from out of his purple, marijuana-smoked lips. She thought it fascinating and beautiful the way the left side of his upper lip would raise when he spoke, each word colored by his New York slang. She cherished the moments when he would call her Ma and say, "Ya na'mean?" He was her thug. She had finally found her protection.

Lola would get lost in his maple brown eyes, which at times would attempt to veil themselves behind a pair of slightly raised slanted lids. The caramel flesh that crowned his tormented soul lacked any blemishes except for the recent scars painted across his slender face. She found it alluring, the way his thin mustache hung over the side of his thick lips. It connected with several small strands of hair dangling from his chin to form a goatee. She adored caressing the sides of his jaw, which were smooth and hairless from years of no growth.

To her surprise, she would observe in awe as he would reflect, with disgust, on the neighborhood he was raised in, his mother's apartment, the criminals in the projects, and his drug dealing occupation. He detested the way he was living. He would remind her constantly that he only committed crimes because he had no other option. He never knew his father. He shared an apartment with his older brother and mother who, because of her lack of education, could only find work at the local supermarket. There she labored tirelessly until suffering a stroke while doing stock duties.

It was at this time that Kane, the elder of the two brothers, became the financial backbone of the family. He was heavily involved in drug trafficking, and while he frequented the streets, Shaheen kept his focus on schoolwork.

This quickly changed, however, when Kane was arrested and indicted on murder and kidnapping charges. It was then after, Shaheen, at the age of fifteen, took over his brother's profession. He couldn't imagine his mother having to go back to work for those wretched Arabs who owned the food store and treated her so terribly. He started exploring the steets daily to provide his mother with money, which he did on a weekly basis until her death two years later.

Every night, he spoke to Lola of his dreams to become an architect one day so he could build more efficient and extravagant housing facilities in his neighborhood for the poor. He would explain to her, "Don't you see, this is why I do what I do. I have to either change all of this or get the hell out of here! While others hustle for Beemers, I hustle for books!"

Yet he would always be left speechless when she would ask him, "Well, why do you have a Benz?"

His answer would come months later when he put his E-class up for sale and purchased a brand-new black 2000 Ford Expedition. His excuse, "This is for the family we're going to have," only came after she informed him she was expecting his child.

But now, at the age of twenty-one, she could not help but wonder where all the love went. It seemed to shadow Shaheen every night he stormed out of the apartment to make more money, so he claimed. Lola's desire for him was to relinquish his occupation, settle down, and finish college. She wanted to have a normal family. At least, she felt that way when he left, but she didn't know how to close and seal off Pandora's box.

The thought crossed her mind to poke her head out the window and scream out for him to come back, yet she knew her attempt would be feeble. Her voice would only reverberate against the emptiness and harshness of New York's November wind. So instead, like always, she awaited his return.

*   *   *

"Man that broad is crazy!" Shaheen proclaimed while coming up for air from what was left of the jerk chicken, cabbage, rice and peas on his plate to fondle his scars.

"Yo, you ate all that plantain already?" Gorilla Leek, his best friend and business partner, inquired while completely disregarding his statement.

"Son! You ain't listening, besides what happened to your food?"

"I ate it all, daddy, I'm a big dog . . . Look out for your dude . . ."

"Blood, you got doe just like I got doe. You better meow your ass over to the counter and order some more. They don't close till eleven tonight, so you got at least two hours to snatch up some more grub. Besides, I got groceries to cop for the crib tomorrow, and this nigga's starving."

Gorilla Leek nodded.

"Yeah, I feel you Blood, but shit, you only got one seed . . . me! I'm holdin' down a family of five including self. Besides, every day, your woman be cookin' up some good ass grub at your crib.

You ain't gotta never come out for food. I mean, I don't know why you be coming to me with a different story 'bout you and her beefin' all the time. Shit, you should be happy you got a chick that cooks and that's that fine. I would trade four of my bitches for her! Word!" voiced Gorilla Leek.

"First of all, you don't know what she be putting me through. Second, as far as you feeding four people while taking care of yourself . . . No one told you to do all that loving or all that prison time. You were as thin as me before you got locked dog."

"Yeah, and you know you a skinny cat," Gorilla Leek retorted.

They both laughed.

Then suddenly, Gorilla Leek ceased his chuckles, and an austere expression enveloped his countenance. "But on the real, what up with Minimart on Rutland? Them Yardy boys still coming through, trying to bogard for doe, I heard . . . thought you said you had it handled?"

Shaheen could see the solemnity in Gorilla Leek's eyes. He purposely attempted to hit his soft spot by attacking his manhood. At the same time, Shaheen realized that most of his friend's eagerness was induced by the fact that Gorilla Leek's family was Guyanese, and he used that as a justification to hold animosity toward most Jamaicans. Not to mention the suspects in his family's murder were Jamaican.

Leek was trigger-happy and hot-tempered. His full name was Malik Moore, but no one would dare call him that, except Shaheen. He was known in the Nineties section of Brooklyn as a terror to be feared. Well built at a height of six foot two inches, he weighed two hundred and forty-five pounds. He had a shiny purple black complexion that surrounded his ever glistening white teeth.

He was completely loyal to Shaheen, who—known in their neighborhood as Sha-Boogie—stood in stark contrast at only five foot eight inches and weighed one hundred and forty-five pounds. He wore a crown of three hundred and sixty degrees waves on his head while Gorilla Leek kept up the cornrolls he grew serving time in Cresson Correctional Facility. While imprisoned for three and one half years for possession and the intent to distribute in Pennsylvania, his best friend took care of his family's financial needs.

They had been close ever since the third grade. The two met when Gorilla Leek tried to swindle Shaheen's lunch but was convinced not to in exchange for half of it. An agreement was then formulated between the two which entailed Gorilla Leek protecting him from the other bullies in the school as a payment for extra food and snacks.

Shaheen was an expert at shoplifting, a skill he acquired from his mother. This talent afforded him more provisions at lunchtime than his peers, so Gorilla Leek was more than happy to accept his offer.

Knowing each other's past and understanding Shaheen's nature, Gorilla Leek knew he would agitate his companion or at least move him to action.

Shaheen attempted to explain, "I'm planning on how to handle it tonight. I just need a . . ."

"No words, let's handle it tonight," Gorilla Leek interjected. "It should've been taken care of already. We look like we giving in to these cats like we're trying to decide on how we gonna pay them. I ain't letting no foreigners, no matter how large they are, extor—"

The words never had a chance to exit his mouth. The sound of gunfire echoing through the restaurant and the shattering of glass interrupted them.

Gorilla Leek pushed Shaheen to the floor, retrieved his Magnum from his pants, and instinctively started discharging toward the front door. He had no need to cock it back as he always kept one in the chamber, and the safety was never on.

His thunderous weapon of death barked across the restaurant like a demonic rottweiler spitting flames. At no time had he the opportunity to view the direction from where the barrage originated, but the smashing of the front window gave him a hint.

As he lifted himself up and ventured toward the door with canon still firing, he felt hot wind from behind streak past him. Shaheen was prone to the ground, lying awkwardly on the side of his left shoulder, squeezing off 9 mm Parabellum rounds at the entrance. They never saw their attacker.

They started shooting from outside the restaurant . . . cowards! Shaheen thought to himself.

Shaheen jumped to his feet and hustled past the frightened customers, who, used to this kind of mayhem, were seeking cover on the floor and under the tables. Gorilla Leek was beyond the entrance still shooting at a black Escalade peeling off from the corner. He hastened down the middle of the street in an effort to chase the vehicle.

When Shaheen finally arrived at the curb outside, he became cognizant of a figure in his peripheral, sprawled out on the floor, groaning. They got one. One of their would-be assassins had taken two of their bullets, one to his abdomen and the other to his thigh. His pistol was approximately six feet away from him. He was bolstered up against a fire hydrant, grasping his stomach with shaking blood-soaked hands.

Shaheen's attention was drawn to Gorilla Leek, who was lightly jogging on his way back toward him. He was out of breath and obviously not agile enough to catch their assailants. When he finally neared his crony, he heeded the maimed long-dread-lock-wearing man lying on the concrete.

"I ain't even see that cat . . . ," Gorilla Leek stated.

"Yeah, you were too busy trying to be the bionic nigga," Shaheen replied sardonically. "You can't go chasing cats down the street, shooting in broad daylight . . . too much attention, we know who they are . . . They missed, we'll get 'em later!"

"Man, fuck that! They need to know I'm a relentless nigga!" Gorilla Leek barked.

"Yeah, and your relentless ass will be locked up and broke again. We gotta be smart."

"What about this yardy cat right here?" Gorilla Leek asked while waving his gun in the direction of their captive.

Shaheen frowned upon the dread and, without laying eyes on Gorilla Leek, commanded, "Leave him for the pigs or let him bleed to death, whichever comes first."

"What about his burner?"

"Man, we have enough guns, plus you don't how many bodies are on that joint."

A menacing smirk crept up on Gorilla's face. He glanced down and surveyed his body with his eyes and his free hand.

"Well, I know two bodies that ain't on it. Who bullets you think he took?"

"I don't know, and I don't care, probably yours, you fired first like a wild man," answered Shaheen while shaking his head. "Let's get the hell up outta here. We got at least two more minutes before five O shows up!"

Gorilla Leek kneeled down in front of the dread until he was eye to eye with him, "Well, I wanna know who got him for sure."

A devilish and sadistic smile appeared on his face, and no sooner than it went away, he quickly shoved his pistol up toward the forehead of the groaning dread and squeezed off a round. Shattered bones and brain fragments burst from the top back portion of his skull. A thick piece of scalp, with wet hair stuck to it, flew up in the air then came back down like a jack-in-the-box. The man's body went limp, then slumped over onto the concrete. Gorilla Leek smiled at Shaheen. Blood slowly covered the ground.

"I guess it was my slug."

Shaheen refused to dignify his friend's statement with a response. As Gorilla Leek stretched his hand down toward the body, Shaheen grabbed him by his black Ecko hoody. He dragged him around the corner and jostled him into the passenger side of his Expedition. He hopped into the driver's seat and examined his rearview for cops or onlookers. He scouted ahead for the same, spun his car into a U-turn, and peeled off down Utica Avenue.

CHAPTER 2

"Yo, girl, how you gonna let that nigga do that to your face?" Kamarsha asked while passing a thick rerolled cigar to Lola.

Lola quickly snatched it from her friend while her eyes scanned the area behind her to make sure little Shane was asleep and the door still closed. Seeing she wasn't being watched by those little beautiful eyes that usually peeked out to catch random curious glances, she gasped deeply upon the tip opposite of the fire. She inhaled the soothing aroma of the purple haze that came out of Shaheen's stash. She always smoked his best stuff up when she was pissed off or sad.

Coughing, she choked out the reply while trying to hold in the smoke. "Girl, I started that shit. He just ended it good." She continued hacking.

"Yeah, a little too good!" Kamarsha disparagingly added.

"Girl, Lo is in love with that dude and ass whippings probably gets her panties wet," explained Qamara.

"Shoot, if Sha was my man, he could beat the shit out of me all night as long as he stuffs some cash in my hand and some dick in my pussy afterwards . . . Hell, that nigga is fine!" Carla said bluntly as she straightened out her red wig.

"Bitch, you better keep those green contacts off my man!" They all laughed.

Lola handed the brown log of fire over to Qamara, who reluctantly received it as if it were diseased.

"Damn girl, you daydreaming about Shaheen's thang or something. You got this wet as hell!"

"Look chick, you can either smoke or hope." Lola extended her hand as if expecting it to come back.

"I'm smoking!"

Qamara took a pull, then immediately began coughing while holding it away from her face.

Carla grappled it from her hand.

"Give it here. It's too strong for your weak ass throat."

Suddenly, there was a raucous and violent knock at the door.

Lola leaped from the couch in a panic.

"Oh shit! Put that out! It's probably them nosy ass neighbors from downstairs or Old Lady Wellington from next door."

Carla gasped two quick pulls, then glanced up at the stick of pleasure with a morbid expression as if to apologize to it.

"Girl, I'll finish this off in the bathroom." She rose and strutted casually down the hall to the restroom with Qamara and Kamarsha hot on her trail.

"Hold up, girl, we wanna take some more hits too. You ain't slick."

After they slipped into the bathroom, Lola began to nervously spray Potpourri air freshener around the living room and onto herself.

She peered into the big brass mirror that hung above the couch to examine her eyes. Assured she appeared sober, she strolled over to the door and looked through the peephole.

"What the hell is he doing here?" she whispered to herself. She glanced over her shoulder. "Girls, you could come out, it's only Redrum's ugly ass."

Carla was the first to burst out the bathroom with a cloud of smoke chasing her. She scrambled to where Lola stood.

"Girl, let that rich nigga in!"

The other two strode out leisurely, eyes low, as if they were half awake.

Lola regarded Carla with disgust.

"I don't know why you sweating him. That dude is hideous!"

"His pockets, girl, his pockets!" Carla replied without shame, anxious for Lola to open the door.

Lola contemplated how ghetto and conniving Carla was. Redrum was far from rich; however, he had more than what Carla was used to, so he was considered wealthy. Lola unlocked all three of the locks. Carla bustled past her as if she wasn't moving quickly enough and swung the door wide-open.

"Hey, Redrum."

Redrum, 5'10", slim, with a scar that crossed from his left ear over the top of his head and stopped in the center, glared past her. His wandering glass eye was drawn to Lola. Unmoved by the attention, he tugged on the red bandanna tied around his right wrist to tighten it, then dispassionately asked, "Where's Sha-Boogie?"

"Don't know."

Observing the marks on her face, he noted, "Yeah, I guess you wouldn't."

Abruptly entering the conversation, Carla opened her scarlet painted lips. "Hey, how's that new Montero riding?"

He evaded her inquiry by simply hissing his teeth.

"Tell him I said to hit me up, I heard what happened" were the only words that escaped his mouth. Without uttering another breath, he about-faced and began heading back out the way he came. Displaying a quizzical expression on her face, Lola violently grabbed his arm.

"What happened?"

Impervious to her questioning, he shrugged her grip off and departed down the hallway. Lola poked her head out the door.

"Redruuumm! What happened?"

He kept walking.

She slammed the door shut, then bolted it.

"My man could be dead, and them dudes wouldn't tell me a damn thing! It's been like three hours now since he left out, and I haven't heard from him."

Kamarsha lifted her head from the couch she and Qamara were now lying on.

"Girl, you know they keep it tight. It's better for you." Then dropping her head back as if it contained a ton of bricks, she began giggling for no apparent reason. Lola watched as her friend stared groggily at the ceiling.

"He didn't even speak to me," Carla said cynically while wiping her eyes to see if she had any cold in them. "He should feel lucky. He could've taste tested this." She paused, then swung her head toward Lola. "Girl, I don't have anything in my eyes, do I?"

Lola, not responding, gestured for Qamara, who was lost in space, to hand her the cordless phone. Noticing that Qamara was in her own world, she walked over to the coffee table, removed it from the base, and dialed Shaheen's number. She waited while it rang for what seemed like eternity and then, frustrated, launched the 2.4 gigahertz Panasonic at the love seat.

"He knows it's me. He got caller ID!"

Carla retrieved the phone. Positioning it back on the base, she pointed out, "Lo, hunny, all cells have caller ID nowadays. Besides, you think he gonna be quick to answer after y'all little tussle? He's probably out getting high with Leek."

"Yeah, but if something bad happened, I want to know. I mean, what if me and Shane had an emergency?"

"Girl, roll up another blunt, so you can forget about it."

Suddenly, the crying of her little one could be heard from the bedroom, canceling their thoughts of getting high. In less than a second, Lola was on the run, scampering quicker than Flash Gordon toward the back of the apartment.

Kamarsha raised her head, oblivious to the frightened sounds coming from the bedroom and asked, "Y'all rollin up again?"

*   *   *

Shaheen, with his left hand on the steering wheel, reached for the cell phone resting on the cup holder. He flipped it open, took in the number on the display, then tossed it in the backseat. Gorilla Leek curiously viewed his right-hand man and smiled.

"It must be Lo," he taunted.

Ignoring his friend's comment, with eyes committed to the road, Shaheen inquired, "Left or right?"

"Right."

He spun the wheel to the right, taking the corner with ease. He cruised down Fifty-first Street.

"Which house?"

"Slow down, the white one, right there on the left."

Shaheen threw the car in to park on the right side of the one-way street, two houses away from their intended destination. He peered through the tinted glass to his left to make sure no one was hanging out on the block. Seeing no one, he returned his gaze to Gorilla Leek, who was reloading his .44 Magnum. Gorilla Leek cocked the gun back.

"Let's do this!"

"I'm ready."

They both exited the vehicle. Shaheen stepped away from the open door, allowing his partner to take the lead. He shut it behind him quietly.

We should've taken care of this already, Gorilla Leek thought to himself.

He led Shaheen across the street and up the porch to the front door.

"You're positive there's only three cats in there?" Shaheen inquired.

"No doubt, Blood, I've been checking out this spot for three weeks."

"Three weeks!" exclaimed Shaheen. "What the hell for? You been planning this?"

"I had crackhead Jimbo watching this spot for a sec but never had any real plans to get 'em. I knew I would one day though. But until now, I just had Jimbo keeping his eyes on the comp. I need to know what and how it goes down when it's this close to my hood."

"And you just spoke to Jimbo?" Shaheen sarcastically inquired.

"Indeed, and he told me he was just by here today, and they expecting five more kis than usual tonight."

Shaheen's curiosity got the best of him. "How many all together?"

"Ten."

Shaheen began calculating the profit in his head. "It's just that I thought we just decided to do this together to get back at them for trying to hit us tonight. I didn't know you had eyes on this spot."

Gorilla Leek detected the accusation of betrayal in Shaheen's tone. "Trust me, dog, I didn't plan to get these cats. It's just that after tonight . . . well, you know . . . I mean . . . I knew about this spot, so I felt it was the best angle to hit 'em. And besides, we ain't never worked ten kis at one time, so imagine how much doe we gonna make."

"A'ight son, whatever. We here already, so it don't matter. Let's handle BI," Shaheen declared.

Gorilla Leek converged on the door. He raised his foot, then forestalling, dropped it to the ground suddenly as if he had a forbidding thought.

"Wait right here."

Shaheen scrutinized him intently. He started to protest but hesitated. Gorilla Leek ran down the five steps of the porch and seized an empty trashcan sitting idly in front of the house. Tiptoeing back up the stairs, he stopped in front of the large window to the right of the door. Peering through the curtains, he could discern the light of a small television set glowing in the dark interior of the front room. It revealed two human forms sitting at a table.

"Yo, Blood, when I start blasting, kick that door in. Jimbo said there's only one lock on it."

Shaheen raised his eyebrow at his partner. "What the hell are you about to do with that trashcan?"

Holding the receptacle with one hand and his Magnum with the other, Gorilla Leek simply simpered. Then without warning, he catapulted it through the window while almost simultaneously launching rounds behind the "rocket" can.

Crazy son of a bitch, Shaheen thought to himself, then with one kick from his Timberland boot, he separated the door from its hinges. He entered, instantly detecting the figure of a baldhead man, wearing a camouflage long john shirt charging down the staircase situated directly in front of him. The man was brandishing a Mocksbird shotgun.

"De blood clot, ya wan romp with mi, ya fossi . . ."

He never finished his sentence. Shaheen aimed for the man's chest and dispatched three shots. One tore through his enemy's left shoulder, spraying speckles of blood across the wall that lined the staircase. The other two ripped through his rib cage, stopping him dead in his tracks. Releasing his weapon, his eyes shot open with an expression of shock covering his visage.

The shotgun exploded when it hit the ground, blasting a fiery meteor shower of pellets upward into his face. The smoking skin on his cheek slowly began to peel downward like a fruit roll-up being stripped from its wrapper until it dangled by his chin. He tried hopelessly to mumble a few incoherent utterances, but instead of words, rosy bubbles of blood burst from his mouth. With eyes bulging down at his leaking chest, he collapsed to his knees and then tumbled down the stairs. His body settled in an awkward position.

By this time, Gorilla Leek had already vaulted over what was left of the window like an athlete jumping a hurdle. He landed on his feet and aimed at the man running toward what appeared to be a basement door.

He lowered his pistol, targeting the man's legs. He sent hot, piercing lead streaking through both of his calf muscles. Flesh flew in opposite directions. The man collapsed to his face.

Gorilla Leek leered down at his feet to assess the other victim who was struck by the first fusillade of bullets that soared through the window. He was grasping what was left of his throat while his legs kicked and jerked violently. Then suddenly, they stopped, his hands still clenched around his neck. He never had a chance.

Gorilla Leek walked over to the other man, who was crawling with his leg injuries, trying to get away. He kicked him in the ribs twice.

"Where's the bricks, Rasta?" Gorilla Leek shouted.

"Gwan suck yuh granny!" exclaimed the dread.

Shaheen came running into the front room out of breath. "Yo, Leek, it's on the table. You ran past it, man!" Shaheen trotted toward the table where their treasure awaited them.

"If you wasn't so amped on chasing blood, you would've seen it! Let's grab the trash can and dump the birds into it, so we can bounce before pigs pop up."

Gorilla Leek emptied the contents of the can and removed the bag that lined its interior. Together they filled the bag up with four kilos of cocaine wrapped in syran.

"These idiots didn't even start chopping it up. Guess we're right on time."

"I thought Jimbo said they would have five more kis tonight? There's only four here. Six are missing," Shaheen observed.

Gorilla Leek turned toward their last surviving victim. "Let's ask my dude over there."

By this time, the dread had sat up against the wall. Shaheen recognized the perfidious smile beginning to form on his partner's face.

"Na, dog, we don't have time. We did what we came to do!"

Gorilla Leek spoke without laying his sight on his friend. "You eat that baldhead nigga's food?"

Shaheen became curious as to how his partner could have known the description of the man who now lie dead on the staircase. Instead of thinking too much into it, he decided to answer his friend.

"Yeah, son dead." Not wanting any extra blood on his hand, Shaheen continued, "Go ahead, I'm headed to the car with the work. Hurry up. We don't have time for you to play with your food." He vanished with the trash bag in his possession.

Gorilla Leek ambled over to the dread, who was cursing under his breath. "Speak up, bitch, I can't hear you."

As he opened his mouth to reciprocate his taunts, he experienced the agonizing torment of his teeth being ruptured from his gums. His jaw exploded with pain as Gorilla Leek violently thrust his pistol past his lips toward the roof of his mouth.

"You told me to suck my granny, rude boy? How 'bout you show me how!"

He squeezed the trigger, sending the dread's head slamming back into the wall, with blood splattering like a bucket of scarlet paint being tossed against a large canvas. Gorilla Leek stood there, with his head tilted, and watched the thick dark crimson fluid mixed with small chunks of brain tissue profusely leak out of his victim's nostrils.

Wow, he thought, *granny always said a man who had to curse all the time had little brains.*

Laughing, he stormed out of the house and jumped into the Expedition. Shaheen studied him but said nothing, thinking, *The worst is yet to come . . . But for who?* They drove off.

CHAPTER 3

"What do you make of this?" Detective Bradford Thomas inquired while viewing the bullet-ridden kitchen wall and the grisly scarlet carcass sprawled across the entrance to the basement.

The middle-aged detective rubbed a handkerchief across his dark and dull-complexioned brow as his bulging brown eyes widened to explore the perimeter. The creases that traveled down the pants of his charcoal black suit were impeccably straight while the gray Egyptian cotton shirt beneath his blazer contained no stains or wrinkles whatsoever. His five o'clock shadow was barely detectable if not for the oil sheen that caused it to outshine his blue black flesh.

"Well, the neighbor in Three Twenty-Four reported the shots about an hour ago. We were the first to arrive on the scene. However, with the three bodies and the bullets found from the same caliber gun used in today's earlier shooting, indicating a possible connection, I would have to assume you would be leading this investigation. So I should be asking you the same question," sarcastically responded Narcotics Detective Archie O'Reilly.

Detective O'Reilly didn't have too much of a liking toward the Detective Thomas types of the world. He detested the fact that Detective Thomas's people thought of their position of employment as a justification for being treated as an equal to the white man.

Detective O'Reilly didn't view himself as a racist or a person who hated anyone. He only believed the world desired to sweep the truth under the rug for the sake of race relations. He recalled a conversation he had with his brother-in-law.

"Sure," he said, speaking to his younger sister's newly wedded husband. "The spades can read and write, so some of them can perform exceptionally well in the same endeavors as us, but that is not natural for them. In order for the niggers to excel in this lifetime, they must emulate us and live according to our standards because they don't have any of their own."

Noticing his brother-in-law's reluctance to nod in agreement, he continued, "This can be seen in Africa, where they kill each other wholesale, some of them becoming killers before they turn six years old. So it is a must that they remain under our customs and, as such, because of the natural relationship between teacher and student. We are indeed their superiors. If a nigger runs the country, it will turn into Africa, and look what they are doing to themselves over there. Look at what they do to themselves over there. I see it every day on the job.

"When one of them acts right, they start becoming audacious, fancying themselves better than a white man. They are fools, and I pity them while at the same time, I am disgusted by their arrogance. If they but look outside their window or turn on the news, it is their people who are causing the destruction of the fabric of this country, and they lend to it by just having more and more babies. It takes too much for us to train them to do right in the first place. Then they want to get all arrogant as if they are better when everything they have they got from us, and they can't even promise us they won't give birth to another criminal because they don't know how to raise their own children."

Detective Thomas simply stared solemnly at Detective O'Reilly as he stood daydreaming off into space without making any expression. He understood quite well the thought process of the old gray-haired man. He knew how he was thinking without knowing what he was thinking.

Without inhaling for air, Thomas declared, "Well, our victims here were Jamaican, just like the one murdered at the restaurant we just left. You also forgot to mention the fact that there were two murder weapons used here as there were also two used at the restaurant. Both of the same caliber. Tire tracks from an SUV peeling off at both scenes. You want to bet there is a connection? This is retaliation."

Detective O'Reilly allowed a sneer to emerge from his freckled lips. *Smart ass nigga thinks he knows it all.*

"Well, Detective Thomas, I might agree that the two are related. But retaliation? That may be so. However, you have to factor in that this is a drug house, owned by Orville Linton Lee-Chin, a.k.a. Chinnah, a major drug dealer. We have had this creep under surveillance for more than three months now. The crime lab geeks have found traces of cocaine here today but only residue. There are drugs missing from this crime scene."

"Under surveillance for three months, really?" Detective Thomas let out a faint chuckle. "So how did the killers manage to kick in a door, smash a window, walk into a drug spot 'under surveillance', murder three supposed drug dealers, then load their vehicle with stolen drugs and leave, all while your men had their ever-watchful eye on the look-out for any suspicious activity?"

Thomas roared with merriment as he leaned his head back and shot his pupils to the sky. "Did you at least get any photos of the perpetrators, seeing you were too busy surveying to apprehend them?"

Detective O'Reilly raised his eyebrow allowing his facial expression to display indifference, hoping to convey his thoughts with eyes rather than words.

Fuck you, you uppity nigger is what he held between his teeth. Instead, he attempted to reply, "My men were loo—"

Thomas interrupted, "Save it. Your men didn't do their job. They only complicated mine. We will know for sure if there is a connection once the geeks get a hold of the evidence."

Detective O'Reilly did not want to tell him that his men were paid not to be there tonight, and instead of surveillance, they were spending the money they earned at a pub in Coney Island.

Thomas abruptly spun on his heels and motioned his new partner to follow him. He made his way past the other two bodies and exited the house with rookie detective Jonathan Torturro right behind him.

Detective Torturro was a graduate of John Jay College and an aspiring criminal lawyer, born and raised in the Bensonhurst section of Brooklyn. He never left home without a suit and tie. This distinguished him from the many detectives in his precinct who dressed mainly in old jeans and denim jackets over faded hoodies.

He reckoned himself the next Rudolph Giuliani. However, his innocence coupled with his ignorance made him the target of many of his coworkers' jokes. His reason for joining the police force was to make a difference in the world. At least, that is what he expressed to others. The truth is he longed for a life of excitement, something different from the ordinary and dull reality he experienced every day in Bensonhurst.

"So what now?" asked Torturro as they approached their vehicle.

Thomas answered him, "You are going to wait until the crime lab confirms a match on the casings found at both crime scenes while I go speak to my CI to see what he has heard. This is obviously not done. It will spill over into more bloodshed. Retaliation, drugs stolen, and men dead . . . yeah, this is far from over. If we don't get a head start, we will be chasing a blood trail. However, we do know one thing that Narcotics doesn't seem to know."

Torturro peered at Thomas quizzically. "What's that?"

A smirk gradually appeared on Thomas's face. "Ford."

"Huh?" Torturro thought he missed the punch line.

"Keep your eyes and ears open for a Ford SUV, Torturro, more than likely, an Expedition."

Torturro did not bother to inquire for further clarification. However, the older detective decided to explain. "The geeks said the tire tracks found at the restaurant belong to Ford and a Cadillac SUV. Judging from the tracks we have here, we have another Ford involved. So I would guess the drivers were the targets of the shooting at the restaurant. Someone had to have seen them inside there, eating or buying food."

Torturro gawked in amazement at the observation of his elder. He chose to ask a question, not so much for information as to show that he understood Thomas's deduction. "So you want me to also go back to the restaurant and question the employees?"

"No," Thomas abruptly retorted, "the employees are poor and fearful of losing a job. They are used to that type of violence occurring in that neighborhood. They will keep their mouth shut in order to stay safe and be able to have a job to go to. Go over the names of the people who were reported as being in the restaurant at the time of the shooting and call them. You probably will get more out of them."

Torturro nodded his head. They both entered the jet-black Crown Victoria that was double-parked in front of the crime scene. Torturro threw the gear into drive, and they peeled off.

*　　*　　*

The clock had two hours and twelve minutes to exhaust before the faintest hint of sunlight would be detectable over Rockaway Parkway. The inner circle of the criminal organization known as the Gully Posse had been in high gear since shortly after four of its members were gunned down.

Chinnah, the leader, had scrambled all of his top lieutenants in the cellar of his Brooklyn storefront located on the corner of Rutland Road and Rockaway Parkway. The elderly man towered over most of the men present, scrutinizing each of them with his fiery red eyes that were glossy from hours of smoking marijuana in a windowless and stuffy basement. The fact that he was high along with the low, slanted-shaped eyelids he inherited from his Chinese father made him appear sinister yet barely awake.

He resembled a tall and lanky brown-skinned Asian with a head crowned by silver dreadlocks that intertwined with several thin strands of black hair. His demeanor was so nonchalant he appeared snobbish. His chin remained elevated into the air when he spoke and his eyelids seemed to touch each other even though they were open. The man wore a very solemn expression.

Yellowman, the lightest in complexion of the group, controlled all the marijuana spots on Rutland Road that ran from Rockaway Parkway to Ninety-fourth Street. The locks flowing from his pale scalp barely touched the floor. It favored a cape as it draped freely from his slender frame.

Cutty, unlike Yellow and Chinnah, kept his hair in a low-cut Caesar and seemed to have a closet full of silk shirts and suede Wallabees in an assortment of colors. He ran Chinnah's cocaine and marijuana spots in East New York, most of which were situated off of Pitkins Avenue and disguised as small convenience stores.

Chinnah's right-hand gunman and executioner was Pauley. He was the biggest of the three, weighing about three hundred and five pounds, with small locks standing erect above clean cut fade. Before arriving in America, he was regarded as one of the most feared enforcers of Claudius Massop, the criminal kingpin who ran the Tivoli Gardens section of Kingston, Jamaica. Pauley had been responsible for the demise of more than twenty of Jamaica's most ruthless gangsters and politicians. Now in America with a new identity, he was Gully Posse's number 1 gunman.

The fourth member of the inner circle and second in command under Chinnah, as well as the youngest of the crew, was his son, Copper. Copper, who was twenty years of age as well as born and raised in America, inherited none of his father's distinguishable traits. He spoke with an American accent, adorned his body with the latest urban hip-hop fashion and always kept his feet covered in the newest Timberlands. However, now in 2003, he decided he would reinvest in a collection of Air Force 1s in an effort to keep up with the most recent American custom.

He was identified in the Nineties section of Brooklyn as a big mouth, with a hot temper, who lived off his father's reputation. Those who weren't familiar with him personally, feared him. However, others who had a past acquaintance with him, such as Shaheen and Gorilla Leek, took him for a joke.

Chinnah was the first to assert his anger, slamming his fist down on the table.

"Wha de Blood! Wha mek dem wan war wit mi? Eh? Mi wan dem Yankee bwoys fi dead, yuh ear? Before dem ed fi get big, an dem eggs up pon de streets, like de pussy-ole chatabax dem are."[1]

He arose from the milk crate, which served as his throne at the head of a wooden table. Upon it rested scattered domino pieces. All eyes were on him as he shambled past his minions over to where his machete lay prone in the corner of the basement floor. He upheld the blade, stared at it in ambivalence, and then returned his gaze upon his comrades.

"Mi might be a foreigna, but dem rassclat edeeats eena mi territory!"[2]

He neared Pauley in a languid stride, machete still in hand. He loomed over the big man inundating him with a callous look from the fervid red eyes that suffocated him with fear.

"I-dren, look pon de grey eena mi locks. When I an I arrive een foreign, it black an shawt like de mon Cutty im ave. Dis ow long I an I run tings yahso . . . an mi continue ta duh so! Cause mi artical!"[3]

---

[1] "What the fuck! What makes them want war with me? Huh? I want those Americans dead, do you hear me? Before their heads get big and they go boasting around the streets like the pussy hole big mouths they are."

[2] "I might not be from this country, but those fucking idiots are in my territory!"

[3] "Friend, look at the grey in my hair. When I arrived in America, it was black and short like the man, Cutty, has. This is how long I have ran things here . . . and I will continue to do so! Because I'm respected!"

Pauley swallowed nervously and began to reciprocate upon his crate. He couldn't understand how Trevor, the man he sent to keep his eye on Gorilla Leek, could end up getting murdered in front of Souljah's Restaurant on Rutland Road. After witnessing Leek walking out of White Mike's store one day, he decided to have him followed to find out what he was up to. He was curious as to why he would be patronizing a store whose owner was an associate of Chinnah. He refrained from informing his boss because he wasn't certain as to what was going on. It was possible that Gorilla Leek was just purchasing something rather than conducting business. However, he had to make certain.

He wondered whether Gorilla Leek knew he was being watched and, in turn, confronted Trevor. That would explain why they robbed one of Chinnah's spots. However, he knew if Chinnah found out Trevor died because he was watching Gorilla Leek, he might, in his insanity, blame him for the robbery. He was relieved when the men who accompanied Trevor, lied and told Chinnah that an argument broke out between the two which led to gunfire. They claimed they had to leave Trevor because the cops arrived on the scene.

Chinnah became aware of Pauley's introspective gaze. "Pauley, mi wan fi dem family's blood ta paint dis ere rachet, zeen!"[4]

"Eeh,"[5] Pauley said, relieved he was given the chance to redress the situation. "Fi shaw."[6]

Chinnah then cast his sight toward Yellowman. "Oonu! Dem fi cause mi badderation. See dat dem Minimart meet wit catastrophe . . . Mi prefa ya mash it up een brawd daylight while it fill wit a wholeheap of dem customers."[7]

---

[4]   "Pauley, I want their family's blood to paint his blade here, understand!"

[5]   "Yes,"

[6]   "For Sure."

[7]   "You! They caused me problems. See that their Minimart meets with a catastrophe . . . I prefer for you to destroy it in broad daylight while it's filled with a lot of their customers."

"Yes, Lion,"[8]Yellowman replied.

"Ave ya top soldyahs galang wit ya,"[9] Chinnah instructed. He brought his attention to Cutty. "Mi yute, mi wan mi kis back wit in wan week's time. Zeen? If na mine's, den deirs. Dem mus be bawn back a cow ta tink dem can cause mi crosses an mi na kya. Mon, dem fi kill mi dead before mi let dem deh fossi-oles tief from mi."[10]

"Dun, sire."[11]

Chinnah returned to his throne, releasing the machete by his feet.

Copper, feeling excluded, pleaded, "Daddy, what about me? I see them muthafuckas all the time at Tilden Ballroom, partying. Me and my locs could get at them. They be up in our territory with their little Blood soldiers spending cash like they're untouchable. If not them, we could take out some of their little slobs to send them a message."

Chinnah recognized what his son was implying was true, not to mention Copper had a bunch of bloodthirsty Crips under his wing eager to earn their stripes. The only problem was their incompetence to handle a job professionally. They hungered for fame more than fortune. He didn't want his son to ruin the organization by involving all those ghetto foreigners. He concluded his son, while eager, was still incapable of leading.

"Easy nuh, mi son. A wha yuh tek dis fa? Yuh tink yuh ca gwan ta some bashment an tump down deir likkle posse?"[12] Chinnah sucked his teeth. "Dat labrish! Dis business ere

---

[8]   "Yes, King."

[9])   "Have your top soldiers go along with you,"

[10]   "My youth, I want my Kis back within one week's time. Understand? If not mine's, then theirs. They must be crazy to think they can cause me problems and I wouldn't care. Man, they would have to kill me before I let those punks steal from me."

[11]   "Done, King."

[12]   "Easy now, my son. What do you take this for? Do you think you can go to some party and beat up their little gang?"

crewtial. A-fe real gunman fi handle. Plus, mi nuh chuck it with no mout-a-massy Crips."[13]

Copper's eyes squinted in disgust. Then suddenly, a grueling sound cut short their discussion. It came from above them, traveling turbulently through the air from the back of the store. It sounded like a woman screaming. Without thinking twice, Copper bolted up the basement staircase.

Chinnah glanced sternly at the ceiling. "Ah, whey dat blasted bangarang ah come from?"[14]

Copper pushed open the door and stopped in the middle of the can food aisle just in time to witness Lennox, the storekeeper, pistol-whipping a teenage boy. The youth was cowering in the corner by the freezer. He was attempting to deflect the blows with his bleeding hands. The boy's jacket was drenched in the vital fluid leaking profusely from the gash above his temple.

Copper observed his homeboy, Killa Kash, who accompanied him to the meeting, calmly guarding the entrance. The door was now locked. Copper had initially ordered him to remain upstairs while he convened with his father and the others.

"Yo, Killa, what's the deal with this?"

Before Killa could respond, Lennox stopped his inflictions and, in between his huffing and puffing, remarked, "Mi ketch dis blackheart mon tryin' fi tief a Heineken from de fridge."[15] By this time, Chinnah and the rest of his cohort had arrived at the scene of all the commotion. "So mi fi tell Killa, lock off de door, so mi can teach dis here tegareg a les—"[16]

---

[13] "That is stupid! This business here is crucial. For real gunmen to handle. Plus, I don't associate with big mouth Crips."

[14] "Hey, where did that blasted noise come from?"

[15] "I caught this untrustworthy man trying to steal a Heineken from the refrigerator."

[16] "So I told Killa to lock the door, so I could teach this here criminal a les—"

Chinnah intervened, "Wha ah gwan? Im try fi tief from me?"[17] Trampling over to the teenager, gripping his faithful machete, he said to no one in particular, "Lif im up an place im and pon de counter dere."[18]

With a grimacing expression on his face, the boy leaped to his feet and began pleading, "Please, don't, sir . . . Please, I'll pay for . . . no . . . I'll pay double . . . Please . . . I'm sorry!"

Lennox and Pauley lugged the thief over to the back counter. Pauley pinned his hands down next to the meat-slicing machine. Copper shifted his eyes to Killa Kash to see him instructing two faithful patrons on the outside of the store to come back in an hour when they reopened.

Chinnah lifted his machete with one hand. "Yuh know wha dem Arabs do eena dem country when dem fi ketch a tief?"[19]

Struggling in a feeble attempt to wiggle out of Pauley's firm grip, the boy tried pleading one last time, "Mister . . . sir . . . please . . . don't do this . . . I know now that I picked the wrong store . . . but I'm broke, and this was the only twenty-four-hour joint open . . . Give me a . . ."

Wham!

The blade came down in one swoop, awkwardly severing part of his wrist from his hand, spurting crimson everywhere. His limb hung from a large chunk of flesh as sanguine fluid sprayed out. The boy howled out in agony. With tears in his eyes, he gawked in disbelief at the flood of blood pouring out of his mangled wrist. He instantly went into shock.

Chinnah, unaffected by the gruesome sight, strolled back toward the basement, again addressing no one in particular.

---

[17] "What is going on? Is he trying to steal from me?"

[18] "Lift him up and place his hand on the counter there."

[19] "Do you know what those Arabs do in their country when they catch a thief?"

"Trow im rass out de back an clean up de counter. Oh, an . . . letoff de Heineken ta de mon."[20]

Before disappearing beyond the basement door, he let out one last remark, "Mo'time."[21]

Copper surveyed the five remaining men. "Bump that, ya'll clean that shit up! I'm gonna light up a spliff!" He pivoted on his heels and followed his father.

*   *   *

"Oh, Shaheen!" Lola let out a long moan, "Harder, baby, harder!"

Shaheen had Lola's naked body straddled from behind with his right arm wrapped around her waist and stomach. With his left knee on the bed, he fiercely shoved his organ up in her as hard as he could, in and out. Lola could feel his manhood spreading the thick lips of her vagina with each inward thrust.

Shaheen released her waist, stood his left foot up, bringing himself in a squatting position, and used both of his hands to fiercely grip and spread her fat, firm, cheeks wide-open. As he pumped in and out, he admired his long brown pride, observing the thick cream gushing out of her and onto him. He loved watching it going in and coming out. While keeping his movement steady, he extended his hand up under her and rubbed his fingers on her clit with each stroke of his penis.

She couldn't bear it. She felt the contractions between her legs increasing. At the same time she reached her climax, she collapsed to the bed on her stomach. He followed her lead. Lying on top of her, he squeezed her throat with one hand and, with the other up under her arm, gripped her shoulder. He continued pushing in her, faster and faster, as if he was trying to penetrate her scalp.

---

[20] "Throw his ass out the back and clean up the counter. Oh, and . . . give the Heineken to the man."

[21] "I'm gone"

He knew once she had her orgasm, she would pull on the sheets in an attempt to crawl away from the dick like she always did. He held on.

"Oh shit, girl, ya pussy is so warm, so . . . Uh . . . so tight . . . uh . . . so wet." *Squish, squash, squish.* He wanted to hear her vagina talk to him. "Oh shit!"

He felt his penis throbbing. "Aaarghh . . . Ahh!"

His tip exploded. He didn't bother pulling out. He released her throat, and his clutch on her shoulder weakened.

"Oh girl, I love you!"

She knew her stuff was the bomb. Shaheen lay limply on top of her, breathing heavily.

She conceded that now was the best time to present her case. "Baby, I'm sorry for starting that argument yesterday, and Lord knows, I don't want to start one today. However, if you love me, you'd stay home with me and Shane all day, instead of going out. It's a beautiful Friday . . ."

Shaheen rolled off her and on to his back. He began staring at the ceiling.

"Ma, you know I want to, but . . ."

She rested her head on his chest and gazed into his brown eyes.

"I know . . . I know . . . if you stay home . . . you can't pay the bills."

Lowering the tone of her voice and imitating his accent, she said, "I'm saying, ma, your dude gotta stay on top of things . . . ya na 'mean?"

He smiled and muttered, "Look, baby girl, I'm twenty-four years old. I'm doing this now so I won't have to be doing this when I'm thirty."

"I can't wait that long, baby."

"And hopefully, you won't. Do you think I enjoy this?"

"Well, from the way you wake up from your nightmares, I would think not."

"Exactly, girl! I hate this life, but what I despise even more is the lame ass nine to five life. I enjoy sitting back and collecting money."

"So why not start a business?" Her head popped up as if a light bulb went on. "We could start one together!" she blurted out excitedly.

Then sitting up, she proceeded, "We could run it together. Think about it. For you, no more bad dreams and an honest occupation. I wouldn't have to worry about being lonely anymore and . . ."

"Ma, you ain't lonely. You have Shane to keep you company, and besides, I already have a business."

Her eyes purposefully revealed her antipathy. "That little grocery store is not a real business, let alone legit. And both Shane and I need you in our life for more than just three to five hours a day."

Shaheen disregarded her comment, then surveyed the room. He stared in contemplation at his son, who was asleep on a small oak bed, which had been converted from what used to be a baby crib. He then glanced in the opposite direction at the electronic clock that rested upon his marble nightstand. It read 11:26 a.m. He didn't realize it was so late. He was supposed to have been at Minimart over two hours ago to drop off the re-up.

He jumped out of the bed and scanned the floor beneath him. Finding his boxers, he gathered them up and made his way to the bathroom without saying a word. With arms folded in frustration, Lola let out a deep sigh.

Shaheen stood in front of the bathroom mirror, calmly brushing his teeth with gentle and fastidious strokes. He observed each tooth intently, making sure they were still white. From the corner of his eye, he detected the door creeping open. It was Shane. He stood in the doorway rubbing his eyes.

"Peace, Daddy"

With a mouth full of foam, Shaheen returned the greeting, "Peace, lil man."

He then loomed over the toilet and ejected the foamy spittle from his mouth. It landed in the water, splattering speckles onto the floor.

"You wanna watch TV?"

Shane nodded his head rapidly, resembling a life-size bobblehead figurine.

"Daddy, Dora dee Splora?"

"Yeah, little man, you can watch Dora, the Explorer. It should be on now. Go ahead up front. You know how to turn the TV on. It's already on the channel."

That was all Shane needed to hear; he was gone, running down the hall, singing the theme song. "De, de, de, de, Dora . . . de, de, de, de, Dora."

Shaheen could hear the television roar to life from the living room. He smiled. The best thing to ever happen to him in all his twenty-four years of living was the birth of his son. He cried when he saw his little head pop out of Lola's womb. It was at that moment he decided to name him after both himself and his brother, Kane, whom he wished could have been there with him.

Every toy that captured his son's attention on TV or whether in the department stores, he made certain Shane possessed it. His son had a larger wardrobe and collection of the latest fashionable sneakers than most of his workers and friends. Shane was his breath, the only reason he remained with Lola after all the fights.

He desired to provide him with the family and life he always wanted but which seem to elude him. All day, every night, Shaheen boasted about Shane's antics: his toughness, the slick ways he made Lola bend to his desires, how he flirted with women and their daughters, and how he inherited his mother's beautiful smile as well as her chinky eyes.

For a moment, while assessing his scars in the mirror and reflecting on his son, Shaheen contemplated leaving the game, living a square life and marrying Lola. Just as quickly as the thought came, he dismissed it. Just hours ago, he and Lola were at each other's throat. Plus, the idea of depending on a check seemed foolish to him. A future in the ordinary life appeared dismal.

He despised the fast lane but at the same time couldn't perceive how complying with the speed limit would get him where he needed to go. *One day,* he contemplated, *I'll be regular, attending parent-teacher conferences, playing catch in the park without looking over my shoulder and teaching lil man about the birds and the bees . . . one day.* He sighed, then said aloud, "But when?"

He felt a tug on his shorts, which caused him to look behind. He wondered how he allowed Lola to silently sneak up on him. *Gotta stop slipping,* he thought. Peering down at the hand that was fumbling through his boxers, he caught a glimpse of a shiny clear glob in her palm.

"Ahhh." A moan escaped his mouth as she, with a tight grip, began stroking his penis. He felt the blood rushing through his organ as it started enlarging. The Vaseline she had in her hands made the sensation feel surreal.

"Damn Ma, keep it slow . . . Uhh."

Her other hand entered from the rear and began caressing his testicles. "You sure you don't want to stay home?"

Leaning over the sink, he settled both of his hands down on the counter. He could see her staring at him through the mirror, smiling sensuously, while biting the side of her bottom lip. She aroused him so well he could feel his love juice beginning to burst again.

"Oh shit, I'm about to . . ."

BLAAAAM!

He jumped back, waist jerking, and swung around toward Lola. They gaped at each other in awe.

"What the hell was that? Was that in here?" she said frantically, wondering where the loud explosion came from. Thinking the same, while holding his crotch, Shaheen's eyes widened. He knew a gunshot when he heard one. However, he couldn't tell if it was inside their home. He just knew the sound traveled from the front of the apartment somewhere. Then it dawned on him.

"Oh shit, lil man."

He exited the bathroom in a panic-stricken run. Lola stood motionless, confused and partly terrified.

"Nooooooo!"

Shaheen's scream seemed to rebound off the hallway walls, striking her ears and causing her to jump. She hastened into the living room to witness him kneeling on the floor, shaking something. She searched the room for Shane.

Shaheen's hollering became sobs. "C'mon, don't do this, lil man, no!"

Lola, still confused but now nervously frantic, darted her eyes over Shaheen's shoulder. Her face turned pale.

"Naw, uh, uh . . . no . . . That's not my baby!"

She saw a puddle of blood and the lifeless body of Shane being shaken by his father. Shaheen attempted to lift his son's corpse up. While he was able to do so, the head barely moved. It was difficult to raise in comparison to the frame and weighed down heavily like a sandbag.

As Shaheen released his son, crimson began overflowing from a fist-sized hole in the head. It kept oozing out faster and faster, reacting to Shaheen's helpless attempt to move it.

Lola recognized that the seat cushion to the love seat had been removed, and on the floor next to what used to be her heaven was Shaheen's Reuger.

"What . . . what . . . how could this happen?"

Shaheen could not hear her. He continued wailing. He endeavored once more to mount Shane up. Failing to do so, he began shaking him more from his nervousness now than in an attempt to revive him. That was impossible.

"Fuck! Fuck! Fuck!" Letting loose of the corpse and falling back into a sitting position, with both arms stiffened on the floor, he moved himself away from his deceased son. His tears ceased, and he just sat their, eyes wide, but seeing nothing. His lil man was gone. He could still hear him singing, "De, de, de, de, Dora . . ." The frantic cries and screams pouring out of Lola's mouth brought him back to reality.

"No . . . no . . . no . . . baby, wake up, wake up. Mommy's right here, mommy's . . ."

"Lola!" he shouted after switching places with her. Now hovering over her, he raised Lola to her feet. Clasping both of her shoulders, he pulled her into his arms and embraced her tightly.

Glancing down at his gun, he struggled with his words. "I'm sorry, baby, he . . . he must've found the gun and . . ." He tried to hold back the tears that were forming again. Lola, trembling uncontrollably, continued her hysterical crying.

"He's gotta come back to us, Shaheen . . . Please try to wake him up . . . He's gotta come back . . . Call the ambulance . . . They can save him." Reality wouldn't register in her mind. "Please, Shaheen, call someone!" she pleaded.

Breaking free of his hold, she dashed to the phone. She picked it up and dialed 119. Too hysterical to recognize the mistake she made, she began speaking into the silence on the other end. "Hello . . . hello . . ." She directed her bewildered gaze toward Shaheen's direction. "No one is answering. No one cares!"

He scooped the weapon from off the floor after which he surveyed the carpet for the shell casing. He didn't see it. *Must have fell under the couch,* he thought. So many thoughts were racing at once in his mind; he didn't realize he was clutching the pistol by the barrel. Yet, it did not burn him as usual.

His nervousness was disrupted by the loud screeching noise escaping from behind the string of mucus that connected Lola's upper and lower lip. He didn't understand her at first because his attention was drawn to the distorted expression on her face. Then it hit him. He understood what she was saying and what she was pursuing. He shoved the gun in his waist, then rushed over to her and snatched the phone from her.

"Baby girl," his tone was more defiant now, "we can't call anyone!" Considering his illegal possession of the weapon and the murder he committed with it the other night, he decided against the idea of calling anyone other than Gorilla Leek. "We will both be arrested."

"I don't care, damn it! We have to save him!"

"Lo, He's . . . he's de . . . We can't save him. God has taken him." He hesitantly glanced down at his son's bloody scalp.

She thrusted her middle finger up in to the air. "Fuck God! I want my baby back!"

Shaheen realized the main lock to his apartment door was halfway turned while the other two were unlocked. Lola had scolded him numerous times in the past about making certain he rotated the lock fully around because it would always get stuck halfway and needed some extra giggling. However, what bothered him most now was the idea of a neighbor hearing the commotion and coming inside to see what was going on. So he ran to the door and quickly bolted it.

Damn, I should've gotten rid of the burner the night we did it, he thought to himself.

After securing the door, he sauntered over to where Lola was now standing with her face in her palms. Once again, he drew her into his arm. She started punching on his chest. He did his best to restrain her.

"It was your gun . . . your fault . . . Why Shaheen? Why!"

His eyes met the ceiling. "I know, baby girl, I know . . ."

Her head fell back as a shriek once again escaped her lips. "Whhyyy!"

She stopped struggling to attack him only to fall to the floor. She sat there, no longer wailing or screaming, just sobbing with her head hung low. A tear rolled down Shaheen's cheek and landed on the tip of her runny nose.

"Baby, look," staring at Shane's figure, "we have to get rid of the body and keep this a secret." He directed his sight to her. "Do you understand me, Lo? Look at me, do . . . you . . . understand?" he firmly questioned.

Without moving and still in the same position, she answered weakly, "Yes . . . I guess."

Shaheen retrieved his cell phone and began dialing Gorilla Leek's number. Then feeling something wet, he peered down to see his boxers soiled with his sperm.

CHAPTER 4

Blades, a five foot five, reddish bronze complexioned, Puerto Rican, was busy counting the hundreds of dollars hidden beneath the cash register's drawer while assisting the clientele that packed the store. There were two types of customers that formed a line inside Minimart on Rutland Road.

There were those few who came in the store purchasing mostly candy, cigarettes, and occasionally, selected items from the outdated food section. They were mainly children sent on errands by parents or grandparents too fearful of the hoodlums, who hung outside of the store, to venture onto the block themselves.

The other group of patrons, who were the reason the store stayed busy after 5:00 p.m., usually made their way straight to the back, only stopping to greet Blades, before continuing toward the refrigerator section. Once there, they would open the glass door and slip a twenty dollar bill or better to the hand of some worker hidden on the other side of the freezer behind the beer racks. In return, he would pass them a small, neatly folded thin strip of aluminum foil.

Before leaving, they would pause at the counter Blades occupied to purchase a store item so as not to appear suspicious to the many marked and unmarked police cars that circled the block casing the cocaine spot.

"Yo, Venom, come up here!" Blades yelled while handing a young teenage girl her change.

"Thank you, Blades," The girl blushed, "Oh, my girl outside told me to tell you that you are cute."

Without removing his eyes from the money, he asked, "Does she have a big ass? If not, she can keep it moving."

The girl glanced in the direction of the door, where her friend had her face pressed hard against the window, giggling. She then shifted back toward Blades.

"I don't know about her, but how you like this?"

She whirled herself around to show off the impeccable figure that outlined her black Parasuco jeans. Pulling the back of her shirt up while tugging down on her denim, she revealed her red thong to him.

Blades halted his counting to gape, then without an expression, returned to what he was doing. "I like that color, write your number down."

Venom, a tall, slim dark-skinned male, with a scar under his eye, came running out from the back of the store.

"What's poppin', Blood?"

"Yo, I'm about to bounce to go drop this doe off with Sha-Boogie. I need you to hold the fort down while Lil Blood Drop handles the back."

"No problem, dog."

The girl frustrated by the lack of attention said, "What about me? I don't have anything to write my number down on!"

"Yo, Venom, give shorty a pen and a piece of that paper bag, then leave the number under the register for me, a'ight?"

"Gotchoo!"

Blades came from around the glass partition and paraded past the girl without uttering a word to her. "Four eyes nigga!" he commanded his young soldier. Not receiving a response, he asked, "Gangsta Dim?"

"Half Glass," Venom reciprocated.

"A'ight then, Peace Blood!" he screamed before exiting the store.

"Peace, Blood!" echoed Venom.

"Washington DC!" were the last words that left his lips as the door closed behind him.

The girl was ignorant as to the meaning of the Bloods' coded language. Completely baffled, she just stared at the young man in front of her.

Venom passed her the pen and the paper bag. He began inspecting her firm breast intently. "Yo, shorty, you got a friend?"

"Yeah, she's right outside."

"Go tell her to come in," he excitedly stated.

"A'ight, here." She passed him the pen back with her number and strutted out to get her friend.

Noticing her backside, Venom squeezed his crotch and said, "Damn! Shorty is thick!"

Outside the store, the two girls began arguing.

"I don't want that ugly ass nigga. I thought you were hooking me up with Blades?"

"I tried, but he kept flirting with me. Girl, he asked me for my number. I didn't ask for his, and I wasn't going to let that fine ass thug go to waste! Why you didn't say something when he came out?"

The girl rolled her eyes, then retorted, "Whatever, skank! You know you had—"

The screeching of a black sedan, coming to a halt at the curb directly across from them, disrupted their bickering. A tall dark figure with dreadlocks and wearing shades eased out of the backseat. His hand gripped a MAC-11. Another man, much lighter, with long locks as well, exited the passenger's side, sporting a thin leather jacket and holding a shotgun.

Before the girls could open their mouths, bullets went soaring at and past them, perforating their chests, heads, and legs. While one girl's body shook and rattled in a dance of death before falling to the ground in convulsions, Yellowman's shotgun bucked the other one off her feet, catapulting her and her torn Parasuco jeans backward through Minimart's glass window. Blood exploded out of her, misting the air around her shredded body.

The two men sent scores of gunshots through the store, tearing apart glass, wood, food, soda bottles, and flesh. The big man stopped firing and retrieved a small round object from out of his jacket. It resembled a large black egg. He hurled the object through the open space where the window had once stood, then quickly jumped back into the sedan where his partner awaited him. They peeled off. Before driving halfway down the block, a teeth-rattling explosion erupted behind them. Yellowman viewed the carnage through the side mirror. He smiled.

*   *   *

"Goddammit!" hollered Kamarsha, with one hand pushing a red laundry cart and the other holding a plastic shopping bag. "Stop running ahead of me! It's getting dark out here, and I don't have my glasses."

Her three children were chasing each other up St. Marks Avenue in the Crown Heights section of Brooklyn, playing tag.

"Gemma, Jamel, and Tracy! You better stop when you get to the house! You hear me? And you better not open the door up with those keys . . . Jah!"

The children, led by Jamel, the oldest at eight years of age, arrived at their Brownstone home and in an instant hurdled the steps, out of view of their mother's sight and into the building.

"Lord, I'm gonna kill these kids," she complained to herself. "They're gonna give me gray hair before I reach twenty-five."

She vigorously labored to tug the shopping cart up the stairs with one hand. "Jamel, come and help mommy!"

There was no response.

"I'm gonna tear his little butt up . . . They never treat Malik like this."

She entered the building, relieved that her children left the front door to the hallway unlocked. As she made her way past the mailboxes, she realized the door to her first-level apartment in the four-unit building was wide-open.

"I told 'em not to go in. Boy, they're gonna get it!"

Suddenly, a sharp shriek roared from the apartment, sliced through the air, and recoiled off her eardrums. The horrifying sound jolted her heart.

"Mommmmy!"

It was Gemma.

Immediately following the scream was a loud thunderlike noise that burst through the hallway with a bright silver flash, lighting up the inside of her apartment.

"Oh my god!"

She released the cart and dropped the bag. She leaped into action like a cheetah chasing a prey she could smell but couldn't yet see. The hallway appeared longer than usual. As she approached the bedroom, she observed the door. It had been kicked open.

"Oh shit!" she yelled out.

A tall dark figure startled her as he jostled her to the side and stumbled out of the room, clutching his stomach. He staggered from wall to wall. Reaching out his free hand to brace himself against the right side of the interior, he collapsed to the floor, his palm leaving a trail of crimson smeared across the plaster. Kamarsha stood frozen in fear.

*   *   *

Shaheen sat in the passenger seat of Gorilla Leek's Black Yukon, staring coldly off into the night. As he waited in the parked vehicle on Rochester Avenue, across the street from Lincoln Terrace Park, he turned the situation over and over in his pain-stricken mind.

The traffic light ahead blinked from yellow to red, reminding him of the bloody scene he had to clean up a little over an hour earlier. He had instructed Lola to go to Carla's house to stay the night. Before she left, he reminded her of their vow of secrecy. A small consolation when pitted against the charges and time they could face. He knew Lola wouldn't totally understand his methodical thinking, but he wasn't sure if he understood it either, let alone accepted it.

What the hell am I doing? He whispered silently to himself, shaking his head. *I'm burying my son in the middle of a freaking park. How am I going to explain his absence? How am I going to get use to his absence?* He slammed his fist against the dashboard. "Shit, lil man . . . shit!"

Tears flooded his eyes. He shook his head. "I'm so sorry. Please forgive me. God, I'm sorry." He pulled a red bandana from out of his black leather jacket and wiped his tears. "God, I messed up."

The thought occurred to him to turn himself in to the authorities as a punishment for his mistake.

"Na, I can't do that, but I promise you, lil man, I'll make it up to you some way."

A moment later, Gorilla Leek shuffled from beyond the shadows of the trees that stood as a dark gate to the entrance of the park. He opened the door to the vehicle and settled into the driver's seat. He eyed his best friend with remorse.

"You a'ight, Blood?"

"Yeah. Is everything handled?"

"No doubt," Gorilla Leek inhaled deeply, then let out a long sigh. "I buried him on Dead Man Hill."

"What about the burner?"

"On the other side of the park by Buffalo Avenue."

"Good, good," Shaheen tried hard to appear unmoved by his circumstance, "You're always there for me man. I would've done it myself, but . . ."

"Look Blood, say no more. I'm your dog for life. You the only brother and family I have." He paused, then scanned his companion up and down. "Man, I love you dog."

A perplexed expression appeared on Shaheen's face. He forced a smile to surface. "Nigga, you ain't getting no ass with that lame ass line."

He released a laugh from his lips as Gorilla Leek followed suit.

Gorilla Leek ceased his chuckles then sincerely stated, "Na, seriously dog, you always looked out for the kid. I got your back forever."

"And I got your front, fam."

"You sure you good?"

"Yeah man, we got BI to handle."

"A'ight, so where to?"

"We need to hook up with Blades and find out exactly what happened at Minimart today. It's best not to go over there 'cause it'll be crawling with pigs. I'm sure they found some of the work in the back, at least what didn't burn up in the fire."

The ringing of a cell phone shot through the air. The two friends shoved their hands into each of their pockets.

"It's mine," stated Gorilla Leek. He flipped the phone open. "Peace!"

Shaheen watched as his friend's expression transformed from anger to relief, then to anger again.

"A'ight, I'm on my way. Peace!" He hung up the phone. He clasped the steering wheel with both hands and gazed at the windshield in contemplation. Shaheen eyed his partner, impatiently waiting for him to finish his brooding, so he could be informed of the latest news that troubled him. Gorilla Leek finally spoke.

"Yo, Blood, we need to make a change of plans."

"Where to?"

"My crib."

"What's up? What happened?" Shaheen inquired.

Gorilla Leek braced the wheel. "I'll tell you on the way. Fasten your seatbelt. I'm 'bout to push this baby!"

The Yukon made a screeching sound, with smoke saturating the air from beneath the tires. They made a U-turn and sped up the hill of Rochester Avenue.

*   *   *

They arrived at Gorilla Leek's apartment within five minutes. Gorilla Leek was the first out of the vehicle, rushing up the steps and into the building. Shaheen shadowed him as they entered the apartment.

"Where the fuck is he?" Gorilla Leek barked.

Kamarsha and the children came scrambling out of the kitchen situated to the right of the entrance.

"Daddy!"

All three of them wrapped themselves around his legs. Kamarsha sluggishly trotted toward him with her head to the ground. Her light brown skin was now pale, her eyes still revealing the shock of what she just witnessed.

Jamel tilted his head up toward his father. "Daddy, I just shot him with your gun." He pointed to the lifeless unstaunched figure lying prone in front of the bathroom at the end of the hall.

The two men glanced at the body. Shaheen drifted toward the back and stood over the dead man, who had a look of surprise imbedded in his lifeless face.

"It's Cutty, Chinnah's coac boy."

Gorilla Leek embraced Kamarsha.

"You a'ight?"

She said nothing.

"What happened?"

Jamel spoke up for his mother. "Me, Gemma, and Tracy came into the house. We saw the man in the kitchen looking under the sink, so we ran into you and Mommy's room and locked the door. I remembered where I saw you put your gun, so I climbed up on the chair, looked up in the closet, and got it. I didn't forget how you showed me to use it." A flash of pride covered his face. "You said I have to protect Mommy and my sisters, remember?"

"Yeah," Gorilla Leek replied with a smile, "now finish telling daddy what happened."

Jamel nodded, then continued.

"So I pulled the top of it back. That's when the man kicked the door open. I told him to get out, and I pointed it at him. He yelled at me, and he told me to give him the gun. I got scared when he started coming to me, so I squeezed the gun, like you showed me, and the man ran out of the room. That's when Mommy came in. The gun made me fall back on the bed, Daddy."

When he finished explaining, he stuck his chest out and lifted his chin up with an air of accomplishment.

"Are you still scared?" Gorilla Leek asked, hearing a trace of fear in the boy's voice.

"Nope . . . I protected, Mommy and my sister."

Gorilla Leek stooped low and peered into Jamel's eyes.

"Check this Jah, never ever tell anyone what happened today. You have to keep this a secret. Make sure your sisters never say anything ever about this. You feel me?"

"Yes, Daddy." Jamel gazed upon his father with worrisome eyes. "Daddy, did I do a bad thing?"

Gorilla Leek rubbed his son's head and forced a smile to surface. "Is Mommy and your sisters okay?"

Jamel acquiesced. "Yes."

Gorilla Leek stood straight up, still staring into his son's eyes and affirmed,

"Well then, you were not wrong."

Gorilla Leek glanced at Shaheen, who was talking into his cell phone.

"Yo, Blades, change of plans. I need you to round up Bloody Papers, Sinnin' Blood, Redrum, and Flames. Tell 'em to meet me over at Gorilla Leek's kingdom in one hour . . . one hour, ya heard? Don't make me wait. Got a cleanup for y'all to take care of. A'ight? Peace Almighty!"

He closed his phone and stuck it into his pocket. Fixing his gaze on Cutty's body, he quietly said, "Stupid dread . . . you got taken out by a kid."

He observed Gorilla Leek, who had his arm around Kamarsha. He thought to himself, *Leek's lucky. At least he still has his family.*

*   *   *

"She still sleep back there?" Qamara asked while reclining idly on Carla's couch.

"Yeah, that chick pretty much out of it." Carla snapped her head toward the closed bedroom door and propped down next to her friend. "She came over here really shaken up."

"I would be too if that shit happened to me. I mean, she probably feel like dying right now. That was her only son."

"That's why when she got here, I told her to go in the room and lie down. She looked exhausted like she had too much on her mind to deal with or something."

"Yo, that gotta be painful for Sha too. I mean, your only child accidentally killing himself with your gun. That would mess me up if it happened to me. I mean, technically that was his fault. That's why I don't believe in keeping guns in the house."

"And that's why you're a square. Shit, they need to keep a burner in their crib with all the shit he's into," Carla countered.

The phone's ringing interrupted their conversation. Carla reached past Qamara's chest and retrieved the cordless phone from the base.

"Hello?"

She listened keenly into the receiver trying to discern what the caller was saying.

"Oh, what up? Na, she sleep in the back. What you want me to tell her?"

There was silence from Carla as the person spoke.

"Hmm? Comin' over where? Why? What popped off? I guess so . . . What about Sha? He ain't doin' too good, you know . . . with the Shane thang and all."

Qamara examined Carla as she spoke into the phone, pondering who she could have been talking to. *Who else knows about Shane?* She contemplated as Carla conversed freely about Lola's personal business. Then it hit her; there was only one person she was aware of who knew about the incident and would have a need to call Carla's house at this moment. It was Lola's sweetheart, her secret lover, her bedroom buddy.

"A'ight. I'll tell Lo you called, and you can . . . Uh, hold on." Carla removed the phone from her ear and peered down at the screen to view the number of an incoming call. She positioned it back to her face and said, "Yo, give me a sec. I got someone calling on the other line. Hold on." She pressed the flash button on the receiver and spoke into the phone.

"Hello? Who this?"

"You'll tell me *who* called?" Lola's voice startled the two ladies who, unaware of the fact she was now awake and standing behind them, jumped at the sound of her question. They both turned behind them to find her lingering in the middle of the doorway.

"Who was that?" she asked while rubbing away any hint of the exhaustion that weighed her eyes down.

"Your dude," Carla retorted, ignoring the person on the phone. "Hold on," she said into the receiver before pressing the mute button.

"Shaheen? What did he say?" Lola's excitement now replaced her restlessness.

"Na, not Sha. Your other dude."

Lola eyelids drooped as she leisurely moved toward the couch.

"He still on the phone?" she asked flatly.

Carla, noticing the change in her demeanor, inquired, "You sure you wanna speak to him? I mean, you seem heartbroken now that you know it's not Sha."

"Heartbroken? No. I just wanted to know what was going on with Shane. What they did with my boy? As far as I'm concerned, Shaheen is the reason this happened, and he barely seems affected by this."

"Lo girl, you know he's hurting too. He's a dude. He has a different way of dealing with it. He's probably scared to death and at the same time depressed as hell," Carla explained in defense of Shaheen.

"Whatever," replied Lola. "He didn't care about us before this, and I'm sure he doesn't care now. This will probably be a reason for him to leave now. I mean, we were on shaky grounds already. I wouldn't be surprised if he was out there tricking on some other shorty."

Carla smiled.

"Yeah well, if you get tired of him, I'll be more than happy to take care of him for you."

"Bitch, watch yourself," Lola shot back.

"I'm just keeping it real, girl. Men are like shoes. If you get a new pair and you're tired of the ones you got, don't let 'em go to waste if they're still in good condition. Shoot, hook your girl up! Especially if they fit her. You know how we do!"

Lola observed her friend with malcontent. She always knew Carla had been attracted to Shaheen. She thought she was better for him because she was from the hood, Brooklyn born and Bedstuy raised, while Lola, to her, was just some little stuck up, bourgeoisie, gullible, spoiled country girl. Carla felt Lola was in no way deserving of a money go-getter like Shaheen, and the reason the two fought so often was because she wasn't used to dealing with a "real nigga." Lola just glared wide-eyed at her friend, wondering how she could speak so blatantly about being with her man at a moment like this.

Not acknowledging Carla's words, Lola uttered, "Like I said before, I love both of them. Pass me the phone."

Carla brought the phone up to her ear and without addressing the person on hold clicked over to the other line. She hearkened into the phone, then tossed it on to the couch.

"He hung up," she stated nonchalantly.

Lola hissed her teeth at Carla.

Carla ignored her gesture and blurted out, "Well, you better at least figure out who's the one if you don't get that visit soon."

"Bitch, that's my business, and it better not get outside of this apartment."

Carla leaned back and folded her arms. "Yeah, 'cause we know it'll be a wrap if Sha finds out and ole boy already think he's the one. I don't know why you told him when you're not even sure if it is true or not yet. You said dude was ready to leave his fam and all. Shit, that nigga crazy."

"Yeah, muthafuckas ain't shit!" added Qamara.

"Girl, you only got about one more month before everything is out in the open. I hope you—"

Carla was cut off by the doorbell. She ceased her preaching, then rushed past Qamara and stuck her head out of the window.

"What up, girl? That was fast! Hold on, let me get the keys."

Carla snatched the keys from off the folding table. She went back to the window and dropped them to the street below. They landed at Kamarsha's feet. Jamel seized them. Carla closed the window, then faced Lola.

"That's Kamarsha. Something happened over at their crib, so Gorilla sent her over here."

"You didn't tell her, did you?" Lola inquired with a burdensome expression on her face.

"Na, girl. What you told us stay with us. Both things!" Carla assured her.

"What do think happened?" wondered Qamara. She was licking the ends of the blunt she just rolled up.

"I don't know Q, but she didn't seem like herself. She sounded down."

"You think Malik said something?" Lola was now sitting on one of the four folding chairs.

"About what?"

"Shit, whatever he knows!" shouted Lola.

The sound of a key turning in the door was heard. It flew open. Kamarsha entered with her three children. They stripped themselves of their coats by the entry, then Kamarsha sat in the remaining chair while the kids rested their bodies upon the cushionless sofa.

"Where's Shane?" asked Gemma, the second oldest of the three.

Carla and Qamara silently viewed Lola.

"He . . . he's . . . Shane's not here." Lola rose up from the chair and ran into the bathroom holding the phone. Kamarsha observed her but said nothing.

Carla spoke up, "She and Shaheen going through some shit."

Kamarsha caught sight of Qamara lighting up the blunt.

"Jah, Gemma, and Tracy, go to the back and play in the bedroom."

The children, without hesitation, dashed into the back. Qamara, after taking her pulls off the marijuana, handed it to Carla. Noticing the blunt wrap unraveling, Carla licked her thumb and index finger and then twisted the end of it to seal it back. She placed it in the corner of her mouth.

"So what happened over there, Marsha?"

Kamarsha let out a long sigh.

"Chinnah is what happened."

Both of the ladies' faces displayed shock. Everyone knew about Chinnah and the fact that the men surrounding their lives were enemies of his.

Ever since Shaheen and Gorilla Leek started out together in their business ventures, Chinnah had been painstakingly attempting to enforce his "20 percent mine, 80 percent yours" rule on them. Each time he would ask, they would decline. At first, Chinnah wasn't concerned with them. They were just small-time street corner hustlers.

However, when they purchased Minimart on Rutland Road and Ninety-third Street, situating themselves only four blocks away from his main store, he was not only furious with them for their boldness in competing with him, but he determined it as a form of disrespect that they did not seek out his approval or at least offer him a piece of the pie.

Besides, Chinnah controlled that section of East Flatbush and Brownsville for over twenty years. Everyone on Rutland, who owned a business, whether legal or illegal, paid him. He was infamous for his green or red principle, meaning either green, you pay, or in red, you will lay. But times had changed, and with the advent of gangs in area, his retaliation for the rejection of his offer, he surmised, would only amount to war. A war he wanted to avoid. It wasn't that he was afraid of the Bloods that Shaheen and Gorilla Leek had backing them as much as it was the comfort of the position he was used to. Chinnah was old. He was pushing sixty, and in the past, he encountered numerous enemies he had to, with much effort, put down.

For the past decade he went unchallenged. The neighborhood was now quiet, so the police never interfered. He became accustomed to the respect he was given. The neighborhood businessmen's pusillanimous attitude toward him over the last ten years left him undecided on how to handle the situation. At first, he sought out an alliance with the two, only to have his messenger gunned down at the hands of Gorilla Leek over a disagreement during negotiations. Then he sent a warning, which was returned by another warning from Shaheen. "Let us live or commit suicide . . . Fuck red or green . . . Fade to black!" So Chinnah decided leaving them alone was the best choice. Besides, they ran a small time operation compared to his own, so he figured it wasn't worth the bloodshed or attention from police.

Now after robbing his spot, they left Chinnah with only one option. This was exactly what Gorilla Leek had anticipated. He wanted him dead since he was thirteen years old. It was then his mother and father were brutally murdered by Pauley for refusing to pay Chinnah in order to keep their small time laundry-mat open. Gorilla Leek would have gone after him then, but he was persuaded not to by Kane, Shaheen's older brother, who was in the middle of making a big deal with Pauley at that time. After Kane's incarceration, both Shaheen and Gorilla Leek decided to sell what was left of his stash. So they left the neighbor transporting 2.2 pounds of pure white to Scranton, Pennsylvania.

One year later, Gorilla Leek ended up getting incarcerated after a raid on one of their safe houses. At the time Shaheen was out enjoying the evening with a pleasure-seeking nineteen-year-old mountain girl. Unwilling to continue hustling out of state without the only person he trusted, Shaheen retraced his steps back to New York. He worked out of a small video store and swore to himself he would only sell weed. It wasn't until Gorilla Leek was released on parole that he was convinced they needed to go back into the coac game.

While imprisoned in Cresson Correctional Facility, Gorilla Leek was introduced to an older gentleman, from Harlem, New York. His name was Papa Tek, a Dominican who had, what seemed to Gorilla Leek, an unlimited supply of white. It was because of him they were able to purchase Minimart. It was owned by a Haitian family who was tired of being extorted by Chinnah. Though the two possessed enough narcotics and money to start up a large operation, Papa Tek ended up falling victim to an assassin's bullet, leaving them scrambling to find a consistent supplier.

While Shaheen had a vision of using their profits to finally leave the game and secure himself a respectable family lifestyle, Gorilla Leek had only one goal in mind: to become large enough to exact retribution, and he wouldn't stop until Chinnah, his son, and his business were in the ground.

Now, after tonight's incident, he was given the green light. He was tired of the little skirmishes he and Shaheen were involved in with Chinnah and his henchmen. Shaheen was never interested in the idea of killing Chinnah and starting an all-out war. Finally, he was in compliance; Chinnah will fade to black. The women surrounding Shaheen and Gorilla Leek's lives were well aware of the fact that someone was about to die.

CHAPTER 5

Blood splashed out of the tub and onto the ivory tile which covered the bathroom floor.

"Aarggh!" Sinnin Blood gripped the crimson soaked saw and with forceful rigor and raked it back and forth over what was left of Cutty's blood-soaked body. He became furious every time the instrument reached one of the bones in the swollen corpse. The arm was almost off, but the saw kept getting stuck. Most of the ligament was torn from the shoulder.

He opted to stand up from off his knees. He snatched the arm straight up into the air and stomped his foot down in between the victim's armpits. Pulling and tugging on the limb, he began pressing his foot down harder. His effort made a sickening sound. *Squish . . . squash . . . splat.* Unable to get a good footing on the arm, he removed it and planted his boot on the chest.

"Yo, how long is this going to take?" Redrum inquired while loitering in the doorway holding a large canister and a rag.

Sinnin Blood stopped struggling and fixed his gaze upon his partner, who had just interrupted him. Still holding the arm up, he pointed to the can. "What's that?"

"Sulfuric acid. Sha said to use it for the body. He said to make sure we pour some down the drain too after we rinse out the tub," answered Redrum. "Did you reglaze it before you put the body in there?"

"Yeah, and I won't forget to peel it up before we scrub down the tub. How does that acid work?"

"He said to put the body into the tub and then pour this shit in and let it sit for about two days. After that, he said to come back and clean it up."

"You mean we gotta come back here? Man, Blood been watching too many movies."

Blades approached the entrance to the bathroom and surveyed the scene. He was always reluctant to get involved in the cleanup process. He could stomach seeing someone murdered, but that was all. Chopping up bodies and burning them or having to subject himself to the smell of the corpse decomposing in acid was all too much for him. His rank as Minister Blood afforded him the power to shuffle off that responsibility to someone else. He couldn't wait until they were finished.

"Yo, can y'all hurry up? This shit is making me sick. I was supposed to been at the club since ten. Y'all got me running late!"

Looking up from the tub, Sinnin Blood asked, "Whose work is this anyway?"

Knowing the answer but not wanting to give it, Blades shouted back, "Man, stop all that yapping and get this done, so I can go hang! The shit stinks!"

Sinnin Blood didn't reply; instead he continued sawing. Blades pivoted on his heels and proceeded out the bathroom. Redrum settled the acid on the floor along with the rag and followed Blades.

Jogging to catch up, he called out, "Yo, dog, hold up!"

Blades glanced solemnly over his shoulders. "What?"

Arriving alongside his superior, he questioned, "Is it true we're going to war with Chinnah?"

Appearing disgusted, Blades hissed his teeth, then retorted, "Focus on what we need to take care of now. You're worrying about the wrong thing. Besides, we won't be doing anything if pigs decide to show up here and we haven't cleaned this mess up." Blades stopped dead in his tracks, then scrunched up his eyes at him, and asked, "Why are you out here anyway, yo? You should be helping Sin, not quizzing me . . . Bounce, yo!"

Redrum opened his mouth but uttered nothing. He was all too familiar with the consequences of displeasing Shaheen's and Gorilla Leek's top soldier; instead he opted to let out an exaggerated cough. Blades proceeded to leave the apartment. His soldier watched as he took out his cell phone, pushed a couple of buttons, and then began whispering into it.

"They're almost finished," he mumbled into the phone as he stepped past the threshold of the apartment.

*　　*　　*

Shaheen held the phone tightly to his ear while he devoured Blades' description of the cleanup status.

"Yo, come by my crib before you hit the club, and I'll have that hard for you to give to the young cat," Shaheen instructed into the phone. "'Bout to cook it up now."

He uttered a few more words, then hung up. He inspected his apartment to ensure there weren't any signs of his son's accident remaining in view for any possible future visitors. It was then he spotted the edge of a white cloth protruding from under the love seat. It was a baby wipe.

He bent over to reach for it, but it appeared to be stuck to something beneath the furniture. He was unable to see anything, so he fumbled with it until he tore it from whatever it was connected to. As he stood to his feet, he realized something about the half torn cloth. Most of it was covered in a dark brownish red color.

He held the baby wipe in his palm and examined it. It was his son's blood. A tear descended from his cheek and onto it. For a brief moment, he relived the incident in his mind and then just as quickly jammed the cloth in his pocket.

He ventured into the kitchen and glanced at the microwave's clock. It was 10:28 p.m. He stretched his hand into the opened cabinet beneath the sink and rummaged through the various household products until he found what he was fishing for. He retrieved a small black trash bag, which was folded up.

He unfolded it and removed a medium-sized ziplock bag containing cocaine.

He reached for a teaspoon that was lying in the middle of the sink, then rubbed it back and forth over his red Polo sweater to make certain it was dry. He opened the ziplock bag and stuck the spoon into it, scooping up a small amount of the powder onto the tip of it. He leaned forward and inhaled it from off the spoon.

He tilted his head back, snorted, and dropped the spoon onto the counter. Once again reaching beneath the sink, he grabbed a small boiling pot. He tossed it onto the stove then meandered over to the refrigerator, opened it, and pulled out a box of baking soda. His fingers explored the top of the refrigerator, and finding a small electronic scale, a plate, and a measuring cup, he took all three items and placed them on the counter next to the stove.

After turning on the scale, he snatched the ziplock bag and spread it out evenly on top of it. The number 28 appeared in red on the front of the screen. Satisfied he still had what he needed, he grabbed the measuring cup and ran the water from the sink's faucet into it until it measured three-fourths. He poured the water into the pot and turned the stove on medium high.

He tore a paper towel from the roll that hung beneath the upper cabinets and blanketed the plate with it. After pouring some of the baking soda onto the teaspoon, he dumped the contents from the spoon into the water. He took the ziplock bag from the counter, opened it, and flipped it upside down, emptying the powder into the pot. The mixture began bubbling.

Shaheen yanked a butter knife from the dish rack and stuck it into the pot. He started pressing it lightly on top of the water to flatten the bubbles. While the mixture cooked, he continued the flattening process until it became solid white.

Using a large metal spoon from the utensil rack hovering above the sink, he removed the cooked substance from the pot. He rested it upon the napkin, which covered the plate, allowing it to drain. Then, he carried the plate over to the refrigerator and inserted it into the freezer.

He leaned against the refrigerator and thought about the situation brewing with Chinnah. He let out a deep sigh. An uncomfortable rumbling in his stomach began bothering him. It shortened his breath each time he thought about his son. He wondered if a war with Chinnah was necessary. He was tormented by the idea of going to the cops and explaining what happened to Shane. There was no way, he fathomed, he could hide his son's death from his family or even his friends. However, the thought of life in a small cell seemed bleak.

For a moment, leaving the state appeared to be the best solution. A war, he contemplated, would only place him in deeper trouble. Besides, he could not focus on another enemy before he faced the one within himself. Then it suddenly hit him like a knife piercing his heart. *Someone will eventually question Shane's disappearance. I can't hide it forever.*

He knew if someone became suspicious, police would get involved, and when he is unable to produce his son for them, he would then become a suspect in his child's disappearance. He would be questioned as to why he was never concerned enough to report his son's absence. This was something he could not conceal forever; it would surface sooner or later. He pondered over the possible consequences of not going to the police.

Exiting the kitchen, he walked into his bathroom and grabbed a blunt and lighter from off the sink. The cigar's original contents had been removed earlier and replaced with purple haze marijuana. He lit it up and inhaled deeply. Blowing smoke into the air, he took four more deep pulls, only to exhale after the fourth. He felt the warmth of the smoke soothing his chest. His shoulders relaxed. He then smothered the fiery tip into the sink, extinguishing the flames.

Out of nowhere the sensation from the weed kicked in. Paranoia raced through his mind. He knew what he had to do. He swung around on his heels and headed toward the living room. Grabbing his jacket from the love seat, he bolted out of his apartment, barely closing the door behind him. As he hustled down the staircase, taking three steps at once, he opened up his cell phone and began dialing 911. He was in such a hurry he had forgotten about the cocaine in his freezer.

*   *   *

Detective Torturro held his twinkie up to examine it under the ceiling light that hovered above him from the Sixty-seventh Precinct. He viewed it curiously, inspecting the makeup of the edible object, then brought it down to his eye level. Pausing as if he had an epiphany, he then tossed it whole into his mouth with ease. He brought his attention to Thomas, who was busy yelling into the phone. Realizing Thomas was too engrossed in his screaming session to indulge in a conversation with him, he turned to Detective Cannon, who was walking by his desk, holding a bottle of water in his hand.

"Hey, Cannon, how do you suppose they get the cream into this cake?" Torturro inquired before opening his mouth to reveal the white and yellow mush that covered his tongue.

Cannon halted and then eyed him in disgust. "What the hell did that used to be?"

"A twinkie!" Torturo exclaimed as if shocked by Cannon's innocence.

"Whatever." Cannon rolled his eyes and waved Torturo off. "Look, I have a missing child case to attend to. The vic's father has been sitting at my desk for over an hour. You know how impatient parents can be. So I don't have time for your 'did the chicken or the egg come first' theories. Some of us here are real detectives."

Torturro blankly stared at Cannon as he trodded away. "Yeah, you're a real dick all right."

Cannon heard Torturro's comment but decided to ignore it. He continued his journey past the dope fiends, prostitutes, thieves, and murderers that occupied the many cells that lined the walls of the precinct.

As he approached his desk, he realized he forgot to get the M&M'S for the gentleman he was assisting. He started to turn around and go back; however, he dismissed the idea, thinking the man would much rather he solve this case than present him with the snack he requested. Cannon approached the man seated at his desk.

"Here you go," Cannon handed the water to him. "The machine was out of M&M'S."

Shaheen glanced over his right shoulder to reach for the water. "Thank you."

Cannon seated himself in his chair, rumbled through a stack of papers and, without casting his eyes on Shaheen, dully stated, "We have what we need so far to conduct an investigation. However, I strongly advise you contact us if you can remember anything else regarding your son's disappearance." Cannon eyed the paper he was searching for, then brought his gaze up to Shaheen and asked, "You are sure you have no reason to suspect kidnap?"

Shaheen swallowed deeply before answering, "No, not that I can think of. I mean, one minute he was in the front room watching TV, and the next, he was gone."

"Well, we are going to need to speak with the mother, and we will be sending two uniformed officers by your house to examine the place for any evidence of foul play. You know, just in case." Detective Cannon stood up from his chair while extending his hand.

Shaheen rose to accept Cannon's hand. "Please, sir, just find my boy."

Showing no emotion, Cannon informed, "We will do our best. Please go home and await our call. We will be in contact with you soon."

Shaheen wondered if the detective believed his story because he appeared to either be unconcerned with his predicament or in disbelief of it. He couldn't tell.

He contemplated whether he may have given himself away by talking too much or by contradicting any of his statements.

In his mind, he replayed what he told Cannon. He couldn't find any inconsistencies, so he dismissed the idea.

Instead he beheld Cannon's eyes and allowed an expression of torment to surface from his face. "Thank you, sir. I know you will help me. I know he will be all right."

It pained him to bring those words from his lips: *I know he will be all right.* He hung his head low and deliberately pivoted around as if the weight of his shoes were too heavy to move. This was all part of his dramatic role. He even amazed himself at how good he was portraying a grieving father of a missing boy. Then again, he questioned whether he was acting.

As Shaheen began walking to exit the station, Cannon remembered he forgot to give the man his personal contact information. He called out to the grieving father, "Hey, sir."

Shaheen, too busy wallowing in his thoughts, didn't hear him. He kept walking. Then noticing that Shaheen was headed toward Detective Torturro's desk, he called out to him, "Torturro!"

Torturro looked up from the conversation he was having with a female officer about twinkies. "What's up?"

"Stop that gentleman in the leather for me."

Shaheen heard the detective but was uncertain if he was referring to him or not. Torturro took in a glimpse of his surroundings but saw no one. He then noticed the young man approaching him.

"Um, excuse me, sir." Torturro extended his hand.

Shaheen stopped. He raised his eyebrow, then curiously eyed the detective. *Oh shit. They didn't believe me. They know what happened.* Still high, his paranoia started to get the best of him. He considered bolting past the detective and running out of the precinct. Instead, he received the detective's handshake.

"Hi, my name is Detective Torturro. Look, I am sure you would like to leave this place as soon as possible considering whatever you are going through. However, there is one more thing Detective Cannon would like to speak to you about."

Both men alternated their attention to Detective Cannon who was fumbling around his desk.

Cannon realized both men were staring at him.

"Torturro, do you have a card with the station's main number on it at your desk?" Cannon asked while tossing paper and folders to the side.

"Sure," acknowledged Torturro. As he scanned beneath him to find a card in the pile of paperwork that covered his desk, his attention was drawn to Shaheen who was rummaging through his pockets. He glanced at the young man and, taking in his scars, stopped his search efforts to assess his face.

"No need for the card. I might have a pen and a piece of paper to write it down on," Shaheen informed him as he continued searching. He was desirous of leaving the precinct as quickly as possible. As he removed his hand from his pants revealing a red ink pen, he unintentionally brought a piece of cloth out with it. It dangled from his right pocket. It was stained with dried-up blood.

Torturro couldn't help but see it. He surveyed Shaheen's person observing to see if anything else appeared to be out of place or wrong. He decided to be blunt.

"Sir, are you still bleeding?"

Shaheen appeared baffled by the detective's question.

"I'm sorry? I don't understand your question."

Detective Torturro pointed to Shaheen's pocket. "You have a bloody tissue hanging from your pocket, and the scratches on you face look recent."

Shaheen glanced down at the baby wipe protruding from his pants. He tried to think of an explanation, but his mind wouldn't move quickly enough. He opened his mouth but had nothing to say. Instead, he appeared surprised by Torturro's discovery, and then it hit him.

"I thought I threw that away. Besides the scratches, I had a really bad nosebleed." Shaheen tucked the baby wipe deeper into his pants. "I was in a small fender bender yesterday."

Hearing the discussion between Torturro and Shaheen, Detective Thomas raised his sight up from his desk. His attention left the phone conversation. He shoved his hand inside his blazer and retrieved his wallet. He opened it up and pulled out a card. He then removed the receiver from his ear and motioned to Torturro.

"Here, I have a card for the young man."

Torturro paid Thomas no attention. His gut feeling was telling him something was not right about Shaheen's answer, but he couldn't put his finger on it. There was something that bothered him about the man in front of him. His thoughts were brought to a halt by the card in Thomas's hand, which was now directly in front of his face.

"You can give him this. The station's main number is on it. He can just ask for Cannon." Torturro calmly grabbed the card from Thomas and passed it to Shaheen. Without saying another word, Shaheen accepted it, then spun on his heels, and made his way toward the exit.

Torturro continued his staring as the young man walked off. "You're welcome!" He exclaimed sarcastically. Without facing the detective, Shaheen threw his hand up into the air and gestured. Torturro turned to Thomas.

"Ungrateful son of a bitch."

A smirk appeared on Thomas's face. "His case hasn't been solved yet, so I wouldn't say he was ungrateful. Suspicious maybe, but not ungrateful."

Torturro squinted his eyes at Thomas as if he was trying to read his mind. "I'm not following."

Thomas smiled at his rookie partner's ignorance, knowing he was about to enlighten him. "This is the father of a missing child, right?"

Torturro nodded his head, hoping Thomas would skip the dramatics and suspense and just explain what he meant.

"He seemed to be in a hurry to leave for someone who doesn't know where his child is." Torturro nodded his head.

Thomas continued, "What was in his pocket?"

Torturro raised his eyebrow. "Are you referring to the tissue?"

Still smiling, Thomas corrected him. "It wasn't a tissue. It was a baby wipe."

"Okay?" Torturro didn't understand where his partner was going with his questions.

Seeing Torturro was having a hard time understanding what he was trying to show him, he decided to get to the point. "This man came in and reported a missing child, yet he also had a baby wipe hanging from his pants that was covered in blood. A baby wipe! When you questioned him, he seemed startled by your observation and took a second before he answered you."

Torturro elevated his eyebrow, and an expression of innocence covered his face. "You know, I could sense something but wasn't sure. He is hiding something, isn't he?"

"Not sure. Not our case."

"Hey, guys!" Cannon yelled out while walking toward the two. "Did you give that gentleman a card?"

Both men nodded.

"Well, there was no need to rush him off. He can't go anywhere."

Both men eyed the detective, not understanding what he was implying. Cannon held a set of keys up to the men's face.

"He forgot his car keys. One of you guys mind running this out there to him. I have a couple of important calls I have to make."

Thomas snatched the keys from Cannon's grasp and, without saying a word, made his way outside.

Cannon cast his eyes on Torturro. "He's in a helpful mood today, I see."

"No, he's just playing detective again," replied Torturro. "He's part bloodhound and part human." Both men laughed.

As Thomas stepped through the doors of the precinct, he ran dead into Shaheen, who was on his way back into the building. Thomas held the keys up.

"You forgot something?"

An expression of relief appeared on Shaheen's face. "Yeah, I was just coming back in there for those." Thomas handed the keys to him.

"You weren't going to get too far."

"Who you telling?" Shaheen could discern a peculiar grin forming on the detective's face.

Both men stood there in silence for what felt like an eternity to Shaheen. He became uncomfortable from the detective's blatant stare. Thomas only smiled but said nothing. Shaheen slightly redirected his gaze, but Thomas motioned his head in order to follow his eyes. He wouldn't let them escape him. Shaheen decided to end the interaction.

"Look I have to go. I have some business to attend to." The detective continued smiling, saying nothing. Shaheen did not bother to extend his hand. He crossed the street and headed toward his SUV. Detective Thomas, noticing Shaheen's vehicle, tilted his head to the side then squinted his eyes. *A Ford Expedition,* he thought. *What are the odds?*

Shaheen revved his engine to life then peeled off from his parking space. The detective viewed the back of the SUV. *ALA 3459.* He took a mental note of the license, then abruptly ran back into the precinct. He needed to discuss this case with Detective Cannon. His curiosity concerning the missing child was heightened.

CHAPTER 6

The constant ringing of telephones and the sounds of various papers being shuffled, along with the sobbing and crying of impatient infants, disturbed Lola's eardrums. She waited furiously while seated in the emergency patient area of Brookdale Hospital. Not even forty-eight hours had passed since the death of her son, and mentally she was in no condition to be sitting in an environment with other children and their mothers.

However, she had been throwing up all morning, which eventually culminated in her becoming faint. At first, she was reluctant to agree with Carla, who told her she needed to go to the hospital. Yet after falling out unconscious, she decided to allow her friend to ride along in the cab with her to the emergency room.

She attempted to clear her mind by remembering moments from her childhood in Georgia. That only depressed her more. *What happened to me? I have changed.* She pondered over whether Shane's death was her fault. *No, it was Shaheen's gun, so it was his fault.* She attempted to deflect the guilt she was feeling, not the guilt from being the cause of her son's untimely death, but she was finding a justification for leaving Shaheen now for her other lover.

She knew it was an irrational and immature idea because her lover was married with children. Not just married, but married to her friend. She felt bothered by the fact she was not only cheating behind Shaheen's back but that it was also with her girlfriend's man. She began to imagine the repercussions of her secret being exposed to Shaheen just as Carla came strutting in the waiting area. Holding an opened can of ginger ale, she approached Lola.

"They ain't seen you yet?" she yelled out.

Lola shook her head, then reached out for the can.

Carla passed it to Lola before throwing her hands upon her hip.

"You need to make some noise up in this piece or you'll never be seen." Carla glanced around and, without looking in any particular direction, said, "That's the problem with y'all country chicks. Y'all too passive."

Lola ignored her. She studied the can in her hand, shook it, and then held it up in the air toward Carla.

"You drunk from this?"

An expression of embarrassment formed around Carla's face.

"Just a little. I haven't had a ginger ale in a while, and besides, I paid for it."

Lola expressed a look of confusion. She then leaned her head forward and as if talking to an infant, appealed to her friend. "Carla, I'm the one sick."

Carla cast her gaze to the floor. "Yeah, you right. You've been through a lot this week. I shouldn't be so selfish. I'll go get you another one."

Lola grabbed her stomach suddenly in an attempt to settle the sharp pain that just struck her. While holding her midsection, she raised the can toward Carla, dropped her head, then said, "It's all right. I'm good. Hold this for me."

Carla accepted the can, then eyed Lola quizzically, "You a'ight?"

Lola shook her head before raising it and revealing a contorted expression upon her face. "Yeah, I'm good."

"Bell, Lola?" A soft voice drew the girls' attention. "Lola Bell," the nurse repeated in such a melodious tone it almost sounded as if she were singing.

Lola's stomach began to settle as her gaze left the nurse for a brief moment. Her eyes wandered across the walls surrounding her. She took a mental note of how dull the white paint was. It was depressing, she thought. It reminded her of the visitation room she waited in when Shaheen was incarcerated for possession of a firearm.

"Lola Bell?" the nurse sung once more.

Carla gently touched Lola's knee. "Hunny, I know what you are thinking and why you are hesitating to go in there, but you need to get up now before she decides to call the next person. We've been here for mad long now. Get up, mommy."

Lola's attention was drawn back to the young dark-skinned blonde. She lazily rose from the hard silver iron chair. She proceeded toward the double doors the nurse held open with her foot. As she neared the woman, she contemplated the consequences she faced if her worst nightmares were true. She stopped just in front of the doors and then whipped her head back toward Carla.

"I'm not pregnant, bitch." She followed the nurse into the room.

*   *   *

The long-bearded young gentleman peered through his dark sunglasses at the constant movement of the many zombies, aimlessly trotting the sidewalks that flanked both sides of his sedan. He lightly puffed on a Newport as he sat alert in the driver's seat. *America is a dreadful country,* he thought as his eyes searched the environment around him. It was a little past noon, yet the sun appeared to be shy as it hid itself from the world behind a gloomy veil of dark clouds.

Pitkin Avenue was busy with poverty-stricken would-be shoppers who bargained more than they purchased. They mingled with countless of teenagers who were either hanging out in front of one of the many shops that lined the block or who were scrambling up and down the pavement marketing stolen merchandise and offering narcotics to nearly everyone whom they passed.

The streets appeared to have its own soundtrack as the chattering of several voices combined with the clattering of the many footsteps marching back and forth resonated throughout the air. The melody was carried to the surrounding blocks as a strong gust of autumn wind swept through the neighborhood.

The bearded gentleman began to turn on his stereo when he saw a familiar face stroll past his car. He followed the man's movement from his rearview mirror as he watched him walk about twenty feet beyond his position before glancing around, then suddenly entering the hallway to an apartment building situated in between a clothing store and a bodega. He found whom he was waiting for.

Gorilla Leek didn't see the bearded man watching him as he made his way into Mama Young's apartment building. He made certain to scan the area about him in search of police or anyone who knew him. He continued past a second door, paused, then waited in the hall.

He wasn't sure if he was making the right decision, but he knew Mama Young's building was the most vacant one on the block. She was the only tenant, and she kept herself locked in her third-floor apartment, feeding off cans of sardines. He knew anywhere else would mean death for him. His face was too known.

Gorilla Leek was positive no one saw him. At least, that is what he thought. If he would have remained outside for just a little while longer instead of rushing to get out of view, he would have seen the tall dark bearded youth getting out of the car, cocking a 9 mm in his right hand.

Gorilla Leek glanced at his watch. If he would've refrained from doing this, he would have caught a glimpse of the bearded man entering the hallway with the gun pointed directly at his forehead. As his eyes left his watch, his heart dropped. It was too late to reach for his gun. His cell phone rang.

*   *   *

Shaheen hung up the phone, wondering why Gorilla Leek hadn't been answering his calls. This was unlike him, unless he was with a woman. *Yeah, he's probably with a chick.* Shaheen smiled.

He contemplated telling him what he had done with the cops, but he figured Gorilla Leek wouldn't understand and would probably just freak out. Instead, he continued walking down Fulton Avenue in Downtown Brooklyn until he came to a pizza shop. He paused, then pondered going in to grab a slice.

He had initially ventured downtown to purchase some new clothes. He always went shopping when he needed to clear his mind and think. He hadn't yet decided what he wanted because his mind would not allow him to stop thinking about his son. The war with Chinnah was insignificant compared to the death of his only child. In fact, it was his lifestyle that led to his son's death and the war with Chinnah. It was the same gun that caused both.

He walked into the pizza shop. He glanced up at the menu but couldn't see past the face of his son, which hovered in front of it. He saw the hole in Shane's head with blood flowing out like a faucet onto the pizza oven below it. He saw his son's lips moving, but instead of hearing the sounds of an infant, he heard the voice of a grown man. *"Not you . . . you, you!"* The words began to fade as they echoed. He didn't understand. He began to reply when his daydream was disrupted by another voice.

"You! You! A . . . You!" Shaheen directed his attention to the husky red-faced man behind the counter who was covered in an apron stained by tomato sauce and wine. "What are you having?"

Shaheen returned his eyes to the menu. Shane was gone.

"Well, I don't have all day. There are other customers behind you."

Shaheen cast a hateful leer at the man who looked down to the ground then back up, but not directly into his eyes. The man then lifted his gaze and focused on the corner behind Shaheen.

"Yo, watch how the fuck you yappin!" Shaheen hardened his eyes even more. "Fuck who's behind me. Ain't no one beefing but you! Open your mouth up again like that, and I'll cut the shit wide-open!"

The man appeared terrified. The customers were silent. He kept his eyes fixed on the back corner of the store.

Shaheen glanced around, then back at the man. His cold expression reverted to warm. His frown became a smile. He wondered for a moment what the man was staring at behind him. Shaheen considered he must have been so terrified he didn't want to take in his eyes at all.

"Now, may I have one cheese slice, please?" he humbly asked.

The man was baffled by the sudden change in Shaheen's demeanor. He couldn't tell if he was going to harm him or not.

"Yes, sir, one slice it is. W-w-would you like th-that warm or h-h-hot?" he said nervously.

Shaheen's raised his eyebrow as the upper left corner of his lip went up.

"The hell you think?"

"I'm . . . I'm not sure, sir. I wouldn't . . ."

"Nigger, I want it hot!"

The man was not sure if he was now scared or furious for being called a nigger. He experienced this once before but not from a *nigger*. When he had first came to America as a boy, he was told by an older American man that all Sicilians came from the Moors, who were niggers. So that made him the offspring of a nigger, not a white man. He was angered by the man's comments, but before he could counter, he was getting his face smashed in by the gentlemen and his friends.

"No problem" is all his heart would allow him to reply.

He hacked a slice from the 18 inch pie, threw it into the open oven, then glanced back at the corner.

"Is that all, sir?"

Shaheen slammed a twenty dollar bill down onto the counter, turned on his heels, and proceeded out of the store.

"I'll be back in a second. Get my change right!"

As Shaheen walked out onto the sidewalk, he didn't recognize the slim short man in the black leather jacket following him out of the store. Shaheen traveled across Fulton Street to the other side of the block. He stood outside of a sneaker store, staring into a window. The slim stalker remained on the outside of the pizza store and watched as Shaheen window-shopped. The man assessed his environment, then discreetly unzipped his jacket, and reached inside. His hand came back out with a small .380 pistol. He cocked the gun, and then positioned his hand inside his outer pocket, concealing the weapon.

Kam began crossing the street and approaching Shaheen. He had spent the evening riding in a cab following behind him since he left his home. He even observed him walking into the police station. He instantly reported it to Pauley, who instructed him to follow Shaheen a little longer, at least until the next day, to find out what he was up to. Witnessing nothing else, which appeared to be worthwhile, he was given the go-ahead with the plan. *One shot to the head, then walk away* is what he thought as he neared Shaheen.

As he came in range of his target, he noticed a young woman walking toward Shaheen. Kam recognized her. Her caramel complexion stood out among the gray and bland faces that surrounded her. Shaheen, not paying attention, gradually began to step backward from the store window. She was approaching him from his left when he backed into her, causing her to drop the two textbooks she held in her hands.

Kam stopped at the curb in front of a payphone and lay hold of the receiver. He pretended to dial while he watched Shaheen scramble on the ground to pick up the young lady's books.

"Damn!" exclaimed the young lady. "You need to watch where you're going, brother."

Shaheen quickly retrieved the fallen items from the ground. "Look, ma, I'm sorry." He handed her the books. "I was in my own world," he said sorrowfully.

The lady detected a hint of sadness in his voice. She had always been good with knowing a person's feelings. She took pride in the fact she could read most people. She stared deep into Shaheen's eyes. They betrayed him. He was lamenting over something or maybe someone, she felt. Her anger dissipated. She was now curious about the soft-spoken gentleman in front of her.

"It's all right," she replied. "I can see you have a lot on your mind."

Shaheen was surprised how quickly she read him.

"Whatever it is, know that life will present you with more of the same, but the Most High will never burden you with more than you can handle. So if you are going through a lot, then it says a lot about your character. You are a strong person. You can get through it."

His mind was blown. Her words while true and reasonable were also erotic to him. As she prescribed her own remedy for him, he watched every movement of her heart-shaped lips. She was different from most females he knew. None ever spoke of the "Most High" before to him.

Kam watched the two interact, convincing himself there was nothing he could do now. The lady would surely recognize him and might even possibly identify him to the cops. He glanced behind him and spotted a cab approaching him. He stuck out his hand and waved it down. The cab stopped, and he entered.

He retrieved his cell phone to contact Pauley but then shoved it back into his jacket upon noticing the battery was dead. Kam watched Shaheen, not sure of how his boss was going to react when he told him the news. He bit his lip while glowering intensely in Shaheen's direction. *You time is limited, young boy.*

Suddenly, for a second, Shaheen became paranoid. He felt as if someone was watching him. His eyes darted up and down the block. His head twisted to both sides, then he swung around and saw a cab pulling off. With his eyes squinting, he attempted to see who was in it. He couldn't make out the driver or the passenger. He took in a deep breath, then let it out. He relaxed. He thought he was going insane. *I'm too paranoid. I can't stay in New York,* he thought.

"Are you okay?" His attention was brought back to the lady in front of him. "You seem very troubled. You know, conscious is a killer."

He cocked his head to the side and allowed his pupils to scan her figure. She was beautiful. Her long locks flowed freely down the back of her thick red, yellow, and green knitted sweater. Her thighs formed sumptuous curves from beneath the tight long green skirt that came down to her ankles. To Shaheen, the pocketbook that hung from her left shoulder resembled a small straw basket. There was a small button pinned to the outside of it. It was a picture of the Ethiopian flag, with a Lion of Judah in front of it.

The sight of her almond-shaped eyes froze Shaheen. Her eyelashes almost seemed too long to be real. She stood the same height as Shaheen, but he could tell from the length of her slim waist; her legs were extremely long. Though she spoke as an American, he detected a slight accent in her speech.

"I'm good." Shaheen came out of his trance. "Where are you from?"

"Flatbush," she answered.

"No, I mean your family. You know, your background."

She let out a deep sigh. "I don't really see my family like that. I am kind of alone out here in New York."

"Where did you live before New York?"

"Miami," she answered.

Shaheen, not wanting to become frustrated by her refusal to answer his initial question directly, decided to be candid.

"What island is your family from?"

"Jamaica."

As she declared forcefully and with pride, his hearing was blocked out by a scent of the Egyptian musk oil that caused his brain to focus on smelling rather listening. Her odor was intoxicating. He recognized her musk but had never experienced it coming from someone's flesh with such a beautifully mild scent. Beyond the pollution of Brooklyn's sewage, hotdog stands, pissed-stained streets, and other foul odors was the invitation the air surrounding her extended to his senses.

"A lot of the people in my neighborhood are Yardy," He explained.

"Where are you from?" It was her turn to do the interviewing.

He lifted his head up and suck out his chest. "Brownsville. But I live in the Nineties now." It was then he realized he was striking up a conversation with this beautiful young lady without even knowing her name. But before he could ask, she threw another question out at him.

"And what is your name? 'Cause you haven't even introduce yourself, but you are asking me all types of questions."

He grinned. "Shaheen," he said while scanning the block, hoping Lola and her friends weren't in the area. "And your name?"

"Sheba," she answered.

Glancing across the street at the pizza shop, Shaheen remembered he had ordered a slice. He decided to cut his conversation short, but he didn't want to let this beautiful woman get away from him. There was something about her he needed to become familiar with. He decided to ask for her number.

"Won't you give me a way to contact you?"

She started blushing. She wasn't certain if giving this gentleman her number was a good idea; however, he was very handsome and didn't seem like a bad guy.

Shaheen could tell she was reluctant to give out her information in the first place, but he also knew she was interested in him. "I have to be out, but I would like to speak to you at another time. You know, to get to know you."

She smiled and then began sounding off the numbers to her phone.

"3-4-7-2-4-6 . . ."

Shaheen hurriedly searched the inside of his pants pocket for his cell phone. Finding it, he flipped it opened, then began typing the numbers into it, attempting to get all the numbers in before he forgot them.

"1-5-5-5"

He typed it in and saved it in his phonebook under her name.

"You have it?" she asked.

"Yeah, I got it," he assured.

"Okay then, you can get back to where you were going, and I can head home to brush off my poor books."

They both laughed.

"A'ight ma, I'll hit you up sometime tonight."

"You do that." She paused to stare into his eyes, then quickly walked off. Without glancing back, she spoke aloud, "Take some time out for yourself to clear your head."

Shaheen watched her hips sway from side to side as she strolled down the street. Her movement was slow and rhythmic like a cat carefully strutting toward its intended prey. She was extremely attractive, but that wasn't what captured his curiosity. There was something else about her, but he couldn't put his finger on it. He had to find out what was behind her mysterious aura and the words that feebly attempted to conceal her wisdom.

He decided to cease his adoring and calmly cross the street. His appetite was gnawing at the inside of his stomach. He had not eaten since yesterday. His mind had been too occupied with his predicament. His nerves shook up the thoughts in his head. He wasn't sure if going to the police was the right thing to do. He decided to try calling Gorilla Leek one more time before he entered the store. After getting no answer, he walked through the doors.

The man behind the counter fetched the bag containing Shaheen's slice when he saw him walk in. He quickly moved toward the front of the counter where Shaheen had stopped.

"Here you go, sir. If it is not hot enough, I can put it back into the oven." He paused and nervously awaited his reply.

Shaheen, addressing him calmly as if he did not just threaten the man earlier said, "It's okay. I'll take it whichever way I get it. I'm starving."

The man, confused by the sudden change in Shaheen's attitude and the forgetfulness of his previous demand regarding the temperature of the pizza, decided to win over his kindness.

"Did you know that guy in the black cow skin?"

Shaheen didn't comprehend. "Huh?"

He could see Shaheen was unaware of the slim short man who took an interest in him. He figured he would inform him he was being watched in order to ensure he stayed on his good side.

"This little fellow in a black leather jacket rushed in here and sat down in the back corner there but wouldn't buy anything. He just kept staring out the window as if he was waiting for someone. Then you showed up, and he couldn't keep his eyes off you. It was then I realized he was trying to get in my store before you passed by. I think it was a coincidence you came into the store he was using to watch you from."

He paused to swallow. "When you walked out, he got up and followed you, then waited by the payphones across from you while you were flirting with that pretty lady."

Shaheen, realizing he wasn't paranoid earlier, inquired. "Where did he go?"

"He got in a cab."

"Which way did the cab go?"

"Down Fulton toward Court Street."

"Did you hear the man speak?" Shaheen knew he only had one enemy, at least he thought. He was certain he was being followed, and it wasn't because he was being admired.

"Yeah. Before you came in, I asked him if he needed some help, and he said some shit in the Jamaican language, then demanded I give him a second. I thought he meant a second to order, not to check you out."

Shaheen smirked at the idea that the man would call it "Jamaican language." Whirling on his heels and leaving his pizza on the counter, he bolted out of the store. He regarded both ends of the block before turning left and sprinting toward his car.

CHAPTER 7

"Ah yuh shaw oonu rawda andel it like dis?"[22] inquired the long-bearded man. Gorilla Leek just stared while keeping his attention to the pistol the man now held down at his side. Gorilla Leek noted the weapon, while no longer pointed at him, was still off safety.

"Man, ya'll swore there would be ten kis, but there were only four. Y'all playing games or what?" Gorilla Leek asked. "You dudes should know what you have in your own spot!"

The man calmly answered him, "Nuh wurri dat. Yuh haffi focus pon de bizness at and . . . settin' up de staw dehso, Jah know?"[23]

"I told you, I don't know what you're talking about! I'm only speaking to him. I don't know you like that! A nigga tired of yapping with you. I'm not dealing with no one else. Tell him I ain't doing no more talking to strangers!" Gorilla Leek yelled.

The man sighed before letting out a slight smile. "Stranga? Ah ooh? Mi? Ney!"[24] He offered his hand to Gorilla Leek, who

---

[22] "Are you sure you rather handle it like this?"
[23] "Don't worry about that. You have to focus on the business at hand . . . setting up the store there, you know?"
[24] "Stranger? Who? Me? Never!"

refused the gesture. "Mi name, Blue Jay."[25] Still smiling, he sarcastically replied, "Now mi nuh stranga."[26]

Gorilla Leek's anger grew. "Nigga, fuck you! I want to speak to him!"

Unaffected by the disrespect that seeped past the lips of the man in front of him, Blue Jay calmly voiced his thoughts. "Im nuh truss yuh. Im tink yuh bandooloo"[27]

"Nigga, you think I trust him?" Gorilla Leek blatantly glowered down at his gun. "Or you!"

Blue Jay grinned once more. It bothered Gorilla Leek he was so emotionless, especially when he spoke, which he didn't do much of.

Blue Jay opened his mouth. "Look mon, seckle down. Oonu an yuh paadi weren't pose ta kill Trevor, ongle Stick, Fats, an Dada. Yuh buckup im fi still make dis deal wit yuh."[28]

"Man, tell that dude I only have one interest . . . and that's his peoples dead!" Gorilla Leek's eyes pierced deep into the man's shades. "Ya heard? Nothing matters more to me than that. No deals, no money, no friends, nothing will get in the way of that. I have been raised, since a boy, solely on that thought!"

Still grinning, Blue Jay said nothing. Gorilla Leek wasn't sure if the man was taking him seriously.

"Yo, man, I'm not continuing this convo with you. If he wants to deal, he needs to speak to me directly"—Gorilla Leek glanced back at the man's gun—"and you need to put that away. You ain't scaring no one."

The young man stared blankly at him as if he didn't understand or just didn't care. Gorilla Leek could tell the bearded killer did not like him, but it no longer bothered him.

---

[25] "My name is Blue Jay."

[26] "Now, I'm no stranger."

[27] "He doesn't trust you. He thinks you are untrustworthy."

[28] "Look man, settle down. You and your friend weren't suppose to kill Trevor, only Stick, Fats, and Dada. You are lucky he is still making this deal with you."

He was there for business, and the person he was scheduled to meet did not show up. Instead he had to deal with this enigmatic fool who appeared like he'd rather kill than converse now.

Blue Jay tucked the gun in his pants. His hand delved into his left pocket and came back out with a cell phone. Opening it up, he began dialing. After typing the number into the device he held it to his ear and waited patiently.

"Eeh, dis bwoy seh im ongle wan chat wit yuh."[29] He paused while the person on the other line replied. Gorilla Leek could hear a voice screaming over the phone, but he couldn't detect what was being said. The phone wasn't loud enough.

"Awight, awight. Mi let im know."[30] He hung up the phone.

"Da baas seh im fi meet yuh tanite at de staw . . ."[31]

Gorilla Leek grew angry. "You mean to tell me, with all that screaming, that's all he said? What? I came out here for nothing?"

Gorilla Leek brushed past him and bopped hard toward the door to exit the building. "I'm out of here."

Blue Jay smiled once more.

"Eh mon!"[32] Hearing the man, Gorilla Leek glanced over his shoulder before exiting. "Next time mi deya,"[33]—he pointed his index finger at his own eyes—"make shaw yuh fi keep yuh windows open. If mi wa ere fi kill yuh, mon . . . yuh be dead!"[34]

Gorilla Leek sucked his teeth and continued out the door. He threw his hand up at him without glancing back. "Nigga,

---

[29] "Yeah, this boy said he only wants to talk with you."

[30] "Alright, alright. I will let him know."

[31] "The boss said he will meet you tonight at the store . . ."

[32] "Hey, man!"

[33] "Next time I'm around,"sa

[34] "Make sure you keep your eyes open. If I was here to kill you, man . . . you would be dead!"

please." The door slammed behind him. Blue Jay's smile gradually became a frown seething with anger.

*   *   *

"I told you!" Carla exclaimed while she walked alongside Lola down her block.

They neared Lola's apartment building. Loud music with a heavy bass line coming from a car passing by electrified the air around them. The children, who were playing football in the street, ceased their game to scatter out of the way of the speeding Honda Accord. If it weren't for the music, the engine would have been the loudest sound coming from the vehicle. Once the car was out of view, the two continued their conversation.

"Bitch, I didn't say it wasn't possible. I was just trying to not think about it. I didn't want to make it a reality by speaking on it. Words are powerful." Lola snapped back.

"Yeah, well, silence must be also because you're still pregnant. You knew you were. You were just in denial. If you didn't believe it, you wouldn't have told dude." Carla said in an "as a matter of fact" tone. She continued, "And since you told him, you must think it's his or you would have said something to Sha."

Lola, becoming nervous, spewed, "Sshh! You don't have to be so loud, girl." Quickly glancing behind her, she searched the faces of the many people hanging out on the sidewalk. "I didn't tell Shaheen because I have more to lose if it is not him. You know, especially now with everything that happened to Shane and all."

The streetlights began to flicker. The lumination in the sky was moderately becoming purple as night began to set in. Carla threw her head to the ground at the mentioning of her friend's son. She felt sorry for Lola for a brief moment. She wondered how she would react if it had happened to her child. She thought about it for a second and, just as quickly, dismissed the thought.

She wasn't able to bear children, and the truth was that girls like Lola were lucky to have a baby daddy like Shaheen. In her opinion, Lola was messing up a good thing by sleeping around.

While Carla herself always chased many men, it was only because she could not find one good one. Hence, she dated a hundred bad ones to make up for it. To Carla, pretty girls like Lola, who were guilty of loving attention but acted innocent, attracted all the good guys.

She decided to change the subject. "So what do you think about the whole Chinnah situation?"

Lola stopped in front of her building.

"I think that Shaheen needs to let it go." Lola glanced around. "It's going to cause too much problems . . . serious problems. I don't need a baby daddy getting killed."

Carla just stared at her friend, not really certain of how to reply and not knowing who she was actually talking about.

"Yeah, I feel you girl."

"Umm, excuse me, ladies." A short and pudgy Caucasian male in a black leather coat and black dress slacks cut the two women's conversation short. He approached the sidewalk, turning sideways to pass through the two parked cars that appeared as sentries guarding the space between himself and the ladies. He was being followed by three other men, two of whom were wearing police uniforms. Carla instantly recognized the face of the tall slender black man who trailed behind the uniformed officers. *He's a homo dick,* she thought to herself.

The pudgy detective's slacks seemed to have somehow gotten stuck on one of the cars' fender. He tugged on it until it tore free. A chunk of his pants was now a part of the vehicle. He heeded the two ladies' chuckles. His cheeks became blazing red with embarrassment as if he attempted to conceal a light bulb in his mouth.

He dug into his jacket pocket and yielded his badge. Presenting it to the women he continued his introduction. "Hello, ladies. Pardon me for interrupting your conversation.

My name is Detective Cannon. I was looking for a Lola Montague."

He could tell by the surprised reaction that suddenly appeared on Lola's face that either she was the person he was searching for or she at least knew where to find that individual.

Carla was the first to speak up. "Why? What did she do?"

Cannon smiled. He thought to himself. *The first thing they think when they see us is "What did I do now?" And they wonder why we come into their neighborhood suspecting everyone. This is the reason we had to burn those civlian homes back in Panama when we were trying to get Noriega out. We did not know who to suspect.*

Cannon took pride in the fact he was once a soldier who saw action. It made him feel a degree of superiority over Thomas and his other colleagues who didn't have any military background. He felt as if he was born to be in enforcement. That, coupled with his insecurity regarding his height, made him staunchly addicted to holding authority. His only regret now was letting his weight go.

"She is in no trouble. Well, at least not with us. We just needed to speak to her concerning her child."

Carla unconsciously took a step back. Lola had confided in her the truth of what happened to Shane and now not only were detectives involved, but a homicide detective at that. She indolently turned toward Lola as if signaling to the detective who she was.

Thoughts began racing through Lola's head. *Could they know? How? Do they think I did it? Should I tell them I'm sorry.* Lola's eyes became watery. A frown hesitantly appeared on her face. Her breath escaped her nose in short spurts while her chest and shoulders began to jerk uncontrollably.

"You must be Lola." Lola did not notice the dark-complexioned gentleman in the long black trench at first. But the deepness of his tone and the calmness of his voice seemed to soothe her. She inhaled deeply and regained control over herself. She wiped her eyes of the tears that had not yet fallen.

Detective Thomas smiled and spoke once more, "At least tell me if I'm correct."

There was friendliness in his words. Lola felt comfortable, yet she didn't understand why. She stuck her chin up.

"Yes, I'm Lola," she said softly.

"We spoke to your boyfriend . . ."

"My boyfriend?" Lola was in awe. She wondered how Shaheen could go to the cops after he instructed her not to do so. Then she wondered, *Did the cops go to him?* She began to panic again. Her nerves started to get the best of her. She felt her heart pounding beneath her breast. Her mouth opened. "It wasn't my fault!"

Thomas raised his right eyebrow in suspicion. Before he could respond, Cannon interjected, figuring he knew why she blurted out such a statement.

"No, ma'am, it is not your fault. We try our best to keep our eyes on our children and to prevent any harm from coming to them." Seeing he had Lola's attention, he continued, "It's not enough that we have to protect them from bullies, drugs, and so forth. But kidnappers also."

The sudden honking of a car horn startled Cannon and the two ladies. The two uniformed officers barely moved. Thomas was unaffected by the noise but instead remained intensely focused on Lola.

Lola was confused by the detective's reply. Cannon probed the inner pocket of his jacket and pulled out a small notepad and pen.

"Can you think of any enemies you or your boyfriend may have?" He flipped through the pad's pages and positioned his pen to start writing.

Lola did not reply. She wasn't sure of the direction the conversation was going. She wondered why the detective mentioned kidnappers.

Cannon tried again. "Anyone you suspect?"

Lola remained quiet. She now pondered over what Shaheen could have possibly told them. Detective Thomas became impatient with Lola's silence and Cannon's sympathy routine.

"What about Chinnah?" Thomas darted his pupils at both ladies. He observed their reaction. Both of their eyes shot open. *Yeah*, he thought, *they know Chinnah.* "Do you know a Chinnah?" He decided to repeat the question to Lola.

The three others appeared baffled by Thomas's question. *I knew this nigger had his own agenda for coming along*, Cannon thought to himself. He regarded Thomas as an excellent and hardworking detective. He was just bothered by the manner in which his colleague would handle a case. He would go overboard in trying to solve a murder. He seemed to search for answers where there were only questions.

Those that knew Thomas personally watched as he became increasingly involved in his occupation after the murder of his teenage son. His wife couldn't take the way he threw himself into every case, so she decided to divorce him. The job was all he had now.

Lola wondered why the detective had an interest in Chinnah when he was suppose to be investigating her son's disappearance. Especially, since Chinnah and her man were preparing to go to war with each other. Cannon began to interject, but Lola's mouth was much faster.

"Chinnah?" she asked hesitantly. "I live in this neighborhood. Who doesn't know who Chinnah is?" She eyed the two men with disappointment. "I mean . . . you guys are cops. I'm sure you probably know more about him than I do."

A sneer appeared on Thomas's face, which just as quickly became an exaggerated smile. He raised his right eyebrow. His behavior perplexed Lola. She couldn't figure him out nor could she understand why he would suspect Chinnah as having something to do with her son being missing. Meanwhile, Carla was still staring at Thomas wondering something else. She decided to voice her concern.

"Why would a homicide detective, looking for Chinnah, be assigned to a missing child's case?"

Thomas continued his long and unusual smile. He wasn't surprised the young lady had recognized him. She was a witness for one of his cases a little over eight years prior. He would see her during his neighborhood patrols from time to time as the years gracefully passed by.

He wondered how the murder she saw affected her, seeing how very young she was when the incident occurred. She was only a child with a fragile and impressionable mind that happened to be with the wrong people at the wrong time. Now she appeared no different from the countless snakes that slithered through this ghetto garden.

Thomas decided to ignore her question. He fixed his attention on Lola.

"Ma'am, unfortunately, Chinnah has had an involvement with numerous crimes that have occurred in this neighborhood in the past. Not to say the least, kidnapping being one of them."

Cannon, becoming uncomfortable with the route his investigation was taking, decided to intervene. "It's not to say we suspect Chinnah of having anything to do with your situation, but we just need to check every angle possible."

Lola, picking up on her friend's question, calmly inquired, "So again, why would a homicide detective be here now interrogating me on the disappearance of my child?"

Lola, realizing the two men had no knowledge of her son's murder, became relieved once again. She decided to entertain their ignorance. "I mean, you think Chinnah has something to do with Shane being missing?" She lowered her focus to the ground. She briefly closed her eyes then opened them while inhaling deeply. She continued her downward gaze.

Thomas answered her. "We are not certain. We are only trying to find your boy, ma'am." Thomas thought to himself, *She admitted knowing Chinnah, but what is the connection?* He knew if there was any connection between her child and Chinnah, it would have to do with something illegal. Chinnah didn't bother himself with just any type of individual. He decided to redirect the focus of his questioning.

"What do you do for a living, ma'am?"

Without raising her head, Lola returned her eyes to Thomas. She softly replied, "I take care of my son"—she lifted her chin up—"and his father takes care of us."

It was the father who originally aroused Thomas's suspicion and prompted him to venture along with Cannon for his investigation. He decided he needed to know more about the father.

"What does he do?"

Lola stuck her chest out. "He owns his own business." She was proud of the fact she was able to say that. She would always nag Shaheen about giving up his occupation but certainly enjoyed telling others that her man was a business owner whenever the conversation came up. Most women would have loved to trade places with her. All she had to do every day of her life was tend to her son and shop. The thought made her quiver. Her blood turned cold. *All I had to do was take care of my son.* It pained her to conceive of a life without Shane.

Detective Thomas could see Lola was beginning to mentally drift away. "What kind of business does your boyfriend own?"

Lola didn't hear the detective. She was still thinking about Shane.

Carla answered for her. "He owns a bodega."

Thomas eyebrow went up. His instincts went on alert. He could smell his prey. "Bodega? Where is this bodega located?"

Carla didn't hesitate to answer, "It's the Mini-mart on Rutland Road."

Thomas couldn't hide the eagerness in his voice. His eyes began darting back and forth between Lola and Carla. "Rutland! Where?"

His question came out like a jolt of lightning, violently tearing Lola apart from her thoughts. Lola took notice of the excitement quickly surfacing on the detective's face. "Why are you asking about his store?"

Thomas dodged the obstacle and went straight for his target. He ignored her question. "Rutland and where?"

Carla once again spoke up, "Ninety-third Street."

Lola snapped her neck toward Carla and frowned.

"Bitch," she cursed under her breath.

Cannon could now see where his friend was going with his questioning. *This nigga is on to something. Guess we will be working together on this one.*

Thomas had what he needed. He could see by both of the ladies' expressions that they knew nothing of Minimart's prior fate. The fact that it was in ruins and now the scene of a murder investigation was unknown to them. The only thing left was to prove a connection between the two because when they began the investigation on the explosion and murder that occurred, they didn't come up with Shaheen's name.

According to the information gathered, Minimart was owned by a Juan Riverez, a Puerto Rican native, who came to the country and opened up his own small grocery store within a couple of months of his arrival.

Originally, Thomas knew he was only a front man but didn't know for whom. He guessed Chinnah at first because he remembered the scared Haitian couple, who used to own the building. They complained to the sergeant of his precinct then about being harassed by Chinnah to pay protection money. After receiving no help from the police, the coupled disappeared. He wasn't sure if they left or were murdered. Now, Thomas may have found the person who Juan was a front for. This would explain why Minimart was attacked. It was a retaliation for the Fifty-first Street murders, where the tire tracks of an SUV, like the one Shaheen owns, were found.

He decided to break the news to the ladies. "The inside of Minimart was just blown to pieces by a hand grenade." Shock appeared on both of their faces. Their mouths hung open. They waited in suspense for the detective to finish his statement. "There were many people standing on the outside of the store as well as within, who were either the victims of fatal gunshot wounds or the explosion."

He strongly penetrated Lola with his eyes. "Did your boyfriend speak to you about this?"

Lola was lost for words. She knew something was beginning to brew between her man and Chinnah but didn't know it was this serious or that it had already started. She had always known Shaheen to talk about getting into some major conflict but just as quickly find a way to resolve it strategically rather than violently. It never became this serious as far as she knew.

Detective Thomas could see she had a lot to say; if not, she at least knew something that could be helpful in his case. He was now interested in the missing child's connection to the shootout at the restaurant and the drug house, as well as the Minimart incident. His mind, for a brief second, drifted back to the baby wipe in her boyfriend's pocket. He decided they needed to go somewhere to discuss the case further.

"Ma'am, do you mind if we continue this in your apartment?"

Lola was confused. "My apartment?"

Cannon followed Thomas's lead. "Yes, ma'am, we need to let the officers, who accompanied us, conduct a thorough search of the apartment to see if there is any indication of foul play. That is the reason for Detective Thomas joining me as well. We need to see the last place your son was last seen"—Cannon surveyed the street about him—"and it is getting dark."

Lola was still in shock over the news about Minimart. She reluctantly replied, "Okay?"

Carla was not certain she should stay. She felt as if the situation was getting over her head. She decided to cut her visit short. "Yo, Lo, hunny, I have to be ghost. Gotta check this dude in thirty minutes. It's real important. A'ight?"

Lola could see she was lying, but she also knew this wasn't Carla's problem. Besides, she felt it would be easier to lie to the detectives without her there. She decided to relieve her friend of her post. "Yeah, you good."

Carla felt guilty for the abandonment. She asked, "You straight, Mommy?"

Lola shuddered at the word *Mommy*. "Yeah, I'm good."

Carla wasted no time. She pivoted on her heels and made her way past the two detectives without saying a word to them. She threw her hand up and, without facing her audience, shouted, "I'll call you later after you get rid of those two dicks!"

Thomas raised his arm and gestured his hand toward the entrance to Lola's building. "Please, ma'am, after you."

Lola led the men inside.

CHAPTER 8

"You goin' to the party tonight?"

Shaheen was too busy contemplating what he had just spoken with the detectives about to recognize Gorilla Leek's words. He sat on the top of the park bench, staring off into the vast darkness of the night, sipping on a half full pint of Crown Royal.

The wind whistled through the noisy streets that surrounded Lincoln Terrace Park. Each gust that blew by seemed to roar at them breaking the silence of the empty basketball court they sat in. Gorilla Leek did not appreciate Shaheen's lack of response. He decided to repeat himself. "The party at Tilden Ballroom . . . Are you goin'?"

The sternness in Gorilla Leek's voice terminated Shaheen's daydreaming.

"Huh? Party?"

Gorilla Leek shook his head. "Yeah, the party. You goin'?" A hint of frustration appeared in his tone.

Shaheen surveyed the park and then shrugged his shoulders. "Dunno."

Gorilla Leek was unsatisfied with the answer he received. "Whatchoo mean, you don't know? Blood, you need to be there. Plus, it'll take your mind off your situation."

Shaheen pondered whether telling Gorilla Leek what he had done with the cops was a good decision or not. He chose to keep it to himself for now. Shaheen felt there might have been some truth in Gorilla Leek's statement. Maybe he needed something to take his mind off things. He decided he would go.

"A'ight, a'ight, man, I'll go." As the words left his mouth, he thought about Lola and how she was holding up. He needed to speak to her as soon as possible so he could explain to her what he did and why. He needed to prompt her on how to respond to the police properly.

"Cool son, you drivin' alone or you rollin' with me?" Gorilla Leek didn't notice his friend's melancholy mood.

Shaheen brought his attention back to the present. "Na, I'll roll for dolo."

"That's what's up!" Seeing he had his partner's attention, he decided to change the conversation. Gorilla Leek swiftly shoved his hand into the pocket of his black denim and brought it back out with a neatly folded thin strip of aluminum foil. He held it out to Shaheen.

"This the stuff we snatched from Chinnah. That is, after we stepped on it."

Shaheen passed his bottle to Gorilla Leek and reached for the foil. He opened it up. It contained a little over a gram of a white powdered substance. He retrieved his keys from his pocket while simultaneously searching the area around him for any life-forms.

He flipped out the biggest key from the ring, dipped it into the foil, and scooped up the powder. He brought the key up to his left nostril while pressing his right finger down on his right one. He sniffed the powder from off the key, wiggled his nose, and licked his lips. He instantly felt the cocaine dripping down the back of his throat. His pupils shot open, and suddenly, he felt his head rush.

"Shit! This some good stuff!"

Gorilla Leek smiled as he watched his friend take another hit. Shaheen scooped up much more this time.

"Yeah, I know it's good. We hit the jackpot on this one, and we've already stretched it."

Shaheen, lowering his eyes in curiosity, tilted his chin up. "Where do you think they got this? I mean this is twice as good as what we're moving."

Gorilla Leek nodded his head in agreement. "Indeed."

"Well, we need to find out who his connect is before we take him off."

"My point exactly, Blood." Gorilla Leek rose to his feet. He took a sip from the bottle, then passed it to Shaheen. "We need to snatch this connect up, so we can cop from them. I mean, we'll get paid, especially once Chinnah is out the picture, and we're the only ones left with this type of product."

Shaheen knew what his partner was saying was true; however, he wasn't certain he would be around long enough to reap the rewards. After all that occurred with his son's death, he was beginning to consider leaving the game alone. Yet he knew he would be unable to do so now because of the war with Chinnah. His friends would regard him as a traitor or deserter if he told them he wanted out now. He decided he would inform them of his decision once Chinnah was out of the way.

Instead of acknowledging Gorilla Leek's words, he settled the foil down on the seat of the bench. He swiftly went into his denim pockets and pulled out a roll of money. He peeled the first bill from the stack and stuck the roll back in his jeans. Holding the one hundred dollar bill from the corner of both ends, he began rolling it up with the thumb and index finger of his two hands. He continued the process until it resembled a cigarette.

Once satisfied he had fashioned the dollar properly, he stuck it between his lips. He retrieved the foil from the bench and opened it wider. He spread the foil out in his left palm. He then used his free hand to grab the dollar bill from his mouth.

Gorilla Leek watched as his friend brought the one hundred dollar cigarette up to his nose. He leaned his head forward, positioning the bill and his face toward the palm of his hand. He snorted loud and long.

He lifted his head up and started making a sort of smacking noise with his throat. He was attempting to rush the drip. He felt the cocaine beginning to cake up at the roof of his mouth, near the back of his throat. He tried to move his tongue back there to taste the powder. Failing to do so, he shoved the foil face down in his mouth, then carefully pulled it out while allowing his tongue to lick it clean. His lips and tongue instantly went numb. His mouth began to tingle.

"Yeah, you're right. We can sure make some doe off this. Where did you stash the bricks?" Shaheen balled the foil up and tossed it over his shoulder.

Gorilla Leek silently gloated over his friend's inability to say no to using drugs. He thought it ironic that Shaheen would always scold him for his recklessness yet never viewed his own addiction to cocaine as a threat to his life. Gorilla Leek would never go near the stuff unless it was to sell it. He considered coac users as fiends, as customers. To him, it was one step away from crack.

"I got it put up in Daffney's apartment over there in Rutland Plaza. I got the key to her crib in my whip." Gorilla Leek smiled. "I take it you like it?"

Shaheen didn't reply. Instead, he licked his lips again and wiggled his nose.

"Well, Redrum will be meetin' me up at the club, so I can hand some of this off to him. We gonna knock off O Zee's for six hundred a pop. That's two hundred less than the normal damage, so we shouldn't have a hard time getting rid of the work. Shit, we got it for free, so we can afford to cut the price. Plus I got White Mike wantin' me to drop off 'half a man' to him over there in Bushwick."

Shaheen became interested in what he heard. "Puerto Rican White Mike?"

"Yeah."

A confused expression covered Shaheen's face. "Bushwick? I thought he was over in East New York?"

"He is. However, he offered me his store on Pitkins. Said we can use it as long as we give him a deal on the work as rent."

"What kind of deal?" Shaheen grew worried at the mentioning of a deal. He sometimes doubted Gorilla Leek's ability to negotiate.

"He wanted fifteen thou per ki, but I got him ta agree on eighteen instead."

"That's not bad." Shaheen realized his friend made a good decision. "Yeah, that's actually real straight. But we only have four kis. I mean, before we can start making deals like that, we have to secure the connect so we can keep that type of weight moving."

"Don't worry 'bout that. I'm getting the hook up on that connect tonight."

"So are we gonna get a good deal on the work since we only charging cats eighteen?"

"Yeah, indeed. And the way I figured, eighteen is more than enough to pay for the store's rent, and we can still make a profit off what we sell him."

Shaheen nodded his head in agreement. "But still, I thought White Mike only messed with trees? Wasn't he copping his work from Cutty?"

A smile crept upon Gorilla Leek's face. As if moving in slow motion, he tilted his head to the right then to the left to better observe his environment. He brought his eyes back to Shaheen and spoke low, "What do you think he said when I told him what we did to Cutty?"

A degree of frustration overcame Shaheen. "We didn't do shit to Cutty! We weren't even there." Gorilla Leek could see his partner's anger was beginning to rise. He didn't care. There was nothing Shaheen could do about it now. He felt as if this war should have happened a long time ago anyway. Shaheen wanted to always be diplomatic about it.

"You're right, we weren't there, so what? What, you scared Chinnah's gonna get at us?"

"First of all, I ain't scared of no one." Spit viciously exited Shaheen's mouth as he barked out the words.

Gorilla Leek smirked at Shaheen's reply. He knew he hit him hard with that question.

Shaheen continued, "It's just stupid to run around trying to get props off a murder you didn't commit."

Shaheen, realizing he was becoming emotional, decided to calm his tone. "No one even knows this cat is dead yet, so why advertise it? The only reason I agreed to robbing Chinnah in the first place was to send a message to him that we were not to be bullied. I didn't expect us to go there and catch three bodies.

"As far as going to war with him, that wasn't really my decision. Once he sent Cutty to your house, I realized it was a matter of time before he sent someone to mine. Plus Cutty is one of his right-hand men, and now, the nigga's dead. Whether I want a war with Chinnah or not, it is going to happen once he finds out his boy got returned."

Gorilla Leek intruded, "I wasn't advertising it to get a rep. I'm takin' the blame away from my son because I'd be damned if he put a hit out on him for that."

Shaheen understood where Gorilla Leek was coming from but also saw the futility in his words. "He already put out a hit on you. That's why Cutty was at your house."

"Yeah, either way, I knew if White Mike knew we knocked off Cutty and snatched Chinnah's work after returning his workers to the essence, then he would feel as if Chinnah's time was limited, and he would jump on board the winning team. I mean, White Mike has always stayed neutral. He was just Chinnah's customer, not his worker, so he don't hold no loyalty for Chinnah."

"Why Bushwick? He doesn't live there."

Gorilla Leek was waiting for that question. "His family is originally from Bushwick. His grandmoms still lives out there. He wants to get out of the way of the beef with us and Chinnah.

"He has a brother out there who has a barbershop he hustles out of. Nothing big. They just be copping big eighths and breaking it down to bump out of there. I told him we'll give him half a man on consignment."

"Half a ki!" Shaheen could no longer contain his anger. "For free?"

Gorilla Leek nullified the tirade that was beginning to start. "Son, it's not for free. Just a loan with no interest other than use of the store. I mean, shit, we got the work for free, and we no longer have Minimart. That was a sweetener for a good ass deal!"

Shaheen thought about it for a second and concluded his friend might be right. "Ok, well, if this is a good deal, when does it start? When do we get to set up shop?"

"Tomorrow."

"Tomorrow? Are we ready for that?" Shaheen wasn't concerned with whether they were ready or not because he knew it was nothing for them to set up shop once they had a location. However, he was more interested in knowing how all this happened with White Mike so fast without his knowledge. It was as if Gorilla Leek already had all this planned.

He couldn't fathom how he would have had the time to think of all this, let alone set it up in such a short notice after the demise of Minimart and the nine or more deaths that have occurred in the last few days. He resolved to thinking Gorilla Leek was always and only worried about making some doe. Besides murder, that was his priority. In fact, he was addicted to blood money.

"Yeah, we ready. I got Blades takin' a couple of young dogs over there to set up shop. White Mike will still have his trees moving out of there. It's just now he won't have to worry about being there, and we will get a 7 percent cut off his gross profit. Chinnah was getting fifteen from him. So son's happy. This will set us straight till we get back on our feet and reopen Minimart."

"So we are going to mix up two products at one spot? That doesn't sound peace," Shaheen interjected.

"Yeah, Blood, we'll have trees and girl moving from there. But check it. We don't have to worry about po po because that is in Chinnah's neighborhood. He got them on smash. They on his payroll, so they barely come through there."

"And you don't think they will come through there once Chinnah finds out we are in his territory. I mean, the reason we have problems with the cat now is because we have always been right in his face."

"First of all, East New York ain't his hood," Gorilla Leek stated with authority. "Second, he won't even know we're there. He don't know Blades, and Blades is Puerto Rican. As far as Chinnah is concerned, he'll think he one of White Mike's workers. And besides, dude ain't gonna be around for much longer, and I have it already planned out how we gonna get his hook up with the pigs."

Shaheen liked the plan. It was on point, he thought. He decided to inquire a little more. "Well, I have one more question."

"What's that?" inquired Gorilla Leek.

"If we are going to take Chinnah off, who will White Mike be coppin' his trees from?"

"That's his business, not ours."

"So we will be making money on the low right in the midst of Chinnah while also being an earshot away from the gossip of his peoples?"

"Exactly!"

"Well, after we take him off, how are we gonna get the connect with the pigs to make sure we don't have to worry about them?"

"Blood, don't worry 'bout it. Trust me. I'm taking care of all that tonight."

"Sweet. So you got that covered?"

"Yeah, indeed. I was handlin' it so you wouldn't have to worry 'bout it. Seeing everything that has happened recently."

Shaheen's heart grew warm at the expressed concern of his friend. "I feel you dog, but still, let me know when something major like this is decided on."

"Indeed, son. Just tryin' to reduce your stress. That's all."

"I feel you, but . . ."

"Yo, Sha-Boogie!" Their conversation was interrupted by the voice of a female piercing through the whistling of the wind. Her shriek traveled across the basketball court silencing the roar of the fall air. Both men glanced toward the direction of the voice.

They could barely discern the figure approaching them from the shadows of the court's entrance. As the body crept out of the darkness, her strut became more familiar to the two men.

With each step she took, the wind began to peel off the blackness of night that veiled her face as if removing a mask. Her eyes were the first to be revealed, then her nose. Her face came to the surface of the darkness like a creature arising out of muddy waters. Both men knew who they were beholding. It was Carla. She neared the two.

"I've been running up and down the hood looking for you."

Shaheen eyed her curiously. "Why?"

"Me and Lo got approached by these two detectives today asking about Shane."

The two men darted eyes at each other. Shaheen became worried. Carla picked up on it.

"I already know what happened. Lo told me."

Shaheen did not reply. He was uncertain of how much she actually knew. He didn't want to entertain her statement because she seemed all too proud to inform him that she knew his business. Seeing the lack of concern he was displaying regarding the words she just spoke, Carla decided she needed some privacy to make him understand the seriousness of her conversation. She didn't want to reveal everything in front of Gorilla Leek.

"Can I talk to you for a sec?"

Gorilla Leek eyed her with suspicion.

"You're talking to me now," Shaheen responded sarcastically.

Carla rolled her eyes. "Look," she said after sucking her teeth, "those dicks went up into your crib with Lo, and like I said, I know what happened. How long do you think it will be before they find some evidence of what took place?"

Gorilla Leek chimed in. "Yo, Sha, you gonna talk to this shorty? You know how big her mouth is."

Carla's menacing sneer didn't go unnoticed by the two. "Yeah, maybe you right, Leek. I got a big mouth. But I'm sure you don't want to see how big it really is."

Contemplating her words concerning his son, Shaheen started to worry, but he wouldn't allow his demeanor or voice to reveal it. He decided to cut in on the dialogue between the two. "A'ight, we can talk." He viewed his partner. "Yo, Leek, you mind?"

Gorilla Leek snatched the Crown Royal bottle from the bench and took a final sip. He decided to let the two talk rather than argue with Carla. "Na, not at all. Besides I have to go handle that before we hit the club tonight." He rested the bottle back on the bench. "I'm out."

He proceeded toward the opposite side of the court's entrance. He approached a large hole that had been cut into the fence surrounding the park. It appeared someone had been dissatisfied with the location of the entrance and decided to make their own. Gorilla Leek squeezed through the hole and then hopped the small gate that stood between himself and the sidewalk. The darkness engulfed his form as he trotted off into the night. In a matter of seconds, he had completely disappeared.

Shaheen brought his attention to Carla. "So whatup?"

Her expression became cold. She brought her chin to her chest while raising her ogling eyes to the top of her lids. She stared blankly at Shaheen. "I know what happened in your apartment."

"Whatchoo mean?" He wanted her to tell him what she knew.

"I know how Shane died."

Shaheen smirked. "What, cause Lola told you something like that?"

Carla cocked her lip to the side and sucked her teeth. "That ain't all, nigga. I know what you did the night before with the same gun that killed Shane."

Shaheen's smirk disappeared. He wondered how she could have known that since he never told Lola about the murders at Chinnah's spot. The only person who knew about what occurred was Gorilla Leek. He figured his best friend must be fucking Carla.

"Who told you whatever it is you think you know?" he blurted out.

She smiled. She knew she had him. "Don't worry about that. Just worry about what I need in order to keep my mouth shut."

Shaheen's face became red. He envisioned putting his gun to her head and squeezing the trigger, but he didn't need any more murders to think about right now. *She's a bitch*, he thought. "What are you talking?"

"Well, seeing I know enough to get you locked up, there are a couple of things I want."

Shaheen interjected, "First of all, you don't know enough to get me locked up. You have no proof of anything."

Once again, she smiled. "Proof? What like the body and the gun buried in Lincoln Terrace Park?"

Shaheen's heart started to race. He wanted to call Gorilla Leek on his cell phone and tell him to return to the park. He wanted to know why he would tell this hoe everything. Instead, he just leered at Carla and calmly questioned, "What do you want?"

She licked her lips and inspected him up and down from head to toe. "First off, I want to fuck."

"Fuck?" Shaheen thought she must have been intoxicated or delirious. He was confused by her demand.

"Yeah. You have a problem with that?"

Shaheen knew there was nothing he could say to her right now other than comply. He needed to give himself some time to think on how to handle the situation. He felt if he told her yeah, she would go home, and he could call Gorilla Leek and figure out how to handle her, that is, after he screamed on him for squealing to her.

"Yeah, that's straight. When?"

She took in her surroundings and then brought her eyes to his crotch. "Now."

"Now?" Shaheen was thrown off by the quickness of her response.

"Yeah, nigga, now."

He wondered if Lola was hiding in the shadows somewhere waiting for him to make a mistake with Carla. He felt as if it was a set-up, then dismissed the idea, knowing Lola wouldn't allow Carla to use Shane's death as part of her scheme. He was well aware of Carla's long-time desire for him, so he reckoned her threat was real. He pondered over her request for about ten seconds.

Oh well, he thought, *I need her to keep her mouth shut, and she ain't that bad looking.* He no longer hesitated. He eyed her intently, grabbed her by her left arm and spun her around in a one hundred and eighty degree circle. While gripping her tightly, he examined her rear end.

His eyes followed the volumptuous curve beneath her jeans from the top of her legs up to the bottom of her waist. He abruptly pulled her toward him. She could feel his penis hardening against her ass. She was now in his embrace. The warmth of his breath shielded her from the wretched wind that was beginning to freeze her blood.

Shaheen reached around her and seized her throat with his right hand while his left one ventured from her breast to the zipper of her jeans. He unbuttoned the first button, only to find out there were several more buttons to undo. She didn't have a zipper. He decided not to waste any time, so he tore all the buttons from their holes at once.

"Uh!" She let out a helpless sigh.

Shaheen wasn't concerned with who was around; he just wanted to get this over with. Besides, he could please himself in the process. He forcefully shoved his hands into her jeans and panties. His index and middle finger crawled into her vagina. It was already wet. He curled his fingers upward and began gently moving them in and out.

"Mmm." Carla began moaning. This is what she always wanted, to feel Shaheen inside of her.

He removed his left hand from inside of her jeans and tugged on them until they fell down to her ankles. He then repeated the process with her panties. Using the same hand, he quickly pulled down his zipper and delved into his pants, bringing out his penis.

The coldness of the brute wind sent chills through the blood in his manhood. He massaged the head of it while releasing her neck to fondle her breast. They were large.

Feeling the warmth return to his private, he poked his finger into her vagina from the rear. She was extremely wet. He moved his finger around in the moisture. He brought it back out and grabbed himself. He thought to himself, *Let's hurry up and get this over with.* He pulled her closer and shoved his manhood into her.

"Ahhh!" She let out a loud and seductive moan.

CHAPTER 9

Lola sat on the couch staring at the ceiling. The apartment had an eerie silence, the type one would experience in a library or a funeral home. No matter how hard she attempted to think away the past few hours, she couldn't.

She kept replaying the conversation over and over in her head, searching her memory for any statement she may have uttered that could have betrayed her. She pondered over the manner in which she carried herself in front of the detectives. She knew they were trained to detect lies. She just hoped whatever she told them didn't contradict what Shaheen may have said.

She held a cigar of marijuana between her fingertips. It was unlit. She wanted to take a couple of hits but was afraid the police might show up at any moment. She wondered whether they believed her or not. She thought for a moment that the only reason they left was to probably get a warrant. She knew she was not ready to be in anyone's cell.

She started thinking about her life, how she should have stayed in college and heeded her mother. This person she had become wasn't who she was, and now, she was concealing the death of her son. Then it hit her. *I didn't do this nor did I commit any murder with that gun. If I hide this, I will get in trouble.*

She thought about being pregnant and that maybe it was another chance at life for her. She knew she wouldn't make it in prison pregnant, and she wasn't going to let her child be born in a correctional facility either. She had to think about herself and the child that was in her. Besides, she and Shaheen had been at odds with each other for years now. Sure, she loved him, but they could no longer stand each other.

She knew what she had to do. Now she felt she was deserving of a smoke. If the police did come, they would be more interested in what she had to say than what she was smoking.

She heard the sound of keys fumbling on the outside of the door. All three of the locks rotated in sequence from bottom to top. The door flew open. It was Shaheen.

"Yo, DTs came by here?"

Lola frowned in disappointment. She barely moved her slumped body. "Yeah," she responded dully, "they said you came to them and reported Shane missing."

Shaheen closed the door behind him and locked it. He removed his leather and tossed it on the floor. He walked over to Lola and fell onto the couch beside her. He noticed the blunt in her hand.

"You gonna light that?"

She glanced down at the cigar in her hand. "Don't have a lighter."

He searched his pants and brought out a red lighter and passed it to her. She eased the cigar in her mouth and lit it. He was uncertain of what to say to her. This was the first time they had been alone together since the tragedy. Though she was silent, he knew she still blamed him for their son's untimely death. The air that filled their apartment was still. He decided to break the silence.

"What did they say?"

Lola took two short and quick pulls from the marijuana. "What did who say?" She held the blunt out to him.

He received her offer and took a long draw. "The pigs. What did they say?"

She laid her head back on the couch. "They said you reported Shane missing and that it might have something to do with a kidnapping." She paused to turn toward him. With her head still on the couch, she continued, "Why didn't you tell me you were going to go to the cops?"

He acknowledged her frustration. "Look, ma, I'm sorry, but I had to go to them. I mean, what if someone would have questioned Shane's absence and went to the police. They would've been wondering why I didn't come to them in the first place."

Lola sat upright. "Yeah, but how was I suppose to know what to say to them. You don't even tell me anything. I mean, why didn't you tell me about Minimart?"

Shaheen was caught off guard by her question. He wondered how she found out. He began stuttering. "I . . . I . . . wa-was gonna . . . I mean . . . you . . . I mean, I want to keep you away . . . You know . . . from all that."

She wouldn't buy it. She was tired of being left in the dark, tired of being ordered to stay at home with her son, and tired of being told what was best for her. She put up with it all for the sake of Shane, and now, she no longer had him. As far as she knew, she may be with child from another man.

"Well, I tried calling you because I didn't know what to do or say to them."

"I'm sure you were on point. I know you handled it."

Her temperature started to boil. She knew he wasn't getting the point.

"They brought other cops here, as they said, to investigate the scene."

She had his full attention now. "What scene?"

"Our apartment!"

"Here? What kind of investigation? Did they find anything?" Shaheen was in the comfort of his own home, so he could afford to lose control of his emotions. He started to panic. "How many was there?"

Lola was unmoved by the worrisome tone in his voice. She calmly answered, "They found a torn baby wipe with blood on it under the couch, next to the spot on the carpet where . . ."—she glanced at the ground and swallowed heavily—"Shane died. They wanted to know why there was a big bleach stain there. Said they were going to come back to conduct a more thorough search. I heard the detective tell one of the cops that they will come back and spray the carpet with something to check for blood. They said it was called Luminol."

"Luminol? What the hell is that?" he nervously chuckled. "What, a new kind of liquor or something?"

She didn't laugh or show any expression. "Shaheen, they said they were going to take samples of the carpet. If they find even the smallest trace of blood, they will view us as suspects. Think about it." She peered at him to see if her words registered within his brain. "They said they expect foul play. They told me to have you call them as soon as you came home."

"Call them?" Shaheen's mind began racing. He felt the walls closing in on him. He started imagining how his life would be if he were arrested. He would be behind bars forever. His life would come to an abrupt end.

He thought about the life he was currently living and how he should have left the streets alone a long time ago. If he had done that, he wouldn't be in this predicament. Deep down within the private recesses of his brain, he wished he could travel back into the past to change some of his mistakes, like for one, keeping a gun in his house.

He felt as if he should have reported his son's death as a murder instead of a kidnap. He could've gotten rid of the gun, so they couldn't trace it. *That's it*, he thought, *I have to get the gun back and throw it away somewhere far from the neighborhood.*

Lola interrupted his contemplation. "What are you gonna do?"

Shaheen threw a disturbed look at her. "Whatchoo mean what am I gonna do?" He took another draw from the marijuana, then passed it to her. "We are both in this," he informed with smoke escaping his mouth.

"Well, they think the explosion at Minimart may have something to do with Shane's disappearance."

Shaheen cocked his head back. "How?"

"They said there was a murder of one of Chinnah's peoples over by Souljah's Restaurant and then that very same night, a drug spot believed to be owned by Chinnah was robbed and three of his peoples found dead."

Shaheen tried to discern the frozen stare Lola was throwing at him. He couldn't tell how much she knew about the murders. However, he was interested in finding out exactly what she had been told because whatever she knew is what the detectives knew.

"What this have to do with Shane?"

Lola continued, "They said Minimart got shot up, then blown up the next day. They think Chinnah had something to do with it in retaliation for the murders. So they think he may have something to do with Shane's disappearance because they know you're connected to Minimart."

His face became distorted. "How they know that?"

Lola sucked her teeth. "Because that bitch Carla told them."

Shaheen instantly thought about their meeting in the park. He knew now she was serious about telling the cops. He felt it was intentional. He didn't know she had revealed his occupation without knowing it would harm him.

He knew something had to be done about Carla. She was too devious.

Her demand for sex was the least of his worries. She wanted twenty thousand dollars in cash to keep her mouth shut, along with a brand-new, rent-free apartment. She claimed to know the location of Shane's body as well as the gun, and it wasn't just a claim.

Immediately after leaving Carla, Shaheen got in touch with Gorilla Leek and let him have it. Gorilla Leek was just as shocked as his partner first was when he heard the news of what Carla knew. He assured Shaheen he never told her anything and that he was definitely not in bed with her. The conversation left Shaheen perplexed.

He believed Gorilla Leek. Even if he was seeing Carla, Shaheen couldn't imagine him telling her about his murders. He had too much to lose. He needed to know who told Carla about the murders and Shane's death, let alone the whereabouts of the body and the weapon as well as how they discovered the truth. He searched his brain for names but came up with nothing.

"So either way, they don't know what really happened to Shane or even suspect that we know where he's at, right?"

She answered him flatly, "No. They don't know anything."

He became elated over the news. He knew that they would rather chase Chinnah anyway. He was bigger fish, and Shaheen knew if he played his cards right he might be able to use this to get rid of his enemy.

Lola observed his change in demeanor with disgust. She could see he thought he was off the hook; however, she knew better than that. Detectives don't get their jobs for being dumb.

"Shaheen, they don't think we know where Shane is at, but they do think we know about his disappearance."

He began to worry again. All he could muster from his lips was "Huh?"

She took three short and quick draws from the blunt, then said, "They think you had something to do with the murders that led up to the Minimart incident."

Shaheen's nervousness started to get the best of him again. The murders were the main reason he went to the extent he did to hide Shane's death, and now, his son's disappearance was what led the cops to suspect him for those same killings.

He didn't want to discuss this with her any further. He held out his hand, signaling to her to pass the blunt. She took one long pull from the cigar, then handed it to him. He brought it up to his mouth and began inhaling. She took in his mannerisms, wondering how much more time he had left to get high.

The muffled sound of a ringing phone startled them both. Shaheen looked toward the ground where his jacket laid. He passed the cigar back to her, then braced both of his hands on the couch and elevated himself to his feet. He journeyed over to where his leather was and snatched it from the ground. Fumbling his hands through the pockets, he found what he was searching for.

The ringing became louder, no longer muffled as he removed it from his jacket. He flipped the cell phone open and spoke into the receiver.

"Whatup?" Shaheen listened as the person on the other end spoke. His face became serious, and his right eyebrow went up. Finally, he spoke, "What else did they ask? Did they ask about me?"

Once again, he was silent, closely following the words coming out of the receiver.

"A'ight, no doubt. I'll come by and check you in the morning. Just stay in the crib for now. A'ight? Peace."

Shaheen closed the phone and placed it into his pants pocket. He ventured over to the couch and sat down. He leaned back, raised his arms behind his head, and began staring at the ceiling. They both sat there doing the same.

Shaheen spoke, "The detectives that came here, was one black?"

She reached for the dusty ashtray that sat idly on the large speaker, which bordered the left side of their couch. She retrieved it and stuck the cigar's fiery end down into the pile of grey and black ashes, smothering the flame. Laying the blunt in the heap of tobacco residue, she returned the ashtray to its previous position. She glanced at Shaheen. "Yeah, one was black. His name was Thomas. The other was Detective Cannon . . . Why?"

"The cat, who we put Minimart's name under, got a visit from the same detective, the Tom dude."

She wouldn't remove her eyes from him. "Did you have anything to do with those murders?'

His gaze dropped to the ground. He thought about Shane. He wanted to wake up from this nightmare. His son was dead, and now, he was being investigated for multiple murders even though he only committed one.

"No," he answered, "not all."

"Whatchoo mean, not all?" she retorted.

"Just that! Look, the less you know, the less you say. Feel me? You don't need to worry yourself with all that," he exclaimed.

To hell I don't, she thought.

Shaheen continued, "We need to focus on keeping these pigs away from the truth of lil man."

She wondered how he could mention their son with such callousness. He didn't even blink when he spoke of "the truth of lil man." She felt he was more concerned with covering up the death than the death itself. He didn't carry Shane for nine months, breast feed him or wipe his first tears. He wasn't missing what she missed. To him, it was just a loss; at least, that is what she told herself.

"What if they find out what happened?" she calmly asked.

He barely opened his mouth. "They won't." Glaring up at the ceiling, he inhaled deeply, sighed, then brought his attention to her. "Trust me, they won't."

She didn't bother to look at him. "They took the baby wipe with them to examine it."

Shaheen shot a quizzical glance at her. "What did they say about it?"

"Nothing."

"Nothing?"

"Yeah, nothing," she repeated.

"You sure they don't think we know where Shane is?"

She finally decided to cast her eyes upon him. "The black dude was more concerned about Chinnah and the murders than anything else."

Shaheen lowered his face into his palms. He lifted his head, tilted it to the right and gazed out of the window. The darkness he saw gave him a glimpse of the inevitable. The blackness of the November night sky resembled death. He could see the reflection of his apartment bouncing off the glass of the window.

He ran through his mental Rolodex attempting to remember everything that took place at the scene of the murders. He searched his memory for any mistakes he may have made. At the house, he deduced there were no witnesses, and he didn't touch anything that was left at the apartment. It was the restaurant that made him uneasy. There were too many eyes. What if someone talked?

Though he did not knowingly commit murder at the restaurant, he was still involved in the shootout that occurred there. Besides, one of the bullets the victim received could have been his. That, coupled with the fact that he knew the cops would be able to connect the shell casings found at the restaurant with the ones at Chinnah's spot, gave him an unsettling discomfort. Plus, if they find Shane's body, they will trace the bullet back to the same gun as the murders.

"What else did the cops want to know?" he asked.

"Nothing, they just wanted to know if you really owned the Minimart. I told you that one cop was more concerned with Chinnah than Shane." Her reply was cut short as she felt her stomach turn. Her breathing became shorter, and her mouth suddenly went dry.

She attempted to rise to her feet, but dizziness overcame her. She fell back into the couch. The knot that was twisting in her stomach began making its way up to her chest. She quickly leaned forward and opened her mouth. Vomit flew everywhere, splashing off the floor and onto Shaheen's denim and sneakers like white water rapids smashing against rocks. He jumped up in an attempt to escape the shower, only to fail.

Lola was now on her knees, bent over toward the floor. Shaheen shot a curious glance at her. She started to covey her thoughts but instead hopped to her feet and bolted down the hallway to the bathroom. He could hear the splashing of toilet water along with her gagging.

He took in a glimpse of the mess on the floor and saw an image of his son lying in a puddle of blood. He wondered whether God would forgive him for what he allowed to happen to Shane. He thought about the murders and, with his eyes open, silently prayed for help out of his situation. His stare left the ground as he made a promise to leave all his criminal activities alone. All he needed was time to handle the Chinnah problem, and he would give everything up.

He fixed his sight on the hallway that led to the bathroom. He then walked into the kitchen and searched through the cabinet under the kitchen sink. Finding the carpet sanitizer, he ventured toward the pantry situated across from a white gas stove and retrieved a small bottle of liquid that was lying on the floor. He went to exit the kitchen but first snatched the dishrag that hung from the stove's door handle, before heading back into the living room.

CHAPTER 10

Copper peered through his dark shaded glasses past the tinted windows of his BMW and into the blackness that blanketed the desolate street they drove down. He had remained silent since he and his two cohorts entered his vehicle. He slowly swayed the wheel to the right, guiding the car onto Pitkin Avenue.

A dark-skinned bearded young man in his early twenties, wearing a black army fatigue jacket and blue denim jeans, occupied the backseat. A blue bandana covered his head.

Killa Kash sat idly in the passenger seat. He spoke, "You sure dealing with this slob is straight?"

Copper kept his eyes on the road. He nodded his head without saying a word.

Killa Kash acknowledged his gesture. "Yeah, but what if this is a set-up?"

Copper decided to explain, so he could alleviate his partner's worries. "Even if it is a set-up, he still had to shed blood for him to get anything big out of this. I wouldn't make any solid deals with the cat until then. Now I have a sword over his head if he decides to think twice."

Killa Kash felt a little easier. Copper quickly glanced at Killa to assess his demeanor. His two-second observation assured him he had persuaded his friend to trust in his plan. He continued.

"Look, I arranged the hit on Fats and Stick after they started becoming suspicious about the extra work we had them distributing. I mean it was the smart thing to do, you know?"

Copper could see from his peripheral vision Killa was hesitant to nod in agreement.

"Look, if they would have went back and told my pops about the cream we been making from putting our work up in his spots, man, my pops would have killed us all.

"I mean, can you imagine what he would do to any of us if he knew we scraped some of his doe in order to cop weight from that cracker cop? And then to top it off, we're moving the work through his spots."

Killa replied, "Yeah, I know what he would do to me and Blue Jay, but you don't have to worry. He's your dad."

Copper grew angry. "Nigga, he don't give a fuck about me! That dude didn't even love my moms. He's the reason why she is dead. He's loves the shit out of my sister because he loves her mother, but the nigga despises me! He think I'm too dumb to run his operation. That's why, I made the connect with that pig."

Killa refrained from uttering a word. He didn't want to upset Copper because he had, on several occasions, bore witness to the violence spawned from his temper tantrums. He decided he would agree and allow his friend to do the talking.

Copper felt he had to make a point. "Man, Fats and Stick had to go. That's why I arranged the meeting between Blue and ole boy." He glanced into his rearview mirror at Blue Jay who sat mute in the backseat. "I didn't want my pops to know we had anything to do with their murder, and I knew Blue was someone to keep his mouth shut."

Killa Kash wanted to remain silent; however, his curiosity would not allow him to. "But why the whole pretend hit drama?"

"That wasn't my idea. That was boy's. I knew both he and I wanted the same thing—Pops out of the picture—so I made the deal with him. I would give him whatever he needed to get at Pops, along with brokering the use of White Mike's store, so they could move into East New York, while we take over all of Rutland.

"I had Blue Jay tell him he had to take off some of Pop's workers before I would begin to trust him and give him access to the store. I didn't say why, just who. Blue Jay told him about the coac in the spot to give him a little motivation.

"Boy came up with the idea to stage a pretend hit at the restaurant. He said he needed a reason to get the rest of his slobs on board with getting at my pops. But, that nigga wasn't suppose to kill Trevor. I used Trevor because I knew he was already keeping his eye on them for Pauley. Plus, Trevor's not a killer.

"I told him to shoot through the restaurant's window to send a message to them but not to aim at them or harm them. I told him two shots through the window, then run. I didn't expect boy to kill Trevor. He said he just needed it to look like an attempted hit, so he could have a reason to talk his peeps into helping him with taking off Stick and Fats. It seemed to work because the same night Trevor got clapped outside the restaurant, Stick, Fats, and Dada were found dead at the spot."

Killa injected, "And that's why you had Blue Jay go and pick up the six keys from the house on Fifty-first, right before it got hit up, so they wouldn't get our bricks? You knew they were going to snatch the work."

A smile appeared on Copper's face expressing the pride he took in being able to conjure up what he thought was an elaborate scheme. While Killa was pleased it was working, he thought it to be basic at best.

"Exactly! I had two of the birds we got from the new connect moving out of that spot without Sticks and them knowing it wasn't from my pops. Told them it was extra work that Pops wanted them to knock off in the same amount of time they been doing the regular stuff.

"About a month after we set everything off, Sticks had started becoming curious, asking too many questions about the work. Dude said he needed to confirm everything with Pops.

So I set up the robbery slash murder, just in case he decided to start flapping his gums about shit.

"Plus I snatched four of Pops' kis from the spot and let them slobs grab the rest. Figured that would start a war between Pops and them. I would show them niggas how to get at Pops, then go after them as a show of retribution to Pauley and the others before taking full reins of the Gully Posse."

Copper brought the car to a stop at a red light. He peered into his rearview for signs of any police that might have been driving behind him. Seeing none, he pulled his shades below his eyes and glanced out his window at the empty sidewalk to his left. He then made the same observation to his right, again noticing no cars coming from either direction. He released his foot from the brake and pressed on the gas. He carefully drove through the red light.

He finished his explanation. "As soon as Blue brought me my work back, I sent Trevor on the fake hit. I told him not to let Pauley know. Told him I would pay him five thou to keep his mouth shut. He never asked a question. He was too busy trying to move up in the organization to worry about telling. So I guess it kind of worked out that he got lit up. Don't have to worry about his mouth or paying him."

Killa scrutinized Copper. "Why Trevor other than the fact he was following Gorilla Leek already? I mean, you could have sent me."

"Because, for one, he was watching them already, and he would have witnessed you doing the pretend hit and would have reported it back to Pauley who would have told my pops. And we both know what the penalty is for going on a hit without the approval of the inner circle. So I went directly to him and appealed to his greedy ass nature. Second, I needed someone who was not a killer because I wanted whoever was going to do it to run, not get into a firefight. Besides, I'm sure you wouldn't want to trade places with Trevor now."

"Yeah, I'm fine where I am at, and you sure this won't get back to your father?" Killa inquired.

Copper directed the car left onto Belmont. He pulled into a parking space behind a black Yukon. He threw the car in park and switched the headlights off. He rested his head on the black leather seat and motioned his eyes toward Killa. "This won't get back to my pops. That's why I wouldn't meet this cat in person till now. Besides, my pops won't be around after this month, and the neighborhood will be ours."

Copper pressed the button on his door handle. The locks flew up. He rotated the key but left it in the ignition. The seatbelts, which were stretched across their chest, automatically moved toward the front of the car, releasing the restraints on the two.

Copper examined his rearview mirror once more to catch the bearded youth cocking back his 380 Raven pistol. "Yo, Blue Jay, stay in the car and keep your eyes out for anything not right. Okay?"

The young man's eyes met Copper's in the mirror. He barely opened his mouth to reply, "Yuh mon."

Copper and Killa Kash exited the vehicle. As Copper approached the sidewalk where Killa awaited him, he removed his cell phone from his navy blue leather jacket. He flipped it open, glanced at it, then closed it, and stuck it back into his jacket. "We about ten minutes early. When I spoke to Mike, he said that slob nigga was on his way."

Killa didn't reply. Instead he followed Copper toward the corner they just drove past. Copper felt the cold wetness of the rain bounce off his nose. It was beginning to drizzle. The silence of the streets was broken by the sound of water hitting the concrete. Copper cursed under his breath. He wished he would have known it was going to rain because he would have worn his boots instead of his brand-new all-white Air Force 1s.

The two men hurried toward the corner, attempting to seek refuge in the store, which stood at the beginning of the block. There were two young males loitering in front of the store. One was black, and the other one was Latino.

They were sitting on a large green dumpster situated beneath the canopy that stretched from the entrance around to the side of the building. They too were seeking shelter from the rain. Their attention was drawn to Copper and Killa Kash, who were quickly approaching them. The two youths hopped from off the dumpster and stood facing them.

Instantly, Killa's instincts went on alert. He felt they were now walking into a set-up. He gripped Copper's shoulder, bringing him to a halt. Killa nodded his head toward the two youths. Copper shot daggers with his eyes at his partner. He didn't have time to discern what his friend was attempting to relay.

"Yo, let's get this over with."

Killa could see he was oblivious to what he was trying to tell him, so he decided to be blunt. "Them kids at the corner look suspect."

Copper didn't notice anything out of the ordinary. "Cuz, calm down. Everyone ain't out to get you." Copper continued walking. "Man, let's go."

Suddenly the explosion of gunshots drowned out the noise of the descending rain. The two teenagers sprinted across the street in the opposite direction of Copper and Killa and kept running without stopping to look back.

Killa and Copper never uttered a word to each other. Copper began running toward the store, hoping to discover the source of the gunfire.

"It came from the store," Killa yelled as he tried to keep up with his friend's pace. "You think that's Gorilla?"

Copper said nothing. He kept running. He was the first to arrive at the entrance of the store. He pulled out his .38 revolver and pulled back the hammer with his thumb. Killa came up behind him, gasping to inhale air. He stood to Copper's right. His pistol was already drawn. Copper braced himself as he grabbed the handle of the door and swung it open. He bolted into the store as the door closed behind him. Three more gunshots went off.

The sound of glass breaking stung Killa's ears. He hesitated for a second, fearful of what he was about to encounter, then leaped through the entrance with his heart racing. The first thing he noticed was the complete disarray the store was in. It appeared someone had trashed the place.

He didn't see anyone. Then, from the corner of his eye, he briefly discerned a moving figure on the ground. He focused his sight. It was Copper. He was shaking uncontrollably. His eyes were in the back of his head. He had a gaping fist-size hole in his cheek. The side of his jaw was almost completely gone. There was nothing there now but a black hole with thick blood-soaked skin protruding around the sides of it. Suddenly, his mouth shot open, and his violent movement ceased.

*   *   *

Gorilla Leek sat in his SUV, smoking a blunt. The chair was reclined as he stared out the sunroof in search of stars. He saw none. The tints on his window along with the black paint of the exterior made his car blend in with the night. It almost appeared invisible. One final pull from the blunt was taken before smothering it into the ashtray that was attached to his armrest. He closed it, then snatched his keys from the ignition and jumped out of the vehicle.

A homeless woman sitting against the wall of an empty building drew his attention. Beneath her was a bunch of old newspapers spread across the concrete. The pile served as her rug. Her pale brown skin was covered in dirt, probably the same as the filth that concealed the dull red color of her wool skullcap. She sat huddled in a thick oversized wool trench coat. Her body was still, but her lips quivered rapidly.

As he passed the lady, he removed two one-hundred dollar bills from his pocket and tossed it to the ground in front of her. Her hand shot out of the trench coat and quickly snatched the money. She gaped at him. "Thank you, sir," she humbly stated.

Gorilla Leek didn't respond. He kept walking toward his destination. He studied the sign that hovered above the store he was approaching. He stopped and assessed his environment, then glanced back up at it. It read Alvarez's Grocery. He wondered how many people in the neighborhood actually knew the name of the store. Dismissing his thought as being irrelevant, he opened the door to the entrance and walked in.

There was only one patron inside the store. The elderly gentleman was rummaging through the freezer for a particular beer. He seemed to be frustrated at the fact he couldn't find it. Gorilla Leek directed his attention to the counter behind which stood a slim five foot ten Puerto Rican male in his early forties.

"Whatup, Mike?"

The man smiled at Gorilla Leek. "Hola, Gorilla Leek! What up with you, bro?"

The conversation between the two interfered with the old man's search. He looked up at White Mike and yelled, "You ain't got no more Ole Gold?"

White Mike turned toward the man and politely spoke. "Na, Pops, no more back there."

The old man cursed a few words under his breath and stormed past Gorilla Leek, making his way onto the street outside. Gorilla Leek closed the gap between himself and the counter. "So everything is good to go for tomorrow?"

A wide grin appeared on White Mike's face. He focused his eyes. The words haltingly left his lips as he slightly opened his mouth to mutter, "You know it, bro."

"What time Copper coming?"

"He called a few minutes ago. Said he should be here soon," replied White Mike. "I told him you were on your way here."

Gorilla Leek grabbed a pack of Doritos from off the green shelf to his right. He tore open the bag, shoved his hand in it, and pulled it out, tossing a fistful of potato chips into his mouth. He widened his jaws to speak, revealing an orange and yellow mixture of mush. "Guess we'll both be early."

"Yeah, guess so. Anyway, you got your boys ready to jump into it tomorrow?" asked White Mike.

"Indeed," he assured, "everything is set. My peoples ready to get it popping."

They discontinued their discussion when the bell attached to the door went off as four teenage boys burst into the store. Two of them were brandishing guns. All four of the boys were sporting black leather gloves. A Latino youth stood with his back to the door, blocking the entrance. The other unarmed youth started kicking and turning over the potato chip racks and newspaper stands. He smashed the glass on two small portable ice cream freezers before flipping them over.

A surprised White Mike jumped back while Gorilla Leek stood still with his eyes on the light-skinned teenager, nearing him, pointing a 25 mm Lorcin pistol.

The other kid, very tall and hefty, was wearing a dark blue hoody with the strings tied tightly around his chin and waving a .44 Magnum. He approached the counter and spoke, "Yo, where's the doe and weed, Poppy?"

White Mike composed himself and, without fear in his voice, declared, "You ain't getting nothing from here. You know who you young niggas' fuckin' with?"

The boy wasn't amused. He faced the weaponless robbers and motioned for them to stop their destruction and go outside to keep watch. The Latino held the door open as the other exited the store.

"Don't let no one in," the leader of the group yelled to the Latino. The boy answered by shaking his head before following his friend outside. He closed the door behind him.

The teenager then stretched his claws around White Mike's neck, grabbed him by his long black ponytail, and demanded, "Nigga, give it up or you'll take two to the head! We know what you got back there!" He slammed Mike's head onto the glass counter below and stuck his pistol to it.

Gorilla Leek went to make a move on the youth but was stopped in his tracks by the teenager holding the 25 mm.

Unafraid, he looked down at the small gun. He relaxed himself then glared at the boy and flashed a smirk.

White Mike attempted to articulate something, but the words came out muffled because of his face being pressed against the counter. The boy released his grip on the pony tail but kept the gun to his head.

White Mike repeated himself, "I said, muthafucka, you might as well kill me because you are already dead!"

The boy didn't respond with words or facial expression. Instead he leaned back and twisted his head to the right while keeping his eyes on him. He calmly squeezed the trigger, causing his captive's head to jerk as crimson splashed onto his hand and the counter.

White Mike started breathing heavily. It sounded as if he was grunting. Then he began hissing in quick spurts. He struggled to bring his head up from the counter as if it was too heavy for him to lift. The boy couldn't believe the shot didn't kill him instantly. He stood in awe at the blood profusely leaking from the hole in the swollen lump of flesh that had now risen around the side of his head. He stepped back, attempting to put distance between himself and the living dead.

The light-skinned youth removed his attention from Gorilla Leek to assess the zombie who was now moaning and almost standing straight up. He watched as White Mike suddenly stopped his struggling and collapsed to the ground. This gave Gorilla Leek just enough time to retrieve his weapon, cock it back, and send two hot slugs slamming into the boy's neck and back.

Blood exploded from his throat as flesh from the front of his neck tore open. The impact caused the muscles in his hand to contract as his fingers went into a spasm and uncontrollably squeezed the trigger sending a bullet spinning toward the ground. It bounced off the floor and went smashing through the denim and flesh that clothe Gorilla Leek's leg.

Gorilla Leek gritted his teeth and clenched his jaw in pain. He spun around and ducked into the canned food aisle behind a three-leveled shelf while the boy's body fell forward toward his friend causing him to stumble against the newspaper stand that was positioned to his left.

Regaining his balance and feeling the dead weight of his partner, the leader shrugged the body toward the ground. It went straight down, slamming the lifeless head against the floor.

He put his back to the counter and darted his eyes up and down the store in search of the shooter. He was unaware of Gorilla Leek's whereabouts. All he knew was he heard three more shots go off after he squeezed the trigger, and now, his friend was lying dead at his feet.

His heart began beating rapidly. He wondered whether the person hiding from him could hear it. His chest was rising up and down with speed. The gun he held started weighing heavily in his shaking hands.

He couldn't figure out how he had lost control of the situation. He was about to yell out for the rest of his partners to come back into the store when the silhouette of a man positioned on the outside of the door's glass window caught his attention. He could see the man was armed and preparing to enter.

The boy swiveled around to the door, lifted his gun, and aimed. He peered over his shoulder making certain the person, who shot his friend, wouldn't surprise him. He started thinking this robbery was a bad idea. He did it because the mother of his newborn child kept urging him to buy some baby clothes. He was only a teenager and could barely feed his family, let alone spend money on shirts and socks.

Prior to tonight, he had purchased weed from the Puerto Rican elder on a regular basis. To him, the man seemed naive and harmless because of his polite mannerisms. He knew he had to have money because he owned the most popular weed spot in that neighborhood. He never saw anyone else in the store besides him, so he thought it would be an easy robbery. He was wrong.

The door flew open, causing the bell to ring once more. The figure walked in as it closed behind him. The boy didn't hesitate. His forty-four launched three large rounds slamming into Copper's face as he entered, causing his cheek to split wide-open as two of the bullets exited. The third bullet went through the window behind Copper to his right.

Flesh and blood flew from the side of his mouth and onto the glass window of the store. He stumbled back, bounced off the door, released his weapon, and fell to the floor on his stomach. He rolled over onto his back and began going into convulsions.

Gorilla Leek stood and watched from behind the canned food shelf. He couldn't believe what he saw. Chinnah's son was just shot dead. He knew if he were found at this spot, Chinnah would think he had something to do with the murder. This was not the way his plan was suppose to work. With Copper and White Mike dead, he would be unable to continue with his strategy properly. This would put him in a defensive position. He needed to escape this environment of death and get some help for his bleeding leg. He remembered the exit in the back of the store. He swung around and made his way to the back on his tiptoes.

Copper's murderer leaped into the corner situated on the left side of the door and pressed his back against the wall, concealing himself from anyone else who might walk into the store. This also gave him a perfect visual on whoever might come out of hiding from in between the aisles. Just as his heart began to slow down, the bell rang once more.

Killa Kash entered and scanned the store about him. He viewed the ground and discovered his friend shaking violently. Suddenly, Copper's mouth shot open and his movement ceased. He was dead. Killa Kash did not see the boy approaching him from behind. The boy raised his gun to Killa's head. The bell rang once more, causing him to rethink his next step. He lowered his pistol and stepped back into the corner.

Blue Jay appeared in the entrance of the store. He looked around at the store and then at Killa. "Whappen?"[35] He brought his eyes upon Copper's body. "Rass! Nuh mon!"[36]

The sound of sirens could be heard from a distance. Killa turned on his heels and went to exit the store. "Let's get out of here. He dead and the cops on their way." He bolted through the door. Blue Jay considered the situation, then shook his head in disbelief. He followed Killa outside.

The two survivors ran around the corner and toward Copper's car. They both entered the vehicle with Killa getting behind the steering wheel. He eyed Blue Jay, who was fastening his seatbelt, and warned, "If you tell Chinnah what happened here tonight, he'll kill us both. Let me handle this. A'ight?"

Blue Jay glanced out the window of the car, then brought his attention back to Killa, and replied, "Eeh, mi ave yuh."[37] Peering through the window once more, he added, "Jus make shaw yuh fi ave mi."[38]

Killa nodded his head, then threw the car's gear into drive without turning on the headlights. He could see the red glow from the sirens in the distance. The vehicle sped down the dark block and through the rain like a salmon swimming upstream in murky waters. The car slowed down and paused slightly at the intersection. Killa glanced both ways and spun the car in the opposite direction of the oncoming police. The cops never saw them.

---

[35] "What Happened?"
[36] "Fuck! No, Man!"
[37] "Yeah, I have you."
[38] "Just make sure you have me."

CHAPTER 11

Chinnah sat silently in the comfort of his black wicker chair as Detective Thomas explained to him that his son was murdered. His hand tightly clenched the edge of the armrests while his blank expression showed no signs of remorse or anger. He did not bother the detective with questions of who or when. He only lent his ear. Detective Torturro kept his sight fixed upon the man posted behind Chinnah's chair. Pauley's deep and serious eyes made him uneasy.

"We suspect there were other perps at the scene of the crime that we have yet to apprehend," Thomas stated. "We found shell casings from a third gun, and my guys discovered blood at the scene that did not match any of the vics there. So we know there was at least one more person at the scene that is unaccounted for."

Pauley rested his hand on his boss's shoulder and gripped him tightly. He cast his focus upon the detective, "So dis mon sim'ow manage ta scape?"[39]

"Yes," replied Thomas. "The suspect we arrested around the corner from the scene is only a boy . . . seventeen years old. He is not speaking much."

"Duz de bwoy ave sinting fi do wit dis oddah mon ooh fi gwan missin?"[40] inquired Pauley.

---

[39] "So this man somehow managed to escape?"

[40] "Does the boy have something to do with this other man who has gone missing?"

"We are not sure, but we will find out. Plus, we just sent the murder weapon to the lab, so we are not certain who your son's killer is yet."

Chinnah spoke, "When yuh duh, mi wan oonu fi contact mi. Mi seh, as soon as possible."[41] Chinnah brought his sight upon Pauley. "Why dem cuz mi dis sufferation?"[42]

Pauley caught his boss's eyes and sadly responded, "Mi nuh know, brethren . . . Mi nuh know."[43]

For a brief moment, Thomas felt sympathy for the old man, but his knowledge of the crimes committed by Chinnah diminished the feelings right away. "Yeah, well, giving it to you straight, you can't expect the dirt you dig to not come back around to you."

Chinnah gawked at Thomas. "Wha yuh mean? Why yuh chat so?"[44]

Thomas continued, "The sins of the father . . ."

"Shall visit pon de son,"[45] Chinnah finished the detective's statement.

"Exactly," Thomas added. "Look, Chinnah, I need you to help me, if you want me to help you."

Chinnah folded his arms and lifted his chin up. "Mi listnin."[46]

Thomas continued, "Your son was murdered earlier this evening. A couple of days ago, there were three murders at the house you own on Fifty-first and Church Avenue. And before that, one of the men known to be an associate of yours met with the same fate in front of a restaurant on Rutland Road."

---

[41] "When you do, I want you to contact me. I'm saying, as soon as possible."
[42] "Why are they making me suffer?"
[43] "I don't know, brethren . . . I don't know."
[44] "What do you mean? Why do you say that?"
[45] "Shall visit the son,"
[46] "I'm Listening."

Thomas let out a sigh. "Listen, Chinnah, you can bullshit me all you want, but it seems you are at war with someone, and you are the one losing."

Chinnah interrupted, "Detective, memba, mi infarm yuh areddi dat de ouse dere may ave bin own by mi, but mi nuh live wan day in it. It's mi rental property. Mi ave paperwuk ta prove so."[47]

Thomas smiled, aware of the game Chinnah was playing. Chinnah finished his statement, "Mi ave nuh idea wha dem deh mon do eena dehso. As far as de yute ooh yuh seh was murdad in fron of dat restaurant, mi noy know im personally. De yute ung owt wit mi pickni's cumbolo."[48]

Thomas gave Chinnah a look of disappointment. "Chinnah, I should have known better than to expect you to help me. The only reason I won't go back and forth over the issue with you right now is because you need some time to grieve. I know what it is to lose a son. May I ask you another question though?"

"Shaw, Detective,"[49] Chinnah answered.

"What does all this have to do with Shaheen Mcfadden?"

Chinnah eyes stood still. He lifted his hands to his head and rubbed his dreadlocks. "Ah ooh dat?"[50]

"Shaheen Mcfadden," answered Thomas, "otherwise known as Sha-Boogie."

---

[47] "Detective, remember I informed you already that the house there may have been owned by me, but I have never lived one day in it. It is my rental property. I have the paperwork to prove so."

[48] "I have no idea what those men were doing inside there. As far as the youth who you said was murdered in front of that restaurant, I never knew him personally. The youth hung out with my son's group of friends."

[49] "Sure, Detective.

[50] "Who is that?"

"Na, mi nuh know im. Wha im ave fi do wit mi son's murda?"[51] sternly inquired Chinnah.

Detective Thomas withdrew his suspicious gaze from the grieving father and cleared his throat before continuing his discourse.

"Chinnah, I know you have no intentions of helping me. However, the more I know, the more I can find out about your son. Do you understand me?"

Chinnah sucked his teeth. "Mon, wha yuh mean? Mi know nuttin bout wha yuh referin ta. Mi jus wan see mi son's murdera fi caught! Zeen?"[52]

Thomas smiled. "Yeah, we'll see." Thomas turned toward the door and proceeded to leave the apartment with his rookie partner following him. As he approached the exit, he stopped and glanced over his shoulder. "Just to let you know, the gun involved in the murders at your rental property and at Souljah's Restaurant was the same one used on one of the vics at the scene of your son's murder."

Chinnah stood up from his chair and trotted toward the detective. "So yuh seh de same mon ooh fi murda mi pickni is de same mon ooh fi kill da bwoys dem ooh live inna mi buildin?"[53]

Thomas made a 180 degree turn.

"No. Whoever murdered those men at the house and restaurant shot and killed one of the robbers. Witnesses reported seeing the boy we have in custody and the deceased robber together with two other kids circling the block right before the shooting. So my guess would be that they were scoping the store out. And I highly doubt the missing gunman was with

---

[51] "No, I don't know him. What does he have to do with my son's murder?"

[52] "Man, what do you mean? I know nothing about what you are referring to. I just want to see my son's murderer caught! Understand?"

[53] "So are you saying that the same man who murdered my son is the same man who killed the boys who lived in my building?"

them, unless he turned on them, because he's the one who shot and killed the friend of our suspect."

Chinnah peered strangely at his cohort; Pauley then aimed his puzzling stare at Thomas. "Scoping owt de staw? Robbery?"[54]

"Yeah, I believe this was a robbery attempt. The boy we have in custody won't give us any information other than admitting to hearing the shots. He claims his friend walked into the store right before the shooting but says he didn't see anything. However, when we picked him up, he had blood splatter on his hands and the right sleeve of his jacket.

So we are going to charge him with the store owner's murder and will charge him with your son's as well, if the lab tests come back pointing at him. We haven't yet informed him but will shortly in order to get the whole story out of him. We need him to tell us what really happened because, unfortunately, the store doesn't have any working cameras. But don't worry, we'll know the whole truth shortly."

A curious and hateful expression covered Chinnah's face. "So, Detective, if mi ear yuh correctly, ya sehin de paadi of de mon yuh ave inna yuh custody was murda by de same mon ooh kilt de tenants ooh fi rent from mi? An yuh fi tink mi son is sim'ow involve wit dem?"[55]

"Not certain if they know your son, but do know that one of the people murdered at the store was taken out by the same gun used on the vics at your property. We matched the shell casings, and we are waiting on the results of the weapon we found at the scene." Thomas glanced down at his watch, then made another 180 degree turn and continued toward the door. Pauley hurriedly rushed past the detectives and opened the door for them.

---

[54] "Scoping out the store? Robbery?"

[55] "So, Detective, if I am hearing you correctly, you are saying that the friend of the man that you have in your custody was murdered by the same man who killed the tenants who were renting from me? And you think my son is somehow involved with them?"

156 PRINCE S. GARRETT

Torturro was the first to exit. As Thomas walked out the apartment, he made one last comment. "I'll be in touch."

Pauley slammed the door behind the detective. He watched as Chinnah indolently paced over to a red oak cabinet, opened the glass doors, and retrieved a small picture frame. It was a picture of him and his son on a beach in Jamaica. Copper was only three years old at the time. He remembered swearing he would protect his son from the lifestyle that entrapped him. He did everything he could to persuade him to choose an alternate life, one that would allow him to earn the same type of income without all the negativity that surrounded it. He now recognized that he had failed as a father. The sins had visited the son. He brought his attention to Pauley.

"Ave yuh eard from Kam?"(56)

"Na, mon. De las time mi chat wit im, im seh im follow Sha-Boogie ta de Babylon station. Since den mi nuh ear from im"(57)

Chinnah showed no sign of emotion. "Wha 'bout Cutty? It bin a whole day since mi sen de bwoy ta retrieve 'mi property. Im fi call yuh 'bout mi coac yet?"(58)

"Na mi nuh ear from im eeda."(59)

"Whey de blood clot could de bwoy be? Im should've contact I an I by now. Fine owt whey im gwan an mi wan yuh fi call Jimbo, zeen?"(60)

---

(56) "Have you heard from Kam?"

(57) "No, man. The last time I talked to him, he said he followed Sha-Boogie to the police station. Since then I have not heard from him"

(58) "What about Cutty? It has been a whole day since I sent the boy to retrieve my property. Has he called you about my coac yet?"

(59) "No, I haven't heard from him either."

(60) "Where the fuck could the boy be? He should have contacted me by now. Find out where he has gone and I want you to call Jimbo, understand?"

"Indeed, mon,"[61]Pauley solemnly answered, knowing what a call to Jimbo meant.

Chinnah's eyes became hardened as his pupils shot ice picks through his friend's worrisome stare. He opened his mouth as the big man's brain swelled with curiosity and nervousness, wondering what words or command would escape. The only sound that came out was "Yuh know wha mi wan im fi do."[62]

*　　*　　*

"I don't know why I allowed you to drag me out here tonight," Sheba griped as she waited on the long line of chattering couples and friends who bordered the outside wall of Tilden Ballroom. Her friend of fifteen years was reluctant to acknowledge her comment. Jada expected Sheba to complain about the club once they were inside but not while they were on line. She was familiar with Sheba's taste and the fact that she could not bear being at a loud party with a bunch of noisy and rude men. She decided to ignore her friend's complaint.

Jada viewed the long line in front of them. She watched as the many umbrellas shook under the rain descending upon them. The people seeking refuge beneath them swayed back and forth engaging in conversation with others while waiting to get inside.

"I knew we should've gotten here earlier. We probably won't be able to get in now," Jada blurted out with frustration.

"Hmm. I wouldn't have a problem with that," Sheba uttered. "This line is ridiculous, plus it's wet as hell out here. I could be in my warm bed reading. I just purchased *Black Women in Antiquity* by Ivan Van Sertima and haven't had the chance to open it up yet. The time it's taking to get into this club I could have been halfway through the book by now."

---

[61] "Indeed, man"

[62] "You know what I want him to do."

Jada rolled her eyes and continued contemplating the long line. She didn't want to engage her friend in an argument and ruin the night. She could care less about Sheba's self-righteous views of the world. She just wanted to meet a nice-looking guy tonight because she had been horny for over a week and needed to release right away. She was out hunting for a one-night stand and only urged Sheba to come along so she wouldn't be alone.

Sheba loathed the smell of the ghetto when it rained. The foul aroma of the sewage and dried blood soaking in dirty water insulted her senses. Yet there was a good side to the rain. It seemed the harder the water fell, the more it muffled out the screams and ignorant chatter that engulfed the neighborhood once night came.

She would sit by her window when it poured and welcome the soundtrack of the streets. The gunshots that went off every other night harmonized well with the splashing sound of the rainfall. Accompanied by the long swooshing melody emitted from the tires of the many automobiles that sped up and down the block hydroplaning through the streets was the ear-piercing, wailing police sirens, which allowed her to gauge the distance between herself and the nearest crime or accident. Every now and then, she would hear the annoying sound of one of the countless crack fiends yelling out the name of someone who was three blocks away with no regard for who they might awaken.

However, this entire concert she was able to enjoy from the inside of her apartment, where the sounds seemed distant enough to be considered unreal or, from the perspective of viewing through her window, only a television program. Yet while she awaited entry into the club, the noise engulfed her and began to close in on her. The sounds became real to her whenever she ventured out of her house at night. This night, however, the melody seemed to be a warning. She could feel it caressing her spine, tapping on her shoulder, trying to tell her something.

Her song was thrown out of harmony as part of the chorus seemed to roar to life and drown out the rest of the music. The chorus became amplified as a group of about ten teenage boys neared Sheba and her friend. They were loud, cursing and laughing. They were all dressed in red from head to toe, except for two of them, who opted to cover themselves in all green. They caught the attention of Sheba and Jada who noticed the red and green bandannas dangling from the boys' back pockets and tied around their necks. One of the boys caught a glimpse of Sheba as he walked past her. He stopped in his tracks.

"Damn, ma, you fine as hell!" The boy ventured closer to her, but Sheba ignored him.

"I'm saying, ma. You got a dude?" He came to a stop right in front of her.

Jada appeared disgusted by the boy's appearance. "Can't you see she don't want to be bothered. Won't you go find you a hood rat."

"Who the fuck talking to you, bitch?" He snapped back.

Jada began rolling her neck. "Nigga, you! What, you think 'cause you Blood someone suppose to be scare of you? Nigga, please."

"First of all, bitch . . ."

"First of all, nothing," Sheba interjected. "You ain't talking to no bitch over here. If you view women as female dogs and you came from a woman, what does that make you?"

Smiling, Jada answered the question for him, "A little puppy!" Jada leaned her head back and roared with laughter.

The boy appeared furious and started to reply but couldn't get the words out of his mouth quick enough.

"You look like a fool running around here trying to be tough with your pants hanging down, cursing out loud and carrying on. Are you gay, brother?" Sheba challenged the boy's ego.

He shot her a puzzled look as his friends began to surround the two ladies.

"Bitch, watch your mouth," one of the boy's cohorts retorted.

Sheba, unaffected by the remark, continued, "That whole fad of letting your pants hang below your backside comes from prison. It was the way the homosexuals would let a man know he was ready to get fucked. Are you ready to get fucked?"

The side of the boy's lip went up, revealing two of his upper teeth, while his malicious stare became intensified. His eyes slowly followed Sheba's long black dress, from the bottom to the top. He could tell from the way it closely outlined her thighs that she was very thick. He contemplated grabbing her by her long locks and dragging her around the corner and proving to her how far from being a homo he was. He imagined himself on top of her while she feebly fought to get him off. Yeah, he would have fun with her, especially if she was a screamer. He wanted to hear her scream.

He began pondering over ways to get her around the corner without drawing too much attention when he heard the sound of car speakers violently rattling the window of an Expedition as it neared them. The vehicle pulled up to the curve next to them. The tinted windows were smoothly lowered as Shaheen's face became visible. Sheba was the second to notice. The boy quickly forgot about her and approached the car.

"What's poppin', Blood?" he yelled as he threw his right hand up in the air, with palm facing downward, and made a gesture with his thumb and index finger forming a circle while his remaining three fingers pointed straight out. Shaheen returned the greeting with the same hand sign followed by series of other finger-twisting movements, which included throwing his thumb and index back up in the shape of an L, then making an O shape with all of his fingers twice before ending it by throwing up a fist with his pinky sticking straight up.

"What that red be like?" Shaheen locked hands with the boy while seated in his car.

"I'm 5 poppin', 6 droppin', crip killin' til my crucifixition." The boy displayed an extreme show of pride.

Their fingers went up into the air forming a five-pointed star by interlocking their middle and ring fingers while allowing the tip of their pinky and index to touch. When they released each other's grip, Shaheen stepped out of the vehicle and bopped toward Sheba. Blades jumped out of the passenger side, walked around the car, then hopped into the driver's seat.

Sheba was partly relieved that Shaheen knew the boy. She could tell from the two's interaction that the group of teenagers held respect for the gentleman she met earlier that day. She watched as the rest of the boys fought to get his attention. He calmly walked through them and approached her.

"Hey, don't I know you from somewhere?" he asked jokingly.

The disrespectful loudmouth spoke before she could answer, "You know this chick, Blood?"

"Na, I know this *woman*," Shaheen stated. "Why? You bothering her?"

The boy appeared worried. "Na, not at all. I mean, I didn't know she was with you. I mean, you know, she on line and all."

Shaheen shot an endearing glance at Sheba, then replied, "Yeah, she is with me."

Sheba swung her head back. "Really?"

"Yeah, really. Unless you want to go off with my lil man, Caesar Red here?"

Caesar Red cast his eyes to the ground and began to blush like an infant.

Shaheen directed his attention toward Caesar. "Yo, you or any of your peeps seen Gorilla Leek?"

The group nodded.

"A'ight, well go on and get up in the club. Now, if any of you see dude tonight, let him know to come check me. I'll be in VIP."

"Indeed, Blood," replied Caesar Red. The crew dispersed and continued their journey down the poorly lit Flatbush Avenue block.

By now, Jada had become increasingly curious about this handsome man who happened to know her friend. She pondered over where Sheba could have possibly known him from. She knew her friend well enough to know that she didn't just meet new people out of the blue nor did she entertain anyone with conversation unless they knew her for a long time or had some degree of intelligence. She couldn't put her finger on where this man could have met her. Who was he?

Sheba outstretched her hand to him. He gently accepted it. As he shook it, he noticed her hand was extremely soft and warm for someone who had been tarrying outside on a cold, damp, and rainy night. Sheba spoke, "Good to see you again, brother. Has your mind cleared?"

"Indeed so, now that I have been graced with your presence."

Sheba smiled, then lightly slapped his arm. "Look at you trying to run game on a lady. Sorry, mister, but I don't fall that easily."

Shaheen returned her smile. "I should have known you were too smart for that." He glanced up and down the never-ending line leading into the club. "You know, y'all don't have to wait on this long ass line. Y'all can walk up in there with me."

Jada watched the two interact as she eagerly awaited her friend's reply. She begged Sheba with her eyes to not turn down the man in front of them. They had been waiting patiently to enter the club for the past two hours, and now, here was a man offering to get them in without having to dodge the rain any longer. Sheba caught her friend's goggle.

"Well, I don't know. We . . ."

"Yeah, we'll slide up in there with you," Jada said while jumping in front of her friend. She extended her hand to Shaheen. "My name is Jada."

Shaheen received her hand. Sheba shook her head and stepped in between the two, causing them to separate their grip. "Please excuse my friend. She has been excited about getting inside there for a while now."

Shaheen recognized her uneasiness. "Na, it's no problem,".

Embarrassment covered Jada's face as guilt muffled her words. "I was only trying to get out of the rain. Wasn't trying to beg or leech or anything like that. I mean, you offered."

He smiled at the lady's self conscious distress. "It's nothing."

He called out to Blades who was sitting in his vehicle still.

"Yo, Blood, hold that down. Just be back here in an hour. I'm not staying long . . . especially if Leek don't show up."

Blades, with the tinted window halfway rolled down, yelled back, "Gotchoo, my dude. I'll try to contact Leek while I'm out. I'm a drop off that work to the youngin', then I'll be back. A'ight?"

"Indeed, dog. Just call when you on your way."

Blades threw the car in drive. The back brake lights lit up.

"Yo, Blades, one more thing . . . Please don't crash up my whip . . . a'ight?"

"You good, my dude. I'll be right back with everything in one piece. Peace Almighty!"

The Expedition rolled away from the corner and eased its way into the oncoming traffic. Shaheen turned to Sheba who was busy whispering to her friend. Jada became aware of his observance. She discontinued her conversation and nudged Sheba in an attempt to direct her attention back toward the man who offered to get them into the club. Then it dawned on her.

"Um, excuse me, but do we have to still pay to get up in there?"

Sheba was instantly embarrassed by her friend's avaricious questioning. She wanted to scold Jada but refrained from doing so to prevent both of them from any further shame. Instead, she decided to apologize for her friend. However, before she was able to open her mouth, Shaheen responded.

"Na, ma, y'all good. Y'all with me." He held his arm out. Sheba was uncertain of how to act. She just met this man, and she didn't want to appear too easy to him. She reconciled that by grabbing his arm she would be accepting more than just a free entry into the club. It almost felt as if she was selling her soul. He sensed her apprehension and decided to be more candid.

"Look, you don't have to take my arm. However, if you don't plan on hanging out with me, it would be best you walk in with me unless you want every Tom, Dick, and Harry trying to push up on you. I mean, I didn't take you for the type to wanna be bothered by a bunch of dudes trying to get at you . . . at least not by the type of crabs that would come here. Ya na'mean?"

"Well, you're here, and if I'm not mistaken, you tried to holler at me earlier." She smiled without revealing her teeth, then continued, "Are you saying you are not my type?"

Shaheen raised his right eyebrow. "I don't know your type. How 'bout we go on up in here and kick it. Then we can see if I'm your so-called type. If not, no hard feelings. We'll part ways. Okay, ma?"

Sheba squinted her eyelids as her pupils shot up to the right and searched the sky above her. She caressed one of the two locks that hung down from her ponytail and over the side of her forehead while exaggerating the act of pondering something important.

After what seemed like all ten seconds, she grasped his arm and said, "After you."

Shaheen did not offer any further conversation. He began walking toward the entrance. Jada followed them. As they closed the gap between themselves and the entrance, the music inside the club started getting louder. Once they arrived at the doors, they felt the bass from the sounds thumping on the inside of their chest. Jada couldn't help but to move her head as the beat traveled from her heart to her head and feet simultaneously.

Shaheen slapped the two bouncers five, who stood to the side of both doors. They admitted him and his guest with no problem. Sheba was in awe from the amount of respect he commanded. As soon as they stepped beyond the doors, the sounds of the crowd and cars passing by on the streets were no longer discernable. They were muffled out by the loud and pulse-pounding fast-paced reggae music being played on the inside. It startled Sheba. Shaheen eyed the two ladies accompanying him and then led them further into the club.

CHAPTER 12

The old abandoned building that stood idly on the corner of Troutman Street and Bushwick Avenue towered the gray and dirt-ridden ground below, which after years of neglect, became a sidewalk portrait of shattered glass, large broken blocks of concrete, leafless withered trees, empty beer cans, and countless garbage that had been left out so long to rot that its original form could not be discerned.

The building was originally erected as a abode of shelter in an inner-city oasis of greenery twenty years prior. However, it quickly became a dilapidated monument dedicated to the numerous lost souls who, entrapped by the decadence of a poverty-stricken life of drug abuse, aimlessly trotted the now-darkened neighborhood as immortal zombies who resembled the dead but never seemed to die.

The inside of the nightmarish structure evoked the grim image of a war-torn ancient ruin complete with half-plastered walls scorched from several fires. The sections that were not plastered held bricks in its place, some of which were brownish in color and others a dull red. There were various depictions of graffiti thoughtfully spray-painted across the decrepit concrete and wooden veils that kept outsiders shut out from the world of its occupants. They resembled the hieroglyphics discovered in the destroyed temples of Egypt.

Out of the twenty or more living dead who sought shelter beneath the visibly broken and burned beams, one displaced soul was searching feverishly through a pile of large scrap metal, molded wood, fragments of stone, and torn pieces of wet carpet that had been blackened by flames. He was dressed in a filthy navy blue hoody, faded from years of wear, and a pair of torn blue denim smeared with brown stains from feces and dirt that had been dry for months.

Though it was extremely dark, with only a small ray of moonlight penetrating the interior through a tiny crack in the wood that covered the glassless window, the man decorated his eyes with large dark shades. That, coupled with his thick bushy unevenly grown beard made him appear threatening. The long thick dreadlocks that hung from the sides and back of his bald head made him resemble the alien from the movie *Predator*. His skin had an ashy and dull dark complexion that made his tiny slits for eyes almost appear nonexistent when they were revealed. The wrinkly bridge of his long and narrow nose seemed to be permanently scrunched up, causing him to display the expression of someone confused.

He stopped his frantic rummaging through the pile and nervously rubbernecked from left to right, scanning the area beneath him. He finally discovered what he was combing the ground for behind him. *How did I miss it?* he thought.

He became relieved at the sight of his gray trench coat lying on the floor. For some odd reason, the coat appeared brand-new in comparison to the rest of his wardrobe. As he took hold of it, an overgrown rat leaped out from beneath it and scurried across the trash that blanketed the floor of the ruin. He ignored it and explored the pockets.

He removed his hands from the coat and held a large blue butane gas lighter and a large metal scooping spoon. He then searched the two large pockets in the middle of his hoody. From one side, he retrieved a small folded piece of aluminum foil and, from the other, a ziplock bag halfway filled with baking soda. Glancing back down at the ground, he squatted on the floor and snatched up an unopened plastic bottle of springwater.

Twisting off the top and carefully pouring the water into the spoon until it attained the three-fourth mark, he emptied out about a half of gram of the baking soda into it as well. He then opened the foil and dumped its contents into the spoon.

Clicking the trigger on the lighter and causing the flame to appear he held the spoon with the water, cocaine, and baking soda in it above the fire. The baking soda began to bubble. By this time, he had seated himself completely on the dirty floor with his back against a brick wall. He patiently waited as the three ingredients started to combine from the heat and the bubbling slowed down. The water became murky in its color as the cocaine solidified into a golden yellow almost-round-shaped substance.

The zombie poured out the remaining water along with the residue floating on its surface, careful to not let the bulk of the product fall out. He then carefully seized the bottled water from the ground and again filled the spoon with it. Retrieving a folding knife from his back pocket, he scooped the substance from the spoon and transferred it to an old metal plate that bordered his feet. After tilting the plate as to let the remaining water escape, he cautiously ran his knife back and forth over the oily, golden yellow clump for about a minute until it resembled a small piece of hard white rock.

Suddenly, before he could finish his process, the sound of a cell phone ringing could be heard from his coat pocket.

"Shit!" he cursed out loud, angry that someone would disturb him at this time. However, he knew better than to not answer it because only one person had his number, the same person who gave him the phone and paid for its monthly bill. He decided to answer it as quickly as possible, not out of fear for the one calling, but to find out what the person wanted so he could get back to his freebasing. He shot his hand into his pocket and answered the phone.

"Yo," he stated emotionlessly.

"Ya, mon. Mi ave wuk fi yuh,"[63] the other voice replied. "Meet I an I in de pawk pon Fulton an Utica near de subway. Dis impawtent, so nuh be late."[64]

The voice on the other end awaited a response but received none. He became impatient. "Jimbo!" he screamed. "Mon, yuh chupid ar sinting? Duh yuh ear wha mi axe?"[65]

Jimbo said nothing.

"Whappen, yuh def ar yuh smokin dat creack sheet rye now?"[66]

Jimbo calmly mumbled, "Na, I'm freebasing . . . There's a difference."

"Well, duh yuh ear wha mi axe?"[67] he inquired once more.

"Yeah, man. I hear you. How much?" Jimbo uttered coldly.

"Tin fi two eads"[68]

"Are these two gonna be in the same spot?"

"Mon, mine ow yuh chat pon de fone. Mi discuss it wit yuh, wonz yuh reach de pawk. Zeen?"[69]

"Be there in one hour." Jimbo didn't wait for a reply. He hung the phone up and dropped it on the floor, next to his coat. Prior to becoming a drug addict, Jimbo was known as James Franklin II, a Green Beret who did two tours in Vietnam. He was a trained killer who, after the war ended, came back home to unemployment and a crime—ridden neighborhood. He found

---

[63] "Yeah, man. I have work for you,"

[64] "Meet me in the park on Fulton and Utica near the subway. This is important, so don't be late."

[65] "Man, are you stupid or something? Do you hear what I am asking?"

[66] "What happened, are you deaf or are you smoking that crack shit right now?"

[67] "Well, Did you hear what I asked?"

[68] "Ten for two heads"

[69] "Man, mind how you talk on the phone. I'll discuss it with you once you get to the park. Understand?"

refuge from the harshness of a financially unstable life in the heroin that flowed so freely throughout his Harlem community.

Nearly ten years after his discharge, Jimbo sought out help and rehabilitation. After cleaning himself up, he moved to Brooklyn in an effort to escape his old lifestyle and running partners. Unfortunately, due to his lack of work experience, he was only able to secure a job sweeping up floors in a neighborhood bodega. The bodega just so happened to be owned by Chinnah, who had recently arrived to America's shores a few years prior. Upon discovering Jimbo's background, Chinnah offered him thirty thousand dollars to murder his rival. Once the job was completed, Chinnah was so pleased with his professionalism and brutality; he offered him a permanent position as one of his enforcers.

It wasn't until Jimbo started getting engulfed by the temptation of money and women that he ended up falling victim to his old habits and graduated to the addiction of crack cocaine. It was then that Chinnah decided to relieve Jimbo of his post, only to use him from time to time when he needed something handled that he couldn't run the risk of being traced back to him. Jimbo became a freelance hit man whose usual payment of thirty thousand or more declined to five thousand dollars a job. Sometimes he only made half of that for his efforts. To Chinnah, it was a good business relationship because Jimbo was still an effective assassin who he now only had to pay a little over 10 percent of what he used to. The fact is no one in the neighborhood, not even Shaheen or Gorilla Leek was aware of Jimbo's occupation. To them, he was just another crackhead.

Jimbo went back to finishing what he started. He snatched the metal spoon from off the ground and used it to crush up the freebase on the plate until it became a fine powder. He then poured the substance into the spoon followed by water from the bottle. He used the knife to stir the mixture for about a minute or so after which he went once more into his back pocket and pulled out a folded up coffee filter. He opened up the paper and poured the contents of the spoon into it. He watched as the water escaped the filter until there was only pure freebase left. He lowered the paper by the metal plate and allowed the freebase to fall out onto it.

He regarded his hands and observed the burnt marks and dried bloodstains on the torn skin of his chewed-up fingertips. He thought about the years he lost getting high and wondered would he ever be able to go cold turkey. Just as quickly, he dismissed the idea for fear of having to cope with a reality he loathed. The fact was he hated himself for the murders he committed, and smoking helped him to alleviate the guilt and forget. Now with another job awaiting him, he could purchase enough rock to last a week. Realizing he didn't have much time to make it to his meeting, he looked down at the metal plate and impatiently waited for the substance to dry.

*   *   *

Sheba sat upright on a couch curiously watching Shaheen as he approached her with two whiskey glasses in his hands. He shuffled past the several men and women shaking their drunken bodies across the dance floor. He cautiously slipped in between couples, obstructing their rhythm, attempting to refrain from spilling the Crown Royal he tightly clenched. She admired the way he strutted with confidence. He exuded a great deal of strength when he moved about in public.

As he neared the VIP section, which was situated to the far right of the club, the six foot six bouncer who stood guard began unhooking the rope that prevented unwanted guest from accessing that area of the building. Shaheen dug into his pocket and pulled out a one hundred dollar bill and subtly slipped it into the palm of the guard as he passed him. The guard pulled the rope back and allowed Shaheen entrance. Shaheen stepped up onto the two-inch high platform meant to distinguish that section from the rest of the club.

He acknowledged Sheba staring at him, so he put on his best walk. He smoothly glided across the surface of the floor toward the couch she sat on. He held in his tough gangsta bop and controlled the motion of his stride. Once in front of her, he passed her one of the glasses.

"Thank you," she said.

He said nothing in return, then propped himself down onto the couch right beside her. He assessed the side of her face. She was gazing out onto the dance floor, observing her friend grinding on one of the Bloods who approached them earlier. He could not help but to notice how beautiful she was. Her cheek bones were very pronounced. They sat high above her slender jaw. Her elongated chin curved outward, causing the shape of her delicate head to resemble a crescent, as her full heart-shaped lips protruded out, inviting him to taste them.

She could sense him staring, so she decided to face him directly. "So are you a Blood?" she boldly inquired.

He smiled, then took a sip from his glass. The Crown Royal warmed the inside of his chest. "I don't bang, ma. I hustle."

She poked out her lips and twisted them to the side of her mouth. "That doesn't answer my question." Her left eyelid drooped as she raised her right brow and focused intently on him. "Besides, you hustle what?"

Shaheen lifted his chin up into the air and let out a laugh. "Why? Are you gonna give me that 'hurting my own people' speech?"

"Na. I won't because it seems you are already familiar with it. However, the negative energy you put out there will come back around full circle to harm you."

"How you figure? I mean, what if I don't care what happens to me?"

Sheba shook her head in disappointment. "What if it is not you, but someone you love or care about?"

Shaheen sat silent and still. The club became quiet to him. He could hear himself breath. He felt the pressure of her statement violently squeezing his heart. It felt as if it was going to burst through his chest. He tried to swallow, but his mouth was too dry, so he took another sip of his whiskey. All he could say was "Whatchoo mean?"

She could see he was uncomfortable now. "I mean, you may not fear death, but everyone fears losing."

"Losing?"

"Yeah, losing someone you love." She paused to analyze his reaction. "Do you have children?"

She caught him off guard. He fumbled with his words under her scrutiny. "Uh, yeah . . . well, na . . . not really."

Sheba appeared confused, and he took notice.

"I mean, I have godchildren."

"Yeah, well, if you plan on having some one day, you might want to relinquish your occupation or else you could be endangering them. What if something happened to your child because of some karma owed to you?"

He tossed the remaining liquor down his throat. *That was it! It was my fault. I'm the reason Shane is dead.* But then another thought crossed his mind, and he voiced it. "But wouldn't that be messed up? I mean, God punishing an innocent child for something I did. I mean, he didn't have anything to do with what I was into."

She seemed perplexed. "What you were into? Who is the *he* you are referring to? I thought we were speaking hypothetically."

He caught himself. "We are. I'm just saying, that wouldn't seem like a godlike thing to do."

"Neither does harming others to gain benefit for yourself, which is what you are doing when you sell poison to our people. You know typically I wouldn't deal with anyone like you, but you seem different. I don't feel you're a bad person, just a person with bad circumstances, I suppose."

He decided now was the perfect time to change the direction of the dialogue. "Yeah, I guess. But anyway, before I went to the bar, you was talking about going to school to be a social worker. Why a social worker? They don't make a lot of money, do they?"

Sheba, aware of his attempt to change the conversation, decided to entertain his questioning.

"It's not about the money for me. It's about helping the youth. We are losing our youth to the streets. I want to be able to make a difference. I have watched too many of our young males wind up dead or in prison. That doesn't have to be their destiny, but most don't know any better or they don't have anyone to talk to or get advice from."

"Have you ever worked with the youth before?"

She took a long sip from her glass. "Yeah, I began working with the youth about two years ago."

"What made you get into that?" He humbly asked.

"My family."

"Your family?"

Sheba let out a heavy sigh. "Yeah, my family." She paused, threw her eyes up into the air, then brought them back down on Shaheen. "My family has done a lot of wicked things and has hurt a lot of people, so I decided to be the exact opposite. I rarely even go around them because I don't want their negativity to rub off on me."

He released a chuckle. "What, you afraid you gonna become like them?"

"Na. I'm afraid that whatever they are into will come back and bite me. So I stay away and just worry about sticking to my plan."

Shaheen leaned back into the couch, grabbed his pants around the knee area with both hands, and tugged on them while raising his behind from off of the seat to straighten out his outfit.

"Your plan?"

"Yeah, finish school and move to Florida."

"Florida? Then how are you going to help the youth? I thought that was the whole point."

She gave him a sympathetic smile as if he was too innocent to understand. "There are children across this entire country that need my help. Not only here. Plus, I want to get as far away as possible from my father."

"Get away? That doesn't sound so good. I mean, you talking about your pops."

"Yeah, but only my fleshly father, not my spiritual one."

"Huh?"

Sheba moved her free hand onto his leg. "You should reverence the womb that bore you, and in most cases, we take that to only mean our earthly parents, but it is also referring to our Heavenly Father."

Shaheen let out a slow and dramatic, "Okay." He was never interested in spirituality, only money. He felt as if God had let black people down and was convinced of this every time he contemplated the dire circumstances that most of them faced. He decided to let her talk while he remained quiet.

She continued her lecture, "That's the problem. Most of us have a greater fear of each other or our oppressors than our own Creator." She shifted her position on the couch, so she could better face him in order that he may see how serious she was. "You know, if you built a better relationship with the Most High, you wouldn't have to worry about making ends meet by doing what you are doing. He can provide all things."

"By doing what I am doing? How do you know what I am doing?" he inquired before sighing, then continuing. "Besides I've tried that already. You know, going to church." Smirking, he finished his statement, "Shit, that just made me even more broke, having to pay tithes and all that."

She shook her head from side to side. "Brother, you have to do a little more than just attend service and give up money. If you do not have a relationship with the Creator, nothing else you do will amount to anything."

She eyed him with curiosity, trying to determine if her words were registering. "Shaheen, you seem to be a good man, who has a lot of potential. Why limit yourself? Have you ever thought about returning to school and getting a degree? Did you finish high school? Don't you want to see more out of life?"

"See more out of life?" A faint smile surfaced on his face. "Why C-life when I can B-life? I mean, Ma, I ain't no dummy.

I just didn't finish college. I actually do want to get a degree though."

Excitement and wonder leaped out from her eyes. "Oh really, for what?"

"Architecture."

"Architecture? I didn't take you for that type. Thought maybe you would want to be a rapper or something."

He frowned. "What's wrong with that?"

Sheba softly sucked her teeth. "We don't need any more entertainers. You can't build a nation with entertainers."

"Build a nation? What? You talking that back to Africa shit? Look around Ma, the only Black Power is white powder," Shaheen retorted. "And besides, on the real, rappers, if they did put something worthwhile in their mouths, could influence youths to go to school, to stay away from drugs, or to become more . . . you know . . . like you . . . spiritual. You know?"

She was pleased with his rebuttal. While it made sense, she knew he was still missing the big picture. However, the fact he had an intelligent opinion on the subject showed he was not just some young and dumb drug dealer.

"Yeah, I see what you're saying, brother, but what we need are nation builders, like doctors, engineers, farmers, lawyers, and so forth. We can't rebuild our nation with a bunch of rappers. The average rapper increases his bank account by glorifying his ignorance and, in return, the youths who follow behind him believe that the crime he brags about committing in his song is the way to go about becoming financially successful.

"Most of those kids don't know that the same brand names he boasts about possessing are owned by companies investing in privately owned jails. Yeah, prison for all those kids who end up getting locked up from running around trying to be like their favorite rapper. So for all the successful and rich rappers that are out there, there are a million other youths getting incarcerated behind the foolishness being promoted in their music. Why do you think they allow them to get so paid? There weren't this many million-dollar deals for rappers when they were kicking positive lyrics. You think they would have paid KRS One a million dollars to say, 'Jesus was an African'? Na, but they'll pay Jay-Z that money to talk all that Cristal shit!"

He could see the flames flickering in her eyes. He was shocked to hear her curse. It didn't suit her demeanor. He could tell she was very passionate about her beliefs. He decided not to push the subject.

"I feel you. I guess I never looked at it that way."

"Yeah, brother, but we have to look at it that way."

The two stared into each other's eyes. Sheba was turned on by the fact he was tough yet displayed a degree of intelligence. It was attractive. Most of the men she met who were brilliant were extremely soft. In other words, they were cowards, and that was a turn off for her. She viewed black men as natural warriors. However, when she met guys who were fearless, they would usually be as dumb as an ox.

She never met someone who had the potential to be balanced. She was certain now she wanted to get to know this gentleman in more depth. She desired to proceed with her speech but was disturbed by the yelling and cursing of a female arguing with the bouncer who stood guard over the VIP section they were in.

Shaheen instantly recognized the face. It was Carla. He couldn't hear the whole conversation but was able to catch bits and pieces. He thought he heard her say something like "I'm with him!" She then pointed right at him. Shaheen didn't want her to approach him while he was with his company, so he decided to walk over to her. Sheba watched as he rose from the sofa and trotted away without saying a word.

By the time he reached the two, the bouncer had his arms around Carla's waist trying to stop her from forcing her way past.

"Yo, what's going on?" Shaheen spoke to no one in particular.

The bouncer, who was so calm he almost seemed high, stated, "This chick said she with you. I told her not tonight 'cause I knew you didn't want to be bothered." He motioned his head toward Sheba as if to tell him, *I got you.*

Carla, taking notice, screamed out but not loud enough for Sheba to hear completely, "I don't care about that bitch!" She then snapped her neck toward Shaheen. "Nigga, tell her to bounce! I need a drink!"

Shaheen shifted his eyes at her with contempt. She was taking the conversation they had in the park too far now. He wasn't about to become someone's personal blackmail slave, and there was no way he intended to let this whore mess up the good moment he had going with Sheba. Plus, he didn't want Carla to blab out anything about him having a woman. "Look, bitch, you crazy if you think you gonna walk up in here giving orders. Ain't no one leaving but you!"

"Muthafucka! Are you forgetting our arrangement?"

"Bitch, we ain't got no arrangement!" he retorted back.

She removed herself from the bouncer's grip and demanded, "Nigga, you either let me up in there and tell that chic to go home or not only will I let Lola know you're up in here with another broad, but I will kindly take my ass over to the precinct and have a nice long chat."

Shaheen's anger intensified. He was more than certain now that she had to be dealt with. He was not going to do any time over this chick. Her words would not let him think straight. He brought his attention to the bouncer and stated with authority, "Kick her ass out the club!"

An expression of awe covered her face. She did not expect him to turn her down. She calculated he would be too concerned with getting arrested than to care about how she came at him. She had played all of her cards. However, if he did kick her out, he would be sorry.

The bouncer made his move and in one motion scooped her from off her feet and tossed her over his shoulder. Shaheen began laughing though he knew there wasn't anything comical about what would come next for either of them. Enraged by his laughter, Carla decided to throw one more stone as she was being prepared to be carried out.

"That's why your Lola been fucking another dude!"

Shaheen was caught off guard by her comment. He was uncertain of how to respond. He did not want to appear bothered by her comment, so he refrained from asking her to elaborate. Instead he glimpsed at the big man and calmly stated, "Get her out of here and don't ever let her back in when I am around."

Carla did not want to snitch on her friend, but she was furious. She was baffled by Shaheen's reaction. He did not seem to believe her, she thought, so she decided to take it further.

"I guess you don't care that it's your boy she's fucking!"

By the expression on his face, she could see she now had his attention. Shaheen raised his hand for the bouncer to stop. "Yo, hold on." The bouncer stood still in his tracks. Shaheen decided to feed his curiosity. "My boy?"

Carla was elated. She knew she had him. "Yeah, nigga, your boy."

"Who?"

She didn't want to give up her goods without getting something out of it. "Won't you tell this overgrown monkey to put me down, and we can go over to the couch and discuss it."

Shaheen sucked his teeth. "Bitch, you got five seconds to give me a name!"

"Man, fuck you, Sha! Tell him to put me down!"

He glanced at the bouncer and said, "Go on, throw her ass out."

The man proceeded toward the exit with the human cargo on his arm.

Shaheen began walking back over to the couch where Sheba awaited him when he heard Carla scream out, "She's fucking Gorilla Leek! Your nigga been fucking your baby mama every Friday morning while you at Minimart counting your doe. They been fucking each other since last year. The dude even got a key to your apartment." She paused for less than a second to see how it registered, then continued, "Shit, and you think I'm foul!" The rest of her words began to fade as the bouncer carried her across the floor.

Shaheen couldn't move. His heart sunk. He wondered whether she was alleging the truth or not. That would explain how she knew where Shane's body was. Gorilla Leek could have told Lola, and she might have told Carla. He came to the conclusion that she was more than likely being honest, even if she had the wrong intentions. He felt too embarrassed to venture back over to Sheba. He pulled himself together and began his journey toward her. His mind was racing between thoughts of Lola cheating with his best friend and murdering Carla, so his secret could remain safe. His desire was to follow her outside and put two slugs in her, but he knew it would be unreasonable.

As he neared Sheba, she could sense something was wrong. She was able to see all the commotion yet heard nothing over the thumping volume of the sounds coming from the large speaker that was hidden in the corner behind her.

"Is everything all right? I hope I didn't get you in trouble with your girl," she stated inquisitively.

Shaheen tried to conceal the trouble that plagued his conscience by painstakingly forcing a smile to surface. "My girl? Na, ma, everything good. That is definitely not my girl."

"So you do have a girl?" she nervously interrogated.

He decided to change the subject to avoid lying to her. He wasn't even sure if he knew how to answer.

"You wanna get outta here?"

She knew he was avoiding the question but was intrigued by his offer. "And go where?"

"I don't know. Maybe we can hit up Brooklyn Diner on Utica Avenue and get some grub."

She thought about it for less than a second. "Yeah, that doesn't sound too bad. But what about my homegirl?"

"How'd y'all get here?"

"She drove."

"Well, I'm sure she won't mind if I take you home, that is, if you feel safe with me."

Sheba bit her lip as if she was uncertain of how to respond. "But she'll be by herself."

"I'll have my dogs watch after her. She'll be safe with them," he assured, pointing in the direction of the Bloods who were taking turns dancing with Jada.

She started to ask him one more question when his cell phone began vibrating. She observed him as he searched his pockets. Finding the phone, he quickly answered. He didn't wait for the person on the other line to address him. "Yo, you hear from Leek?"

Sheba noticed a different person coming to the surface of his personality now. He seemed more dangerous, a lot angrier.

"Yo, never mind that. Are you outside? A'ight, I'm coming out now. I'm gonna drop you off by the spot and then go handle some BI."

He closed his cell without uttering another word. He peeked at Sheba, who was staring at him with worrisome eyes.

"You ready to go?"

She didn't know how to turn him down. She wanted to be around him for the rest of the evening, so all she could say was "Yeah, I'm ready, King."

CHAPTER 13

"Do you think he will cooperate?" inquired Detective Torturro.

"Not sure. Doubt it," responded Thomas as he guided the Crown Victoria down Sutter Avenue. "More than likely he'll try to handle it himself. Chinnah lives in his own world where he is the law."

Torturro glanced out of the passenger window onto the dark street they drove down. The sidewalk was packed with several teenagers hanging out and engaged in loud dialogue. Every now and then, Torturro would notice a fiend scurrying through the crowd of nightwalkers, stopping only to ask for change or whatever else he imagined. As they passed Blake Avenue, he witnessed a woman, probably in her forties, wielding a pocketknife at an older gentleman. They appeared to be lovers. The couple was screaming at each other and seemed to be drunk. The man's beige fatigue coat was covered in filth and soaked with his own blood.

Though bleeding, his quick and agile movement betrayed the seriousness of his injury. Torturro turned away from the scene as they drove by and dismissed it as an ordinary and nightly conflict the inhabitants of the ghetto were use to. He reasoned the couple will probably be back to loving each other later on after they finished getting high. That is why he sometimes felt it to be a waste of time helping the degenerates in the neighborhood. They didn't even want to help themselves.

"Well, if this is the world in which he wants to be the law, he can be it. Unfortunately, these folks would probably respect him more than they do us."

Thomas shot a quick glance at Torturro before placing his eyes back on the road. He was preparing to reply when he felt his cell phone vibrating on the side of his waist. He fumbled with the flap on the holder while he kept one hand on the steering wheel. Bringing his phone to his ear, he spoke into the receiver.

"Hello."

"Man, where have you been. I've been trying to reach you for over an hour now," Cannon excitedly shouted from the other end of the phone. He was so loud that Torturro could hear his voice through the receiver although he couldn't make out the full content of the conversation.

"Trying to reach me? For what?" Thomas asked calmly.

"I have a location on the missing child."

"And? That's your case. I just wanted to know how it was connected to Chinnah. I mean, I am still working my murder case. Don't get me wrong. It's good you were able to close your ca—"

Cannon interrupted his peer, "You will want to work this one. I think it's a hommie. I have a lead on the whereabouts of the child. According to the information received, the child was murdered, then buried."

The excitement in Thomas's voice exploded into a high pitch shriek. "The child is dead! Are you sure? Is your lead credible? Do they know the father's involvement?"

"Not sure if it's on the money. The tip came from a call in. It was a lady who claims to know where the body is hidden."

"Do you have her contact information?"

"She hung up without identifying herself. I ripped the number from the caller ID. I have the rookie getting info on it now."

"Look, don't go anywhere! I will be there in fifteen minutes!" Thomas excitedly yelled into the phone before placing it on the seat in between his lap. Torturro eyed his partner with intense curiosity.

"Was that about the Chinnah case?"

"Kind of. It's all connected, just not sure how yet."

"So I guess we're headed back to the station?"

"You know it, brother."

Torturro relaxed and leaned back into the seat as Thomas drove the rest of the way in silence.

*   *   *

"Well, where the fuck is he!" screamed Shaheen into his cell phone. "Yo, dude was 'pose to be handling our BI. Nobody's heard from son?"

Sheba's pupils diligently searched his contorted expression for any hint of the emotions that were pervading his thoughts. She could discern from his tone that whatever he was discussing was bothering him. She tried to appear uninterested in his conversation, but the truth was she was avidly listening to every word. She wanted to know the type of man she was sitting at the table, eating with at three o'clock in the morning.

"Yo, go and look for dude. Check out his crib. Maybe he went back there to clean up more. Just find him! We got too much going on right now for him to be doing a disappearing act." Then as if wondering whether his next thought was logical or not, he hesitantly commanded, "Go by my crib and see if he's there."

He pressed his ear to the receiver as the person spoke.

"Nigga, don't worry about that. Just go over there!" He was obviously vexed.

Sheba watched as his tongue lashed out venom with each word that escaped his twisted lips. Up until the recent phone call, they had been enjoying each other's company, talking through the night about their ambitions, goals, and perceptions on life and its tribulations. Their conversation became so in-depth at one point that it felt like they had known each other for years.

They surprised each other on how much they had in common, considering how different their lives were. Every now and then, Shaheen's mind would drift back to the words Carla hurled at him earlier regarding Lola's infidelity. He decided to not allow his thoughts of insecurity overwhelm him, so he forced his mind to focus on what was in front of him, a beautiful young lady.

They both had taken long and slow bites of their food, attempting to prolong the night. Finally, they were finished and prepared to leave when he received the phone call. It changed his whole demeanor. Now, the perfect gentlemen transformed into a deadly criminal right before her eyes. She contemplated what the consequence would be for those who seemed to be the cause of his displeasure at the present.

"Peace!" shouted Shaheen into the receiver. He hung up, then brought his eyes upon Sheba. She could tell he was now distracted by the manner in which his deep-set eyes remained fixed on the thin air that transparently veiled her face. He was staring right through her yet regarding nothing in particular. She brought him back to reality.

"Is everything okay?"

He pondered over how to best answer her and decided on "Yeah, I'm good. Just everyday trouble, that's all."

"If that's everyday trouble for you, I wouldn't want to be in your shoes. Seems like a lot to deal with."

"I suppose. Guess I'm built for it."

"Yeah, I guess so. I mean, between the drama at the club and phone conversation you just had, I would say you have a lot on your plate."

Shaheen's memory was jolted by the mention of what happened at the club. His mind was so consumed with the possibility of Lola cheating that he had, for a moment, forgotten about Carla's threat. Now that the Crown Royal was wearing off, his mind raced over the possible disaster that could ensue if Carla had left the club and went straight to the police. He calculated the odds of her going through with the promise.

Instead of seeing Sheba's beautiful full lips sympathetically smiling at him, the image of a judge's gavel slamming down upon a bench hovered in front of him. He quickly decided he needed to leave and take care of the situation that was brewing.

The only words he could force from his lips were "The club, uh . . . yeah . . . You know, I just remembered . . . I'm sorry, but I have some important business to take care of. Do you mind if I drop you to your crib now?"

"Um, na." Sheba was caught off guard by the sudden change in plans. While disappointed that their night had to end, she was elated he was not trying to get her to go back to his place. She respected him for that. "You can drop me by the house. That's fine, but you say you have business? At this time of night?"

"Yeah, something I forgot about that I need to handle." Shaheen's only thought at the moment was getting back over to Lincoln Terrace Park and removing the body and the gun. His thoughts were moving a mile a minute, causing him to be indecisive about which action he should take.

He figured if Carla went to the police, they would instantly go to the park in search of his son's corpse. So the best option, he reasoned, was moving everything to another location. He decided he would do it while he still had the darkness of the early morning as an ally.

Shit! he thought, *I should been doing that instead of going out with ole girl tonight.* He decided he needed to get her home as soon as possible. He wasn't going to allow Carla to ruin his life. He figured he would pay her a visit after he moved the body. The only problem was he didn't know exactly where in the park Gorilla Leek had buried the body or the gun. Sheba just watched her company as he sat staring off blankly into the air.

"I guess you're ready to go now?" she asked.

"Yeah," he informed as he snapped his mind back to reality and refocused his vision in order to better observe her. "Let's bounce." He threw two twenty dollar bills down onto the table, overpaying as usual, and then lifted his coat from the chair as he eased out of the booth. He stood fastening his coat as Sheba smoothly glided out of her sitting area. They both made their way past their waitress toward the exit of the diner.

*   *   *

Bright white searchlights flooded the wooded section of the northern side of Lincoln Terrace Park. Several voices could be heard chattering along with the sound of branches breaking and leaves shuffling as the many uniformed and plainclothes officers search the grounds and shrubbery of Dead Man's Hill.

The hill received its name back in the nineteen eighties when the park served as the neighborhood's headquarters for prostitution and drug trafficking. It became the local criminal's choice of location whenever they needed to dispose of a corpse. However, during the early nineteen nineties it served as a place to perform death-defying stunts as Shaheen and the neighborhood children dared each other to ride their bikes full-speed down the steep and dangerous obstacle.

Now at four o'clock in the morning it resembled the stage at a Madison Square Garden concert, with the blinding brightness uncovering the dark and gloomy atmosphere that pervaded the area. The countless living corpses of the damned that usually paced back and forth aimlessly through the park were nowhere in sight now. If they were present, they blended in with the twenty or more policemen and women who canvassed the scene in search of Lil Shane's body.

Several dogs sniffed and poked their wet noses in and out of the various bushes and trees that surrounded the hills. The men who tended to them eagerly waited for the all-familiar tugs on the leashes from their excited canines. So far, the search yielded nothing. The park was filled with blue uniforms, black dress suits, men, women, dogs, and all types of technological devices being wielded by geeks with badges. The noise from the many voices would increase in volume only to lower and then get louder again as someone would yell out to the others that they discovered something of interest before finding out it was of no importance.

Detective Torturro stood on the sidelines and viewed the cooperation among the different city employees while Cannon and Thomas interacted with a couple of crime scene investigators who were using a prong-like instrument to probe the ground beneath them. Torturro took notice of his peers convening and decided to approach them.

"What's that for?" Torturro innocently inquired as he neared the group, pointing at the instrument one of the investigators held. He did not want to disturb an important conversation; however, he was becoming bored with waiting as his more experienced partner conducted the majority of the investigation.

Thomas decided that answering his rookie partner's naive questions was his responsibility. "He is using it to check the density of the soil to see if the dirt has been disturbed."

Torturro slightly raised his head, then gradually allowed it to sink as he, in the same time frame, let out a long and dull "Ohhh."

Thomas could see his partner did not understand what they were doing, so he decided to explain. "If the body was buried, then the dirt would have been tampered with and weakened from the digging and refilling."

"Okay," Torturro replied lazily. Torturro felt his eyes becoming heavy. He had been awake for more than twenty-four hours trying to keep up with his mentor and partner. The investigation was beginning to wear him down. He really could care less about the instrument's use. He was only attempting to throw out hints of his exhaustion.

Suddenly, a loud bark echoed repeatedly from beyond the purple shadows of the wooded area that sat atop of the hill. The bark was vicious and relentless, causing the other canines to follow suit. Thomas and the rest of his cohort took notice. They could not see the animal or the officer holding it. It was difficult because of the thickness of the night that shielded that section of the park from the floodlights that shone in the opposite direction.

The men started leisurely heading toward the location where the dog was heard from. Thomas began to squint his eyes as he heard someone yell out, "I think we got decomp!" The men started jogging lightly up the hill, only to increase in speed as the barking became louder and closer.

While they ran, Torturro turned toward Cannon and asked, "Did he say decomp?"

Cannon glanced briefly in his direction and answered, "Yep, looks like we might have a body!"

CHAPTER 14

Carla sat idly upon her couch with her head tilted back, slowly exhaling a thick gray cloud of marijuana smoke. She let out a light cough before dumping the ashes onto the floor beneath her. Frustration pervaded her mind. She had to figure out a way to induce Shaheen into liking her. She did not want to be the cause of his incarceration because that would defeat her purpose, which was to be with him forever, yet the event that occurred earlier that night left her aroused with anger.

She had spoken to Lola earlier and, from their conversation, knew that Shaheen had not addressed her about cheating yet, so she still had some time left before she would have to deal with an angry friend. Yet from what Lola told her, she might not be around to discover the betrayal.

Suddenly, there was a loud and disturbing knock at the door, causing Carla to leap out of her skin. The fist on the other side of the door continued to viciously slam against it, turbulently vibrating the hinges, provoking the doorknob to rattle. She stood to her feet staring at the shaking frame as if she was waiting for the person knocking to enter. The knocks became kicks causing the door to have a murderous pulse, a heartbeat of death.

"Open the fuckin' door!" the person screamed from the other side.

Carla instantly recognized the voice. She bolted over to the entrance and nervously unlocked it. Shaheen shoved his way past her and slammed the door shut. She watched him as he erratically paced back and forth.

"Bitch, you went to the cops?"

Carla's expression displayed a lack of comprehension. "Huh?"

Shaheen sucked his teeth. "Bitch, you went to the cops!" he stated rather than asked this time.

"Went to the cops about what?" she timorously inquired. "What? About Shane? Na, I didn't go to no one."

Shaheen retrieved a 9 mm automatic pistol from his waist. "You Triple 9 bitch! You gonna tell me everything you said to the pigs. I just drove by Lincoln Terrace, and the shit was swarming with po po. What the fuck did you drop on them?"

At the sight of the pistol, Carla began to shake uncontrollably. She released the blunt she held in between her fingers. Her lips quivered rapidly as her chest pulsated with each quick and short breath she took. "I swear, Sha, I ain't said shit to no five O," she pleaded.

He aimed the weapon directly at her forehead as he closed the distance between them. She began to ease backward away from him in small steps. Fuming, he waived the gun in front of her as he screamed, "Tell me what the fuck the pigs know or I'm a blow a hole through your fuckin' dome!"

She began crying convulsively. "I didn't go to the police. I came straight home after I left the club. I'm telling you the truth! You have to please believe me," she begged in between her loud and frantic sobs.

"So how the fuck did the pigs know where to look?"

Her tears had now totally drenched her face, causing her to appear as if she just stepped out of a swimming pool. Her bawling gradually became a sniffling whimper while she pleaded with her captor.

"Sha, you have to believe me. The only person I can think of that knew is the person who first told me."

"And who might that be?" he asked with a tone of disbelief.

"Lola. Lola is the one who told me everything 'cause Gorilla Leek told her."

Shaheen's eyes widened as he removed the pistol from her. "Lola?"

He glanced to the ground, then raised his sight back up to her eye level. "You think Lola went to the police?"

"I dunno. I just know I didn't go."

"Why would she go to the police? I mean, we could both get locked."

Carla shrugged her shoulders, then slyly replied, "Maybe because she pregnant."

Shaheen's eyelids shot open as he tilted his chin to his chest. "Pregnant?"

"Yeah, she just found out yesterday."

He was so consumed by her words he barely felt the gun slipping from his grip.

"By who, me?" he asked.

"She's not sure if it's yours or Leeks. That's why she is getting ready to leave."

A perplexed expression overcame his face. "Leave?" The pistol almost fell from his hand. He tightly clenched it as it began to drop and secured it in his grip.

"Yeah, she's going back to Georgia. That may be why she decided to go to the cops."

Shaheen couldn't believe what he was hearing. His woman was possibly a snitch and pregnant by his best friend. His heart sank. He wanted to collapse to the floor in a fetal position and weep his problems away. In less than three days, he lost his son, woman, and possibly, even his freedom now. He wondered what he had to live for and just as quickly reasoned that if he could no longer have his family, he definitely was not going to relinquish his liberty. *No matter what this bitch had to go*, he reconciled. The fewer people that knew, the better his chances of escaping a prison sentence were.

He wondered whether the police found anything. When he drove past, he didn't slow down to assess what was going on.

He actually sped up upon seeing the cops searching the area. It was then he knew he had to pay Carla a visit to see how much she revealed to them and to see what she really knew. He came to the conclusion that she still had to go.

After her threats, he reckoned she was too dangerous to be walking around freely with the information she had. She appeared to be telling the truth regarding not tipping the police off to anything concerning Lil Shane. Even though she might have said nothing thus far, Shaheen knew he couldn't trust her with keeping that information to herself.

Carla's tears were now hanging from her chin. While her blubbering had ceased, her eyes were still flooded. He motioned for her to sit down. As she walked toward the couch, he methodically dragged his feet behind her. She sat upon the couch and retrieved the blunt she dropped earlier from the floor. Lighting it up, she did not pay much attention to Shaheen walking around to the back of the couch. He stood erect directly behind her, towering over the smoke that rose to his nostrils.

After positioning the weapon back in his waist, he gently placed his hands on both of her shoulders and started to massage them. His grip went from delicate to rough as he apologetically stated, "Look, I'm sorry for wildin' out. Just a little stressed over her dealing with my dude." He leaned over and kissed her on the back of her neck. "How long have they been messing around?"

Relaxing from his touch, she quickly rolled the answer off her tongue, "About ten months now. He comes over every Friday like clockwork." Relieved that she was no longer in danger, she continued, "She started dealing with him 'cause she said y'all always fighting and you never be in the crib. You always out. They hit it off pretty fast and been on the low since."

"Where the hell is Leek now?"

"Dunno. She had been trying to get up with him too."

He began caressing her neck with both hands while she slumped further into the couch and exhaled smoke from her nose.

"So you said every Friday, he over at my crib?"

"Yeah. Except for this past Friday . . . I mean I saw him go up into the building that day, but he came right back out running. He wasn't up there longer than five minutes. Guess he knew you were at home and turned around . . . obviously."

"You said this Friday? About what time?"

"Yeah, this Friday. Close to twelve in the afternoon."

The first thought that came to his mind was that was around the time he was home and when Shane's death had taken place. He wondered whether Gorilla Leek, not knowing he was home, came to see Lola and ended up witnessing the incident. A million thoughts scurried through his mind. He couldn't believe his woman was having an affair with his best friend. The betrayal was suffocating him.

He felt as if his whole world had come crashing in. There was nothing left but tears now even though they never fell from his eyes. Hatred began to replace his despondency as he carefully moved his right hand from her neck to her chin and placed his left one on the top of the back of her head.

In one quick and sudden motion, he pulled her chin to the right and pushed her head in the opposite direction, causing her neck to snap instantly. It made a sickening cracking sound before her body went limp and collapsed into the couch. The lit cigar fell onto the cushion. Shaheen seized it, brought it up to his lips, and inhaled deeply before tossing it onto the floor. Barely heeding the corpse, he exited the apartment, closing the door behind him.

*   *   *

Lola dragged her heavy and shivering legs up the staircase that led toward the entrance of her apartment building. Her quick and sporadic breathing displayed her exhaustion. She could not remember the last time she gassed out so quickly from walking up the stairs. Though tired, she moved as fast as she could to get away from the cold, wretched air that chased her.

She shoved open the door, which was unlocked as usual, probably by one of the neighbors running out to the corner store. As she entered the small foyer, the door closed behind her causing a gust of brutal morning air to forcefully push its way past her, blowing her red cotton scarf across her eyes. She removed the material from her view.

Before venturing past the second door and into the hallway that led to the apartment units, Lola ceased her movement to search through the several envelopes that lay across the small green wooden table situated to the right of the entrance. She had been so consumed with the weekend's events that she neglected to collect Friday's mail. Seeing nothing addressed to her or Shaheen, she proceeded to walk past the second door and into the corridor. With her head sunken low, she languorously marched up the stairs.

As she trotted, she thought about the consequences of her most recent actions. She pondered over whether severing her ties with Shaheen should have been handled in the manner in which she just did.

Earlier that morning, around 3:00 a.m., she had awoken, called her mother, and informed her of what happened. She told her everything, from Shane's murder, which occurred two days ago, to finding out she was with child. She begged for a way back home, for she was without money of her own. Panicking, her mother paid for the first Monday morning flight back to Georgia, then instructed her to pack lightly, and leave before Shaheen came home. She warned Lola not to tell anyone of her movement. She just wanted her daughter safe and sound back in Georgia as soon as possible.

Unfortunately, Lola called Carla and blurted her plans out over the phone. Carla was elated. She knew she would now be able to have Shaheen with no problem, regardless of how long it took him to see the light. So she supported Lola's decision and even offered to drive her to the airport the next day. Lola declined and stated that her mother sent her enough money through Western Union to stay the night at the Marriot Hotel in Downtown Brooklyn, and that from there, she would take a cab.

As Lola envisioned being back in Georgia around family and familiar faces that she could trust, tears began to descend from her long blinking eyelashes. As she converged on the last step leading to her floor, she quickly wiped away the evidence of her emotions. In reality, she did not want to abandon Shaheen, but the walls were closing in and what she treasured most, their family, was no longer a possibility.

She retrieved the house keys from the Chanel bag that dangled from the crease of her left elbow and stood in front of her doorway. She exhaled deeply as she contemplated starting life all over, with her new child, minus Shaheen or even Gorilla Leek. She wanted to be back at home in the country, raising her baby. Finally, she was able to see a ray of hope, a new beginning.

She inserted the key into the lock and tried to rotate it. It didn't move. She then grabbed the door handle and gently twisted it to see if it was unlocked. It was. *Shit,* she thought, *Shaheen must be home.* She knew he would sometimes forget to lock the door when he came home. She did not expect him to be there. She wondered how she would be able to pack her things and get out of the apartment without him becoming curious.

She cautiously pushed the door by the knob, peeking through the opening, as it slowly widened. In silence, she hoped he was in the back room. As she stuck her head into the entrance and around the side of the door, she became startled by an unfamiliar body sitting on her couch, staring right at her. She perceived a shiny silver gun pointing at her. Her head jumped back in fear.

"Bitch, get in here now!" The now familiar face ordered. Her brain told her to turn and run, but the fear would not allow her legs to do so. Instead, she moved further into the apartment.

Jimbo smiled. "Close the door and lock it. You won't be going anywhere."

CHAPTER 15

"Are you serious?" Detective Thomas inquired into the receiver of his cell phone. Torturro handled the steering wheel of the Crown Vic with the dexterity of a NASCAR driver. He sped through red light after red light, causing the streams of rain to appear as streaks of lightning, flashing past the car's windows. The gray sky hung low, masking the brilliance of the morning sun.

"The same gun that was used in the murders at the store? You have to be shitting me," Thomas unbelievingly stated.

"That's some fucking connection! We're on our way now to pick up the boy's father. I didn't see that one coming. What about the source of the tip? Did Cannon pull up the person's information yet? Well, when you do, make certain to contact me."

Thomas spoke a few more indistinct words before removing the phone from his ear and placing it in his coat. Torturro quickly eyed his partner, then fixed his sight back on the road.

"What's the news?" asked Toruturro.

"The gun used on the child was the same gun used during the store robbery."

Torturro's calm expression suddenly became replaced by awe.

"Are you serious? What, the gun we found buried in the park?"

"No. According to the lab, the weapon we found buried didn't match the bullet used to kill Shane Mcfadden nor the casings we discovered at the scene of the store murders."

Thomas searched the side of his partner's face to see if he realized the importance of the newly acquired information. "I'm guessing the father knows who the killer is. We need to hurry up and get to him before someone else does."

Torturro was perplexed. "What do you mean?"

"I am not sure whether he has anything to do with the murders, but one thing is almost certain . . . He is involved in a major conflict, and there's someone out to get him. This guy has some answers, and I am going to get them out of him."

Torturro stepped heavily upon the gas pedal, sending the automobile speeding down East New York Avenue. Thomas smiled at the rookie, knowing he was now beginning to understand the importance of time. Detective Thomas shoved his hand into his coat and fetched his cell phone. Deciding to contact Lola, who he felt he could get more of the truth out of, he began dialing her number. No one answered. After about three or more attempts, he gave up.

Just as he started to return his phone to his pocket, it began to vibrate. He reviewed the number displayed on the screen. It was the station again. He quickly pressed the talk button in hopes of it being a call about additional information concerning his case.

He spoke into the receiver, "Hello."

The voice on the line came in clear. "Tom. This is Cannon. We have an ID and address on the person who called in the tip. We're on our way over to her house now to talk to her and see what else she knows."

"Really," Thomas stated flatly. "Well, I'm on my way to pick up the father of the vic. My ETA is about three minutes."

"Okay. Good deal. As soon as you get a hold of him, give me a call."

"Sounds good." Just as Thomas began to say his goodbye, his curiosity struck him. "Cannon."

"Yeah man, what's up?" responded Cannon.

"Who was the source?"

Cannon hesitated before answering, "You know her well. We were with her yesterday."

"Really, who?" Thomas grew impatient with Cannon's suspense routine.

"Carla Brianna Johnson. Your witness from the Barker case back in ninety-four. She was with the mother of the missi . . . uh . . . child when we visited her home."

"So this woman knew where her friend's missing son was the whole time? Naw, Cannon, we don't need to just pay her a visit. We need to get her down to the station for interrogation. She is a possible suspect. She could have informed us of the boy's whereabouts earlier. Go and get her ass. This case is starting to unravel more and more. Since Thursday, we have had over ten people murdered. That's about three a day. A war is going on."

"Yeah, who you telling? Your case load is heavy, brother."

"Yeah, exactly. But I guarantee you I will be closing every last one of them because they are all connected in some way or another. We have the murders at the restaurant and Chinnah's rental property, the deaths at Minimart, the dead child and the killings at the store, in which the same weapon was involved. Not to mention the gun used at the restaurant and at the house was used during the robbery attempt as well."

Thomas realized that the car was slowing down. He eyed his partner. Without returning the gaze, Torturro heeded his mentor's stare. "We're here." He parallel-parked alongside a brown 1979 four-door Chevy.

"Look, Cannon, we're at the parents' apartment now. I'll call you when we're on our way back to the station. Speak to you later."

Thomas hung up. Torturro removed the key from the ignition, and the two gentlemen exited the vehicle.

*   *   *

Lola struggled to separate her bound hands in an attempt to tear apart the duct tape that secured them. She feebly endeavored to force the blue rag from her mouth with her tongue. The gag was firmly held in place by a tight knot tied around the back of her head while she lay helplessly on her stomach with both of her feet anchored to each bedpost connected to the headboard.

Her legs were spread apart as her naked trembling body lay stretched out across the mattress that had become soaked with her urine. She was scared. No tears fell from the terrified eyes of hers which she kept on Jimbo as he sat at the edge of the bed with his penis in his hand and his pants hanging by his ankles.

Jimbo desired Lola for the longest, and now, he had his chance. The only problem was he couldn't get his dick to stay up. It remained soft as he vigorously shook the little limp creature in between his thumb and index finger. Becoming mad and ashamed at the same time, he stood up and faced Lola then began gyrating his waist in front her face.

"Go head. Suck it, bitch." He tore the rag from her mouth and brought himself closer to her. He rubbed the wet tip of his filthy penis against her lips. She couldn't bare the smell and tried to turn away. He grabbed her by her hair and held her head so she was unable to move it. "Come on, bitch, get it goin'!" he squeezed the head of it, causing yellowish colored pus to seep out.

Lola tucked her lips in. He smeared it across her chin. He kept shaking his hips side to side hoping to arouse himself. It wouldn't work. With his pants down he penguin-walked over to the nightstand where he placed the pipe and crack Pauley had given him earlier at their meeting. It was at that meeting he was instructed to go to Shaheen's house and wait for him to arrive. He was given the job of murdering both Shaheen and Gorilla Leek. He could not locate Gorilla Leek, so he decided to pay Shaheen a visit first. He supposed Chinnah thought it would be easier to keep the bloodshed under the radar if he handled the job as opposed to any of his bloodthirsty and reckless soldiers, who could be traced back to him.

Jimbo seized the burnt glass pipe and the small bag of rock. He lodged the rock into the pipe and proceeded to light the end of it. He took a long and deep pull from the pipe and held the smoke in as long as his lungs allowed him to. When he exhaled he instantly felt his heart race as a tingling sensation overtook his body and waves of euphoria bolted through his flesh. He put the pipe back down upon the stand and began slapping the little worm in between his legs.

"Shit, I can't get hard," he said to himself.

Lola just scoped him in fear, hoping he would get so high he would forget about her and leave. She was petrified of being raped and possibly murdered. She regretted coming back to the apartment and instead wished she had ventured straight to the hotel. Suddenly, her train of thought was broken by the buzzing of Jimbo's cell phone. He quickly answered it.

"Jimbo?" Pauley said into the receiver.

"Yeah,"

"Yuh murda im yet?"[70]

"Na, he hasn't popped up yet. But I got his ole lady here tied to the bed," answered Jimbo.

"Good, good, mon. Ave she fi call im an ave im ta cum ta de ouse. As soon as er dun chattin wit im . . . kill er. Zeen?"[71]

"Gotchoo. I'll handle that now."

"Awight, call mi when it ova."[72]

Jimbo said nothing in return and hung up.

He stumbled over to the bed where his victim lay bound. With worrisome eyes she took a gander at her tormentor as he snatched the cordless phone from the receiver and glanced down at the bed.

"I need you to call your man and get him to come home. Do you understand?"

---

[70] "Did you murder him yet?"

[71] "Good, good, man. Have her call him and get him to come to the house. As soon as she is done talking to him . . . kill her. Understand?"

[72] "Alright, call me when it is over."

Lola said nothing but shook her head in compliance. Jimbo pulled out a torn piece of paper, glanced down at it, then dialed the number. He aligned the phone to her ear and mouth. It began ringing. Lola prayed Shaheen would answer. She needed him now. The other line picked up.

"Peace," answered Shaheen.

Lola hesitated before pleading into the receiver. "Baby, I need you to come to the apartment."

"What? Now?" he asked.

"Yeah, now. It's important." Instantly his interest was piqued. At first, he thought for a moment she was ready to confess the pregnancy and the affair until she mentioned their son. "It's about Shane."

His next thought was that she was going to tell him about her snitching to the police. He decided not to pry too much into her statement and reasoned that meeting her in person so he could question her was best.

"A'ight, I'll be there. You there now?"

"Yeah."

"Okay, I'm coming."

Just before she went to remove her head from the phone she spoke once more.

"Shaheen," she pleaded, "please hurry home."

Jimbo snatched the receiver from her ear and hung it up. She gaped as he revealed his pistol and aimed it at the back of her head. She dropped her face into the pillow. She could feel the cold barrel pressing against the back of her skull. She tightly squeezed her eyes close. Her tears began to pour.

Jimbo spoke. "Too bad I couldn't get a chance to fuck that fat ass first. But business is business. Night, night, bitch!"

She braced herself for the impact. The sound of two gunshots went off, causing her body to jerk suddenly from the noise. Seeing nothing but darkness, she felt wetness trickling down her cheeks. Her eyes remained closed. She couldn't feel her head. In fact, she didn't even feel the impact of shot. She heard a loud thud like sound hitting the floor and then a harsh coughing noise which turned into choking. Though she had her eyes sealed shut, the room began to spin. She heard footsteps approaching her, then felt the gentle touch of a hand caressing her head.

"Lola," a familiar and calming voice spoke, "Lola, open your eyes."

She reluctantly raised her eyelids. Her face was soaked from the tears. The first sight she saw was the body of Jimbo awkwardly sprawled out on the floor going through convulsions. She brought her pupils up to the man who stood over his body, holding a revolver. It was Detective Thomas.

"Get her some clothes!" he yelled out to his partner who had just entered the room.

*   *   *

Shaheen peered through the windshield of his SUV, which was situated at the corner of his block, staring at the numerous marked and unmarked police cars that were parked outside of his apartment building. He was somewhat taken aback when he saw Lola exiting the building, escorted by two detectives.

She was in tears as the black detective walked beside her with his arm around her shoulder. The gentleman spoke a few words to a couple of the uniformed officers posted outside, then proceeded to direct Lola toward a black Crown Victoria. He helped her into the backseat of the car, then passed her a cell phone before closing the door. He and his partner stood outside the car conversing while she began dialing into the phone. They seemed to be giving her some privacy.

Shaheen's temperature was boiling. He was infuriated by the thought that Lola not only went to the police and told them about Shane but that she even tried to set him up by calling him to the apartment while the cops awaited him. He was relieved he saw them before they got the drop on him. He began weighing out his options. He wasn't certain if he should leave the state or try to find Gorilla Leek. He had questions that needed answering. He also knew if he was going to leave he would need a portion of the work they stole from Chinnah in order to set him straight financially when he relocated. Suddenly, his phone roared to life. He fumbled his hands through his jacket, then answered it.

"Peace!"

There was a silence on the phone. He repeated himself. "Peace!"

"Peace," Lola gently spoke from the other end. "Shaheen, where are you?"

"Not in jail yet, no thanks to you," he said facetiously.

"What do you mean?"

"You called me to come to the crib to have me arrested? Your ass actually went to the cops and told them about Shane?"

"No! I didn't go to the police. They just showed up at the apartment. They actually saved my life. Jimbo—"

"Saved your life. I'm suppose to believe that shit? How did they know where to look for Shane's body?"

"They told me they got a tip from a call in," she nervously spewed.

"A call in? Yeah, 'cause you called them. Where are you right now?" He was testing her to see how far she would go with her lies.

Lola began to answer but hesitated. She was uncertain of whether telling him where she was currently at would be prudent. She then resolved that he already knew there were officers at their home so he might also be aware of her whereabouts. She wondered whether he was just testing her. She decided to tell the truth.

"I'm in the detective's car on my way to the station. They want to question me, and they asked me to call you and have you come down to the station."

"For what, to lock me up!"

Lola glanced outside of the window to make certain the detectives were no longer paying her any mind. Seeing she was not being watched, she quickly spoke.

"No, not to lock you up. They want to know what we know about the connection between Shane's death and Chinnah's son's murder."

Shaheen almost dropped the phone. He removed it from his ear and raised it to his lips. Keeping his eye on the car Lola was in, he asked, "Did you say Copper got murdered?" He placed the phone back to his ear.

"Yes. They said the same gun used at the scene of his murder was used on Shane."

"How?" Shaheen was completely baffled. "Leek buried the gun. It's been in the park the whole time. Did they find it?"

"Yeah, they said they got a tip on that too, but it wasn't the same gun used on Shane."

"I'm not following. Did they tell you what kind of burner they found in the park?" His tone displayed a great deal of confusion.

"No, but I overheard the cops talking, and they said Shane was shot with a .44 Magnum."

Shaheen's mouth shot open. His heart began to race. He couldn't believe what he just heard. There had to be some mistake, he thought.

"Are you sure they said Shane got shot with a forty-four?"

"Yes."

"That's not possible. I don't own a four four."

"I know."

Then suddenly, as if having a jolting thought, he ceased his conversation.

"They listening to us?"

"Huh?" Lola was thrown off by his question.

"The pigs. They got you calling to get me on tape?"

"No. They aren't even paying attention to me. They just wanted me to contact you and ask you to come down to the station."

He listened closely into the phone as if to make sure there wasn't anyone monitoring them. He glimpsed in the direction of the car Lola was in to see if the police were focused on her.

Seeing they weren't he continued, "So are you saying Shane didn't kill himself with my gun?"

Lola said nothing. Shaheen quickly brought his memory back to that day's events. He painfully relived the incident. He searched his confused mind for answers, something that made sense out of what he just heard. Then it hit him. He remembered the day Shane was shot; he discovered the door was unlocked, and when he seized the gun from the floor, he didn't feel any heat as one usually would from a pistol that was just fired. He also thought about the fact that he never found the shell casing. He thought to himself for a moment, *What if Shane was murdered and didn't kill himself? But my gun was on the floor.* He was brought back to reality by the sound of Lola's voice.

"The detectives are searching the crib again with some other investigators to see if Shane was killed inside our home or not. They think you know something but that you are trying to cover it up. They want you to come down to the precinct for questioning."

Shaheen ignored her last statement. "So they told you that Shane was murdered with the same weapon that killed Chinnah's son? When did Chinnah's son get hit?"

"I think Saturday night. But they didn't say he was killed by the same gun. There were three people murdered there. They didn't say which one or if all got shot by the burner that . . ."—she swallowed deeply—"took Shane's life. I just know that Copper is dead, and they have one dude in custody and looking for another. They think a war with Chinnah's been going on since about Thursday or Friday."

The mentioning of Friday brought the conversation he had with Carla to mind. "Friday? Hmm."

According to Carla, Gorilla Leek had been visiting Lola every Friday like clockwork for the past six months except for the last Friday. The Friday his son was murdered. He recalled that on that same day the door to his apartment was unlocked. He remembered how Carla said his best friend kept a key. And to top everything off, he knew he also owned a .44 Magnum, his favorite weapon. For a brief moment, Shaheen prayed that this was all a mistake. He reasoned that dealing with his son accidentally shooting himself was easier than having to confront the betrayal of who he thought was his best friend.

He decided to feed his curiosity. "So did they say where Copper was murdered?"

"Yeah, in East New York at a bodega on Pitkin."

His heart dropped. He knew Gorilla Leek was suppose to go to White Mike's store on Saturday night and that the store was on Pitkin Avenue, but he did not want to believe his best friend had anything to do with the murder of his only son. However, it all added up. He thought about Gorilla Leek's reasons for committing such an atrocity and reconciled that pussy could make you do anything. He just could not fathom Gorilla Leek, no matter how he felt, being so calloused as to kill a child just to get what he wanted. Whatever his reason, if he did it, he would pay for his crime, Shaheen promised himself that.

"Shaheen." Lola brought his attention back to the matter at hand. "I don't have too much time. They gave me privacy to call you. They're about to get back in the car and drive me down to the station." Lola looked out the window once more. "I'm scared. I can't go to jail. I need your help."

"Well then, you shouldn't have been fucking Leek! Maybe that nigga can help you."

Lola was in shock. She did not return the reply. The thought crossed her mind to explain, but her mouth wouldn't open.

Acknowledging her silence, Shaheen became infuriated. "Leek owns a .44 Magnum, you dumb bitch! He was probably on his way over to fuck you, got startled by me being in the house, and then decided to leave. But before turning back around, he must've thought killing Shane would've been a good way to get y'all closer!"

"What? Na, that's crazy. You said it was your . . . your fault . . . Shaheen. I'm . . . I mean, I . . ." she attempted to relay her thoughts.

"Save it, bitch. You fucked the nigga, and I hope it was good for both of y'all 'cause when I get to him, it's a wrap! I'm eating that nigga's food!"

Lola tried to get her words in once more. "Shaheen, baby, you have to understand, I was weak because of . . ."

"Bitch, please. For all I know, he killed Shane to be with you, knowing you wouldn't leave me because we had a child together. I hope you're happy. Our son didn't die because of me. He died because of you!"

Shaheen watched as Detective Thomas opened the door to the car Lola was in. He shot his hand inside the vehicle. Shaheen could hear a small scuffle through the receiver of the phone. He observed the detective's hand come back out the car with a phone in it.

"Hello? Mr. Mcfadden?" Thomas inquired as he brought the phone to his ear. Shaheen said nothing.

Thomas decided to continue anyway. "Mr. Mcfadden, we need to speak to you concerning your son. We have found his body."

Shaheen still did not reply. Suddenly, the roar of a siren from an ambulance speeding and nearing the cross section where he sat parked, drowned out the sound of the detective's voice. It startled Shaheen. The vehicle changed its course and veered down the street toward the numerous police cars.

Almost simultaneously, Thomas heard the siren coming down the block while also through the receiver of his phone. He removed his ear from the phone and rubbernecked toward the corner of the block. He now knew Shaheen was not only in the neighborhood but on the block, possibly watching them. The sound of the ambulance over the phone and on the street brought it to his attention. Thomas began a slow stride toward the corner. He recognized the parked black Ford Expedition. His strut became a light run.

He called out to his partner. "Torturro! That's him! The father's in that car right there!" He screamed pointing in the direction of the car Shaheen sat in.

Shaheen took notice and threw his vehicle in reverse. The car sped off backward, making an eerie screeching noise as he maneuvered out of his parking space and into the middle of the cross section. He spun the wheel to the right, causing the car to turn in reverse. He then slammed the gear forward as the SUV peeled off down Rutland Road. Thomas ceased his running and decided to venture back to his peers so he could get the young lady down to the station for questioning. Out of breath, he swung open the door to his car and asked Lola, "What did you say to him?"

CHAPTER 16

Shaheen's vehicle sped down the FDR expressway, wobbling each time he took a curve on the narrow lane. He wove in and out of traffic, dodging automobiles moving much slower than his. Not long after he left his neighborhood, he received a phone call from Gorilla Leek. He was in Harlem recovering from a gunshot wound to his leg. He informed him of everything that happened at the store.

Shaheen had now confirmed that his best friend was at the store, which meant it was his gun that killed Shane. Now, all that was left was for Gorilla Leek to explain exactly how it happened and why. However, what bothered him the most was the fact that from what he was able to gather from Gorilla Leek, it seemed as if he was doing business with Copper, their enemy.

Gorilla Leek was reluctant to travel back to Brooklyn because he knew the police would be looking for him sooner or later for the killings that took place at the bodega. He decided he needed to stay on the low for a while. For this reason, he besought Shaheen to journey uptown to Harlem to pick up the key to the apartment where the cocaine they took from Chinnah was stashed. He reasoned it would be easier and safer for him if Shaheen gathered the drugs from Brooklyn and brought it back to Harlem.

Gorilla Leek was in a state of panic. He briefly uttered to Shaheen his concern about being sought after for the murders.

He also made mention that he wanted to sell off as much of the work as possible so he could have money to stay on the low. He claimed to have a connection that could get more work for them, but they needed to get rid of what they currently had in order to purchase it. Shaheen was more than happy to venture uptown to meet him, not only because he could finally get his hands on Gorilla Leek, but he also needed the drugs to secure some cash after he left the state. *Yeah!* He decided now was the best time to get out of the dodge. It appeared he had lost Lola, his son, and his occupation all in one weekend. He wasn't ready to lose his freedom.

Shaheen was oblivious to the black sedan following him. Pauley had been watching him ever since he arrived at his apartment. Initially, he was there keeping an eye on Jimbo to make certain he went through with the hit. He knew that Jimbo was on friendly terms with Shaheen, so he wanted to make sure he didn't have any second thoughts. He also had lost contact with Kam, who he had trailing Shaheen, so he decided to stay close to Jimbo until the job was completed. Because of Chinnah's mood, he had to be sure the plan was successful.

When he witnessed the detectives exit their car and enter the building, he became worried. Sure enough, within fifteen minutes the building was swarming with police. He waited outside to see what had become of Jimbo. Just as he was preparing to leave, he saw Shaheen's vehicle pull up at the corner.

Pauley decided to double around the block only to come back and park a few feet behind his enemy. He figured Jimbo might have failed, but he wouldn't. He stayed and watched Shaheen watch the police. When he pulled off, Pauley decided to follow him. He reasoned he might get lucky, find out where Gorilla Leek was, and kill two birds with one stone. He was hoping Shaheen would lead him to the drugs also but knew that was the furthest thought from Chinnah's mind right now.

Pauley attempted to stay as far away from Shaheen's vehicle as possible. He quickly spun the wheel to the right, trying to get behind his prey as he exited the freeway. The Expedition cautiously made its way off the ramp, veered right, then pulled into a gas station. Pauley drove past, unsure of what to do. He didn't have anywhere to stop on the busy two-way street, so he slowed down as he approached the corner. He checked his rearview mirror for Shaheen's vehicle. Seeing it parked alongside a gas pump but seeing no one in the driver's seat, he decided to whip his car into a U-turn.

He neared the gas station and pulled into it. He still did not see the person he was following, only the vehicle. He slowly brought his car up to the side of the SUV. As he drove past, he rolled down his passenger window and snuck a glimpse inside of it. *Whey de bloodclot im gwan?*[73]He swung his head to the right, then the left in search of Shaheen but saw no one.

As soon as he brought his sight back in front of him, he caught a glimpse of a shiny metal instrument in his peripheral. It came from the passenger side of the vehicle. Before he could turn toward the object, fire and thunder leaped out from it and slammed into his face. The bullet sent his head crashing into driver's side window, causing it to crack, as dark crimsom splattered everywhere, tinting the glass. Another loud roar ripped through the air as his head fell forward landing hard on the steering wheel. He was gone before his body slumped over. The first shot did it.

*   *   *

Shaheen carefully steered his vehicle off of the expressway and onto the ramp. He directed the SUV to the right and pulled into a gas station. As he parked alongside a gas pump, his instincts went off, causing him to become suddenly paranoid. He was uncertain as to why, but for some reason, he felt something was wrong, so he shot his eyes up and down the block.

---

[73] "Where the fuck did he go?"

That is when he became aware of Pauley's sedan. He watched as the vehicle decreased in speed and drove past him before coming to a halt at the cross section. Shaheen wasted no time. He leaped into action, ducking out of the vehicle with his gun in hand. He concealed himself behind the side of the SUV. Raising his head up to better observe his prey's movement through the window of the Ford, he curiously watched as the sedan made a U-turn and headed back toward him.

He awaited the car's approach. He ducked his head as it cruised past his Expedition. Suddenly, the car stopped. That was all the time he needed to give him the advantage. Hunched over, he crept around his vehicle until he came up to the passenger side of Pauley's ride. Without hesitating, he raised his gun at the same time he stood up and fired two shots into the car. Pauley's body jerked as he fell over dead.

Shaheen turned on his heels and hopped back into his SUV. The rubber wheels peeled off from the scene as the screams of an elderly woman alerted the gas attendant who, hearing the shots at first, dismissed them as a tire blowing out. He instinctively ran outside just in time to get a full and clear view of the driver and the license plate. Once Shaheen had retreated from the scene, the man made his way back into the station and dialed the police.

Shaheen pushed his car through the many red lights that stood between him and his destination. He stopped for nothing. Knowing he was being careless, he opted to slow down significantly. He drove below the speed limit until he arrived at the apartment where Gorilla Leek was holding up. He parked directly in front of the entrance, then reached beneath the seat he sat upon and brought out a 9 mm Browning pistol. After cocking the gun and loading a bullet into the chamber, he stuffed the weapon into his pants, then stepped out of the vehicle.

He searched the trash-filled street. The afternoon air blew a turbulent breeze that howled out a warning to anyone who decided to venture onto the streets that day. The coldness sheltered the neighborhood from the flames of heated barrels that usually exploded during winter wars. The frigid air made the criminals stay indoors that day. It was the coldest it had been all week.

Shaheen eyes followed the tall apartment building all the way up to the roof. As he strutted up the staircase, which led to the first door, he thought about how elated he was over never having a need to come here for himself. The apartment was being rented out by his brother's ex-girlfriend, Tanya, who was now a doctor. She had stayed close to Shaheen after his brother's incarceration, only to later on work for him as an underground physician.

He knew Gorilla Leek was upstairs having his bullet removed and getting stitched up, so he figured he would be an easy target. His only concern was getting him out of the apartment in order to put a slug in him. He did not want to involve Tanya, so he decided he would ring the bell and have him come downstairs.

He scanned the list of names taped to the side panel of the entrance. Finding the name he needed, he pressed the buzzer next to it. He received no answer, so he repeated the process. Finally, a voice crackled over the intercom.

"That you, my dog?" Gorilla Leek shouted through the speaker.

"Yeah. Come downstairs. I need to yap with you."

"Can't do that. I got someone up here you need to meet. Come on up."

Shit! Shaheen thought to himself, *Why he making this hard?*

"A'ight, Blood. Buzz me in."

The buzzer went off, sounding more like a howl than a bell. The clicking sound that came from the door informed Shaheen that it was now unlocked. He pushed it open and stepped into the hallway, gripping the pistol that was concealed by his shirt and pants. Making his way up the staircase he pondered over who Gorilla Leek could have waiting upstairs to meet him.

Maybe it was a set-up. Arriving at the second floor, he carefully and lightly walked down the corridor toward the apartment he was searching for.

Contemplating a possible trap, he imagined himself kicking down the door and shooting everyone in sight. It wasn't that he was bloodthirsty; he just reasoned it would be safer for him to go in blasting. Standing in front of the apartment, he ceased his pondering and knocked upon the door.

It opened, revealing Tanya, who motioned for him to enter. He hesitated, then calmly stepped in. Gorilla Leek was not in view. However, the first sight he saw startled his nerves. It was a tall red-faced Caucasian man standing in the middle of the living room. He sported an NYPD badge around his neck, which hung from a slim silver chain that dangled over his black leather jacket.

"What the fuck!" Shaheen let out as the door closed behind him.

*   *   *

"So what do we have?" asked the young uniformed officer who was dawdling in the hallway of the precinct conversing with Detective Torturo.

"Well, right now, Thomas is in there interviewing the vic's mother. Not sure what to make of it so far," answered Detective Torturro. "All I know is this has been the longest weekend."

The officer gave Torturro a quizzical stare. "You think the father did it?"

"Not sure. I don't think so, but my money is on him knowing who did."

"Really?"

Torturro began to reply, but the sound of the steel door of the interrogation room opening stopped him. Thomas walked out and strolled toward the two.

"Grayson."

"Yes, sir," the officer quickly answered.

"Do you mind getting the young lady some water?"

"No, not at all." The officer marched off without uttering another word.

Torturro kept his eyes on his partner. "So what is the deal? Is she staying?"

Thomas let out a deep and slow sigh. "No. It doesn't appear she knows anything. If she does, she is not speaking a word of it."

"Does she even have an idea of why this happened to her child?" asked Torturro.

"She is playing stupid right now. We need to get a hold of the father."

"Well, what happened when she called him? Didn't she speak with him?"

Thomas released another sigh. "Yeah, but she said he became frightened when he heard what happened and hung up the phone. He has not answered since."

"Well, what do we know so far?"

Thomas's eyes shot up into the air as he pondered the situation. "Well, we now know that the murders at Mike Alvarez's store and Shaheen Mcfadden's apartment are connected. Ballistics revealed that the same weapon was used at both scenes."

Torturro decided to chime in. "And though we found no fingerprints, we know the pistol used at Chinnah's rental property was the same as the one we found buried near the boy. And we can't forget the restaurant shooting. Coincidence?"

"Na, not at all, partner. Let's see. We have a dead child, more than seven deceased adults, a store blown to pieces, a grieving father on the run, and a possible suspect sitting in custody. All connected somehow to the same weapons."

"And the perp we caught at the Alvarez's Grocery still isn't speaking yet?"

"No, not yet. He thinks he is tough. But he'll break once we send him to the Island. It doesn't take long for Rikers to do that. Is he on his way back to the interrogation room?"

"Yeah," answered Torturro. "He doesn't yet know he is about to be questioned regarding the death of the three-year-old."

Then, as if he had a sudden flash of revelation, Thomas blurted out, "You know something? We need to know if the mother knows him."

He slammed his index finger into Torturro's line of sight. "Go and get that boy back upstairs soon as possible!"

His partner was startled by the abrupt change in Thomas's attitude. He couldn't bring his lips to utter anything other than "Okay, will do."

Just as Torturro moved to obey his senior's command, Thomas's phone went off. Answering it, he held one finger up in the air toward the rookie, signaling for him to halt. Thomas greeted the incoming caller and then became silent as the person spoke. His facial expression went from being solemn to displaying excitement.

"What? Where? In the wall? I'll be there in fifteen minutes. Don't have anyone touch anything! How many did you find? Okay, I'll be there!"

Thomas shoved the phone into the case that was attached to his belt. His eyes moved from side to side as his head hung to the ground. He lifted his chin and spoke. "We are going to have to let the mother go soon. We have nothing to hold her on. But I need her here long enough to see the boy. I want you to handle that. I am going back to their apartment to check on some additional evidence."

Torturro stood seemingly confused. "Additional evidence?"

"Yeah, the geeks found a bu—"

"Thomas!" screamed Cannon as he came running around the corner of the precinct's corridor. "I've been killing myself to get here." Cannon stopped running as he closed the distance between himself and the detectives. He was huffing and puffing heavily while his chest jumped rapidly. "I . . . need to . . . speak . . . to . . . you . . ."

Thomas smirked. "Are you okay?" He let out a small laugh.

"Yeah . . . We went to the home of the person who called in with the information. Ms. Carla Johnson. She was dead."

Thomas and Torturro looked shocked. Thomas was the first to open his mouth. "Dead? How?"

Cannon swallowed nervously, then replied, "Her neck had been snapped."

CHAPTER 17

"Hello, Sha-Boogie," Detective O'Reilly greeted the startled Shaheen as the door closed behind him.

Shaheen quickly glanced behind him to check for an ambush.

"Calm down, dog. Ain't nobody out to getcha," said a smiling Gorilla Leek as he limped around from behind Shaheen. "I wanted you to meet Detective O'Reilly. He's the reason we were able to run up in Chinnah's spot without having to worry 'bout police." Gorilla Leek stepped closer to the detective and placed his hand on his shoulder as Tanya exited the room for the kitchen.

Shaheen immediately took notice of Gorilla Leek's torn pants leg that had been cut open up to the thigh. A blood-soaked red bandanna was tightly tied around the spot where his wound was.

"He's also the connect for that shit we took from Chinnah."

Shaheen did not open his mouth. Instead, he allowed his ex-best friend to do all the talking. He only had one reason for being there. He could care less about securing a new connect.

"I told you I would handle gettin' a connect," Gorilla Leek said.

Shaheen gave the detective a disbelieving look. "Well, why are you dealing with us?"

Detective O'Reilly brought his sight upon Gorilla Leek, then back to Shaheen before uttering, "Because I need the money, and Copper is dead."

"Huh, what Copper got to do with this?"

Gorilla Leek abruptly interjected. He rushed his words out. "Copper was copping extra work from the detective and had his pops' peoples moving the weight out of his spot without him knowing."

The detective added his two cents. "Copper was trying to go for himself. He no longer desired being up under his daddy. Besides, the narcotics I was getting from the station was twice as good as Chinnah's."

Shaheen gazed at both men. He felt left out as if Gorilla Leek and the cop in front of him were the real partners to this business venture. "So we robbed Chinnah that night . . . or Copper?"

"Both," Gorilla Leek answered, unwilling to reveal his relationship with Copper or ambitions they shared. He understood that with Copper out of the picture, while his plans may have taken a detour, he would be able to profit more from the new connection he now had directly with the detective.

"So where are you getting the work from?" a curious Shaheen inquired.

Both O'Reilly and Gorilla Leek looked at each other with unscrupulous grins.

"Like I said, from the station. All the narcotics we take off the streets go into lockup as evidence. If the case never goes to trial, then the drugs just sit there in storage. I have access to that area of the building, which means an unlimited access to a drug storehouse," O'Reilly stated with an air of accomplishment.

"Yeah," interjected Gorilla Leek, "that's why he givin' it to us for so cheap."

"How cheap is so cheap?" Shaheen facetiously inquired.

Gorilla Leek glanced at O'Reilly as if giving him his cue to interpose.

"Ten per ki."

Shaheen's eyes lit up. His mouth dropped. His avaricious nature began to take over. Instantly, the idea of profit overtook his desire for revenge. He began to calculate the potential earnings. Gorilla Leek took notice of his partner's contemplation and smiled. He knew he was on board.

"Yeah, but we have one issue," O'Reilly pointed out.

"What's that?" asked Shaheen.

Gorilla Leek's demeanor became serious as his upper lip stiffened. He barely opened his mouth to say, "You."

"Me? How?" Shaheen attempted to discern the two men's expressions to determine what may have been on their mind.

O'Reilly spoke first. "Yeah, well according to my intel at the station, it seems you are being investigated for your connection to the death of your son as well as four of Chinnah's henchmen."

Shaheen's face became a portrait of stone. Suddenly, all of his thoughts of making money were gone again, only to be replaced by the remembrance of what he initially came to do.

The detective continued. "They haven't mentioned Gorilla Leek yet, but the word is that the case can be solved if they can find you. They believe everything is connected to you somehow, so trying to set this spot up with you having all this heat on you will prove to be a problem."

Shaheen beheld his friend, who said nothing in return. He wanted to scream out how unfair it was that Gorilla Leek was not a suspect and everything occurred because of him. Instead he decided to completely ignore the cop's statement and change the subject.

He stared icily at his ex-partner. "So you in bed with Copper?"

"Whatchoo mean?" Gorilla Leek's guilt surfaced instantly when he opened his mouth.

"Why were you at the store when he got killed?

Gorilla Leek did not want his friend to know he went behind his back and made a deal with their enemy without consulting him first.

"Coincidence?"

"Did you kill dude?" Shaheen threw the question out so suddenly Gorilla Leek almost felt as if he had to lie even though he knew he had nothing to do with Copper's murder.

He stuttered, "Uh . . . na . . . no . . . Some kids came up in there waving burners. They were trying to rob White Mike when Copper stepped in the store. One of the dudes panicked and popped him like three times. I was hiding behind the canned food aisle when it happened."

Shaheen couldn't tell whether he was lying or not, so he decided to ask, "Well, what happened to White Mike?"

"They popped him too."

Shaheen grew concerned. That was the first time he had been presented with the news of White Mike's death.

"Then, where are we gonna move the work out of?"

"We're handling that now," stated the detective.

Desiring to get back to the topic at hand, he asked once more, "So you didn't kill Copper?"

"No, neither did I kill White Mike." Gorilla Leek was becoming impatient with Shaheen's questioning.

"But you were there when it happened?"

O'Reilly, noticing the suspicion in Shaheen's voice, interjected. "They have the person who shot them in custody."

"Really?" Shaheen did not believe the two. He thought about the fact that if his friend could murder his son, he could lie also and would not hesitate to murder him as well. He decided to cut the conversation short so he could no longer be lied to.

"Yo, Leek, the business arrangement sounds good but can we talk in private." He glanced in the direction of the cop. "You know, without the extra ears."

O'Reilly was preparing to reply when Gorilla Leek raised his hand and indicated for the officer to give them some privacy. The detective, taking notice, began to venture into the hallway, but Gorilla Leek planted his palm on his chest, forbidding him from moving any further.

"Yo, you stay here. We'll go outside."

The two made their way toward the door. Gorilla Leek walked out first with Shaheen on his heels. Once arriving in the hallway, Shaheen made sure to close the door behind them. As Gorilla Leek trotted in front, Shaheen retrieved his pistol and cocked it, before aiming it at the back of his friend's head. He paused in his movement and stood on the edge of the staircase.

Gorilla Leek never noticed. Instead he started up the conversation without glancing back as he went to journey down the staircase. "Yo, dog, can you imagine how fat we'll be once we set up shop? I mean, this is what we been waiting for. You know?" He took in a glimpse over his shoulder. The gun sent shockwaves through his nerves. He instantly spun into a 180 degree turn, bringing his face directly in front of the weapon.

"What the fuck is this, Blood?" he nervously demanded.

Shaheen's palms became sweaty. His grip around the pistol tightened, causing his hands to tremble. His lips shook as he felt his biceps begin to twitch.

"Nigga, you shot my son!"

Gorilla Leek's expression became extremely contorted as he jerked his head back in confusion.

"Huh? Shot Shane? Are you okay?"

"Nigga, stop lying! The pigs told Lola that the same gun used in Copper's murder was used to kill Shane."

Gorilla Leek raised his palms in the air. "Blood, I don't know what you're talking bout. I ain't kill no Shane."

"Nigga, I thought you were my dude. How you do this shit to me?"

"Blood, I don't know what you're getting at, but I didn't kill him."

Shaheen cocked the gun back and forcefully pressed it into Gorilla Leek's forehead. It sent pain through his skull.

"Leek, I know you was fucking Lo! So keep lying to me, and I will not only put a slug in you, but I will put one in each of your children!"

Gorilla Leek's eyes shot open. He glanced back at the door to the apartment they just left, hoping someone would come out and rescue him.

"Carla said she saw you the day Shane was murdered leaving the apartment. Said you be over at my crib every Friday banging out my shorty."

Gorilla Leek took a deep breath. "Look, Shaheen . . . I . . ."

"Save it, nigga! Lo already admitted the shit. I just want to know why my son. You could've fucked the shit out of my girl if you wanted . . . but my seed?"

Gorilla Leek began pleading, not so much out of fear of losing his life as that of losing his friend. "Look, Shaheen, I'm sorry about Lo. The shit with me and Lo just happened. But I swear I could never—"

"Well, what the fuck were you doing at my crib this Friday . . . the same day Shane was murdered?" Shaheen was fuming.

Gorilla Leek swallowed nervously. He glanced once more at door. He looked back at his friend, then hesitantly opened his mouth.

"I heard it happen."

Shaheen sucked his teeth. He was growing impatient. "Heard what happen?"

"When I unlocked the door, I saw Shane in the living room playing with your gun. I peeped your coat on the couch so I closed the door back. When I went to walk away, I heard the shot. I couldn't tell if it came from your apartment or not, so I opened the door to check. That's when I saw him lying there bleeding. I panicked, turned around, then ran."

Shaheen eyeballed his friend. He did not care to assess his behavior or words to see if he was telling the truth. The story did not make sense.

"So if you turned and bounced, how did he get shot with your gun?"

Once again Gorilla Leek swallowed deeply. "My gun?"

Frustration overtook Shaheen's emotions. Gorilla Leek's feigned innocence infuriated him.

He steadied his pistol, lowering it toward his captive's groins.

"How 'bout I blow you dick off and then maybe that'll jolt your memory."

Shaheen's eyes became intensely focused upon his friend. He raised the gun back up to Gorilla Leek's forehead.

"You know what? Fuck all this yapping! Just die, bitch!"

Gorilla Leek braced himself to receive the shot. Just as his accuser went to squeeze the trigger, a gunshot from above went off. Shaheen felt his flesh tear open as the impact of the bullet striking his shoulder launched him down the flight of stairs.

*   *   *

Police of all sorts, in uniforms, dress suits, as well as sweatshirts with hoods and denim jackets, canvassed Shaheen's apartment. They were performing several tasks, ranging from cutting out pieces of carpet that covered the floor to bagging and numbering different items they felt were of interest to them. The living room buzzed with the mumbling and chattering of officers attempting to keep their voices down so as to not disturb their peers while they were engaged in their respective duties.

Detective Thomas stood motionless, observing the wall nearest to the dining room table. His head was tilted awkwardly to the right. He traced his finger along the wall, randomly glancing over his shoulder toward the foot of the couch where two officers in windbreaker jackets were huddled.

His eyes scanned the floor that surrounded him. Noticing broken chips of paint and plaster speckled about his feet, he stepped back a couple of inches. Searching the area to determine where the chips fell from, he discovered a crack in the plaster that covered the wall. Allowing his eyes to follow the lines of the breakage up to its point of origin, he let out a sigh before poking his latex covered index finger into the hole positioned at the end of the broken trail.

He felt the inside of the hole to gauge how deep it was before walking backward toward the couch. Arriving at the location where Shane bled out, he bent down while keeping his eyes on the hole and placed his right hand in the exact spot the body had laid just a few days ago. A female officer approached Thomas from behind disrupting his observation.

"So am I right?" she proudly asked.

"It appears so," the detective retorted. "Thanks for the call, Smith."

The female officer smiled graciously. "Just trying to do my job. Besides when I take and pass the exam, it would be good to have someone in my corner who could attest to my potential for being a good detective."

"Keep up the good work, and you will have nothing to worry about."

Thomas stood straight up and glanced around at the many faces pacing back and forth, conversing in the apartment. He brought his attention back to the female officer.

"I need you to lay hold of another officer, so you two can accompany me."

She appeared baffled by his request. "Accompany you?"

"Yes. Go grab another officer." His eyes became stern as his chin sunk to his chest. "You are taking up time we don't have the leisure of wasting."

A short and slim Caucasian male in uniform, was preparing to pass the two when the female officer suddenly seized his arm, causing him to cease his movement. He regarded her with bewilderment.

"Huh? What?" A hint confusion rattled from his voice.

"The detective needs us to walk with him."

The officer could not hide the helpless curiosity that blanketed his face.

"Okay" was his only reply.

Thomas whipped around and urgently marched out of the apartment with his sidekicks shadowing him. As he exited the dwelling unit, he abruptly shifted his direction to the left and came to a halt in front of the entrance to the apartment situated next to Shaheen's. He retrieved his badge from his belt clip and knocked on the door with authority. There was no answer at first.

He lifted his fist to bring it down upon the door once more, just as the soft hoarse sound of an elderly woman could be heard pleading, "Hold on, I'm coming."

The trio waited as the locks began to turn and the door struggled to open. Thomas attempted to assist the lady by gently pushing the stuck door open.

"This door always gets jammed," the lady stated as she poked her head out from between the halfway-opened entrance. Her frail body remained hidden while the bifocals that hung below her pupils appeared to mask her whole face. Deep-cut lines ran beneath her eyes and formed creases in the dull and dark skin that loosely sagged from her tiny bones. Recognizing the police uniforms she widened the door. She stood about five feet tall, shivering beneath a salmon-colored robe decorated with illustrations of pink and green bouquets that had been faded from years of wear.

She adjusted her glasses on the bridge of her nose as she looked up at the officers. "May I help you?"

The two uniformed cops glanced at Thomas, unaware of what he was going to say. Thomas took in the eyes of his peers and flashed his most innocent smile at his elder, who was staring in oddity at him from behind her large frames.

"Well, what is it, son?" she demanded.

"Um, yeah . . . um . . . ma'am, My name is Detective Thomas. Do you reside here?"

"Well, I am answering the door, son."

"Yes, I know, but . . . um . . . ma'am . . . well . . . I'm sorry, but what did you say your name was?"

"I didn't say my name, honey. However, if you would like to know, it's Ms. Martha Wellington." She pulled the collars of her robe closer together. "And why are you knocking at my door, son?"

Uncertain of how to properly address the lady without offending her, he stated, "We have a murder investigation going on next door. Is it okay if we came in and asked you a few questions? We also need to take a quick look around your apartment, if you don't mind."

"Murder investigation? Oh my god, who? When did this happen?"

"A couple of days ago, a three-year-old boy from next door was shot and killed. We are trying to find out answers as to how and why this could have happened."

The lady clasped her hand around her mouth while her remaining one held onto her robe. "Oh no! Not that little handsome boy? Sweet Jesus . . . his mother must be devastated." Then it dawned on her as she peered deeply into Thomas's eyes. "But my apartment? For what?"

"Well, ma'am, before answering that, I need to know if there is anyone else in there with you."

"No, my grandson is outside somewhere." Her eyes went from the female officer back to Thomas. "You know how hard it is keeping up with that boy? Especially since he started hanging with all these new friends?"

The three officers glanced at each other.

The lady continued. "My grandson didn't hang out with anyone next door. They are much older than he. Although I wish he did 'cause that Shaheen is a good man. Known him since he was a little boy, before his mama died. I would have preferred for John John to have made friends with Shaheen and his wife rather than that damn Anthony."

"Anthony?" Thomas was fully aware of the fact that Anthony was the name of the suspect they had in custody for the Copper Lee-Chin murder.

"Yeah, ever since he started hanging out with that boy, he has changed."

"Changed? Like what? His behavior?"

"Yeah, he has been trying to be some sort of tough guy now."

Thomas shot a quizzical expression at the woman. "Ma'am, I hate to ask this, but do you know if your grandson owns a gun?"

The woman seemed baffled by Thomas's inquiry. She studied the detective's expression, wondering what sort of trouble her grandson was involved in. She did not want to see him in anyone's jail cell. He was too smart for that. He was only fourteen but had been an honor roll student for his entire academic career. He was well on his way to becoming someone great until the death of his parents, which caused slight but sure changes in his attitude. She was uncertain of whether she should continue her conversation with the police or not.

The only words that were able to escape her mouth was "Gun?"

Thomas spoke up as his two cohorts remained quiet. "Yeah, gun. Like I said, would you mind if we stepped in to talk and take a look around?

The lady, not certain of how to reply, stated, "Sure." She opened the door and stepped to the side, allowing the officers room to enter. As they began walking past, curiosity overtook her. "But why my apartment?"

Thomas stopped directly in front of her and flatly stated, "Because the bullet that caused the murder came from here."

CHAPTER 18

Detective O'Reilly eyed Shaheen's bodily language intently. The eagerness induced by his anger and intentions was visible to the officer. However, each time he spoke, his hands slightly shook, making himself appear nervous rather than impatient. As the two friends went to exit the apartment, O'Reilly eyes followed them, attempting to discern the suspicious behavior of Gorilla Leek's right-hand man. Something on the inside of his gut was warning him about Shaheen. He could not put his finger on it, so he decided to follow behind the duo after they walked out of the apartment.

His senses immediately went on alert as he stepped out into the hallway and the door to the apartment closed behind him. He couldn't believe what he walked into. The man who Gorilla Leek just spent hours trying to convince him was a loyal and trustworthy business partner was now holding a gun to his head.

O'Reilly slowly retrieved his revolver and raised the nozzle up to Shaheen's back. He crept alongside the banister out of sight, controlling his breathing as he neared his target. There were few words between the two before O'Reilly approached them and squeezed off a round into Shaheen's flesh.

Releasing his weapon, Shaheen tumbled past Gorilla Leek, causing him to lose his footing and accompany him down the steps. The two landed at the bottom of the staircase with Gorilla Leek on top. O'Reilly swooped down upon them with pistol still drawn as Gorilla Leek seized a hold of the banister that lined the stairs and lifted himself from off his friend.

"Shit, dude! What the hell was that?" screamed Gorilla Leek.

O'Reilly extended his hand and assisted him to his feet. "That was called saving your life. Are you not grateful?"

Gorilla Leek glanced down at his friend, who was sluggishly moving about on the ground moaning.

"You didn't have to shoot him. It was a misunderstanding. I could have handled it."

Detective O'Reilly laughed at the naïveté of his new partner. "Hah! Handle it? You were about to be where he's at right now. He came here to kill you not discuss business. I thought you were a better judge of people. This was supposed to be someone you can trust. I guess you learned a valuable lesson, eh?"

Gorilla Leek was still in awe from what just occurred. He glanced back at his friend who was struggling to bring himself to an errect position. "Why? What, for ole girl? Or do you really think I had something to do with Shane?"

O'Reilly, impatient with the slow movement of the injured man, decided to violently pull him to his feet with one hand while he held his weapon with the other.

"Get up!" he yelled as he grabbed hold of Shaheen's jacket and lifted him partially up.

Shaheen stumbled to get up but made it to his feet. He leaned against the banister as the two watched him closely. He searched the ground for his pistol. It was at the feet of the officer. He told himself to dive down and snatch it up from the ground; however, as the thought scrambled through his brain, he felt his right arm becoming extremely heavy.

Feeling a great deal of throbbing pressure squeezing the life out of his ligament, he attempted to raise it to alleviate the discomfort but couldn't. As he tried to lift it, the weight of his arm increased, causing him to abandon the idea of moving it. Numbness engulfed the nerves in his flesh while the sensation in his fingers began to fade. The pain he was experiencing subsided as he lost the feeling in his wounded body part. He told his hand to constrict into a fist, but it wouldn't. He started to panic, but controlled his fear upon seeing the barrel pointed directly at his face.

"You picked the wrong time to start a war with your partner," O'Reilly calmly warned as he held his weapon to the face of his injured victim.

Shaheen remained silent without removing his eyes from the pistol pointed at him.

"Hold on, hold on!" Gorilla Leek stood in between the cop's gun and Shaheen. "I need to know why the fuck he think I killed his seed. I mean, this is crazy. This is my boy."

Shaheen spat blood from the busted lip he received from falling down the stairs. It landed at Gorilla Leek's feet. "I ain't your boy, bitch! You murdered my son and fucked my woman! So don't talk that boy shit with me."

O'Reilly was becoming apparently impatient with the interaction of the two, so he decided to cut them short. "Well, there you have it. Your boy said he is not your boy. You people turn on each other in a heartbeat." Pushing his weapon to the temple of his victim, he continued, "Let's hurry up and get rid of this monkey so we can finish off our business. He is obviously not concerned with being a part of this relationship, so forget about him!"

"Wait yo! This is my dude! Not some cat off the street. I ain't just gonna return him like that!"

"Your dude. You guys kill me with your fake loyalty. Didn't he just say you were sleeping with his woman? Did you consider him your dude then? Look, we have serious money to make, and nothing can interfere with that. Besides, you have Chinnah after you. Minimart is gone, and White Mike is dead. Can you really afford to let your feelings for your so-called boy get in the way of you making this money? Do I need to find another partner to handle the work?'

Gorilla Leek swallowed deeply before answering, "Na, we good. It's just that . . ."

"Good. That's what I want to hear. Now you can feel sorry for him and allow him the opportunity to come back and try this shit another day or you can handle it now so it won't bite us in the ass later on. Which is it?"

Gorilla Leek let out a deep sigh. O'Reilly opted to decide for him. "To hell with this! I don't have time to waste." O'Reilly seized Shaheen by his leather jacket and tossed him across the hall. Shaheen let out a groan as his wounded shoulder slammed against the wall. He gripped his arm tightly and glared wickedly at his attacker. The detective swung him around and pressed his face further into the barrier. He brought his pistol upon the man once more.

"I could give two cents about the concern your friend holds for you. From what I have seen here today, you would only cause trouble. You should have left your feelings about your girlfriend at home. I will not allow you to ruin this. My daughter is on her way to college, and this money is needed. Plus, I don't need another Larry Davis on my hands."

The detective glanced over his shoulder at Gorilla Leek. "Are you all right with this?"

Gorilla Leek humbly asked. "Would it matter if I wasn't?"

O'Reilly smirked. "Na, not really."

Bringing his attention back to Shaheen he stretched out and stiffened his arm that held the pistol, aiming it at his head. He stepped back a couple of steps, and while keeping his eyes on his mark, he cocked his head slightly away then inhaled.

As he went to exhale, Gorilla Leek yelled out, startling the two. "Oh shit, po po!"

O'Reilly pointed his weapon to the ground and faced his new partner, who was staring out the elongated windows positioned in the center of both doors of the entrance.

"What?" asked the detective.

"Police. They walking out there around Sha's whip," he said as he pointed beyond the door and onto the street. "They looking through his window and all that."

O'Reilly ventured over to the door just in time to see one of the officers, motion for his partner to walk toward the building the three were now in. Shaheen propped himself up against the wall. He began feeling weak and light-headed.

O'Reilly watched as the officer nearest to the SUV suddenly grabbed his walkie-talkie from his waist. He listened for all two seconds before holding it up to his mouth and talking directly into it. He then quickly shoved the instrument back into its holder and retrieved his pistol. He yelled out something to his partner who was approaching the stairs to the building.

O'Reilly fingered his weapon as he observed the officer nearest to him stop to look back at his partner. The officer pulled out his 9 mm and cautiously ventured up the stairs. O'Reilly tentively backed away from the door.

"Something is going on. They're coming up here."

"What! Man, I'm not staying around to get arrested. We need to bounce," shouted Gorilla Leek.

O'Reilly wouldn't take his eyes off the window as he proceeded to move backward. "And go where? Is there another way out?"

"Yeah. Through the basement there's another exit that leads to the back of the building," answered Gorilla Leek.

"All right, well, get ready to run." The detective pivoted around to face Shaheen, who was leaning against the wall holding his right tricep. He lifted his gun up to the man once more.

"Yo, what are you doing? They'll hear that shit! Them boys are on their way in here. We don't have the time!" Gorilla Leek's voice revealed his nervousness.

Shaheen thought he would never hear those words leave his ex-friend's mouth when it came to murder.

Without removing his eyes from the side of Shaheen's skull, he replied, "That's why I said get ready to run!"

Once again, the detective took in a deep breath. As he began to let it out and squeeze the trigger, a loud thunderous bang riveted the hallway. O'Reilly's head violently jerked forward as if it was about to leap off his neck. He stumbled toward the wall, just missing Shaheen who ducked as soon as he heard the gunshot. For a fraction of a second, he thought he had been shot until he saw O'Reilly's body fall against the wall.

The wounded detective attempted to regain his balance after which he released his weapon and lifted his hand to the back of his head. He fumbled through his wet hair in search of the wound. Suddenly his searching stopped, and he dropped to the ground. Shaheen watched as the man's eyes rolled to the back of his head and blood began to ooze out of his skull and onto the floor.

Shaheen's instincts went on alert. He shot his left hand down to the floor and scooped up the dead man's weapon. Losing no time, he drew it upon Gorilla Leek, who was still aiming his forty-four at the body sprawled out in front of them.

As soon as he heard the shot, the officer that was closing in on the entrance hopped over the side of the staircase and sought cover from the view of the shooter. His partner was crouched behind the SUV calling in for back up.

"Shots fired. I repeat, shots fired!" the officer screamed into the walkie-talkie. "We were investigating a call that came in reporting a gunshot going off at 130 Lenox Avenue about three minutes ago! When we arrived at the scene, we noticed the same vehicle that was reported as being involved in a gas station homicide that just occurred. We have a location on the vehicle but not the suspect. We were getting ready to look around when gunshots went off! We need back up!"

Gorilla Leek glanced out the window to see the top of the officer's head bulging above the hood of the Ford. He shot his eyes toward his friend who was now pointing a gun at him. He knew he did not have an ample amount of time to aim at his predator because his gun was pointed to the ground. Shaheen would get him before he could get a chance to raise his arm. However, he realized his right-handed ex-partner was barely holding the weapon in his left hand and it was shaking uncontrollably.

"Whatchoo gonna do, shoot me?" Gorilla Leek defiantly inquired.

Tears started flooding Shaheen's eyes as his lips shook rapidly, causing his flesh to move along his cheeks like the waves of an ocean. His left eye repeatedly twitched as he felt the muscles in his left palm tighten. His heart thumped voraciously within his chest each time it rose to capture the silent air that now reeked of the feces and urine that soaked the dead cop's pants.

Gorilla Leek eyed his friend. "Look dog, we can handle this some other time. Right now, we have to get out of here." Looking down at O'Reilly's body, he continued, "Besides I could've let that pig kill you, but I didn't."

Shaheen stood with the pistol pointing at Gorilla Leek but said nothing.

Gorilla Leek became impatient. "Blood, either you can return me to the essence right now or we can get the fuck up outta here! Either way you need to make up your mind before them pigs reach up here. Whatchoo gonna do?"

"Did you cum in her?" Shaheen's voice held no trace of emotion.

"Huh?"

"Nigga, did you cum in my woman?"

"Son, we don't have time for this. We have to go!" From his peripheral, Gorilla Leek could see the figure of the officer creeping up the steps once more. "Son, for real, for real, we have to bounce. They coming now!"

"Then answer the question! I know she's pregnant!" Shaheen seemed unmoved by the idea of getting caught by the police. He had only one concern on his mind.

Gorilla Leek let out a deep and exaggerated sigh before answering, "Yeah. I let loose in her but not on some put-a-seed-in-her shit. It was just the moment."

A confused smile appeared on Shaheen's face. His lips began moving with no sound as if he was enjoying a conversation with himself on the inside of his head. "Just the moment, eh? So is that why you murdered my only boy?"

"Dude, I'm telling you, you're wrong. I didn't . . . I wouldn't kill . . ."

"Man, fuck you! You always wanted my wifey, dude! You been jealous of me since we were shorties. But my fucking son?" Shaheen began crying and screaming uncontrollably.

His strong authoritative tone was washed out by his feminine sobs. "I loved him, man! He was my firstborn. I ran around this whole time thinking he died by my gun. An-an-and you . . . you . . . helped me . . . bury him! I murdered that bitch Carla over this shit, and come to find out the only reason she even knew anything was because you told Lo, and she told her! Dude, I went to the cops and told them he was kidnapped when I should've just told them you killed him!"

Gorilla Leek's eyebrow went up in shock. "You went to the cops?"

"Yeah, and now, they think Shane's death has something to do with Chinnah!"

Gorilla Leek kept glancing out of the window in search of the cop, who was now closing in on the last four steps of the building.

Shaheen continued, "They said the gun used when Copper got shot was the same one used on Shane. They said it was a forty-four, not a nine, that murdered him. I don't own a fucking forty-four."

Gorilla Leek looked confused. "You sure? How you know?"

"Lo told me that's what the pigs told her."

"And you believe her? How the fuck would they know what he got shot with?" Gorilla Leek said glancing once more onto the street outside.

"Because they found his body!"

Gorilla Leek's face became distorted with awe. "What! How? You told them?"

"Fuck no! Lola snitched. They was all over the park looking for him. And they found my burner too! Said it wasn't the murder weapon. Nigga, you already admitted to being there when he and Copper got shot. Muthafucka, one plus two equals you, bitch! Now fuck all this bullshit convo. Tell me why!"

Gorilla Leek could discern in his friend's eyes that he wasn't about to let up. He considered for a moment the idea of attempting to get a shot off first. His palms started to sweat profusely even though the air in the hallway was uncomfortably frigid. He viewed the officer from his peripheral and decided whatever he was going to do had to be done now.

Without pondering any longer, he quickly raised his pistol. Shaheen took notice. He told his finger to pull the trigger, yet it did not respond right away. It took a second to get there as he watched Gorilla Leek lift, then point his gun at him. At first, he thought he was about to become his ex-friend's next victim until he saw him turn, aim at the window, then let off three shots. As the gun exploded in the other direction, Shaheen's finger received the message from his nerves and decided to react. He quickly thought about not shooting, but it was too late. His finger jerked from the sound of Gorilla Leek's gun. The bullet exploded from his barrel, then went straight through Gorilla Leek's left shoulder.

"Argghh shit!" Gorilla Leek cried out.

His body barely moved from the hit. Blood began trickling down the side of his arm. He appeared to have not felt the impact as he kept firing out the window of the hallway. Both officers returned the fire. The churning and smashing of wood and glass combined together with the explosion of gunpowder to make a horrific sound of destruction and chaos.

Shots tore into Gorilla Leek's chest and stomach as he stood his ground, firing his weapon. Without looking at Shaheen, he screamed, "Run, nigga, run! I got these muthafuckas . . . argh!" He stumbled backward as another bullet slammed into his already wounded shoulder. He braced his right foot behind him to keep from falling. He kept firing. "Run, nigga!"

Shaheen gaped at his friend in awe as bullets riddled his torso. It seemed as if each time he blinked another bullet went through his friend's body. He posted himself against the wall so as not to receive any of the shots fired by the officers. Gorilla Leek kept firing wildly through the door and window. His body shook from the constant impact of the bullets tearing apart his flesh and clothing.

To Shaheen, the gunfire seemed never-ending. He almost felt sorry for his friend as he kept pulling the trigger with nothing coming out. Gorilla Leek seemed to be unaware of the fact that his weapon had ran out of ammunition. The barrel of his pistol popped out and locked on him while he kept squeezing. The police officers had ceased their firing upon realizing there were no longer anymore gunshots coming from the building.

Gorilla Leek stood in a bloody puddle, huffing and puffing heavily. His shirt was ripped to shreds and soaked with his blood. His face had become a portrait blood-splatter. Crimson leaked from his mouth and nose while his neck twitched repeatedly. He almost lost his balance as he dropped his weapon to the ground. He struggled to turn his head toward Shaheen, who was plastered against the wall. His head fell back as his eyes viewed his friend from the corner of his lids. He haltingly opened his mouth as if it was torturous to do so.

"Get . . . the fuck . . . outta here."

Shaheen wanted him dead but didn't consider the fact it would be so painful to watch. This was the only friend he knew. If he had befriended a different person growing up, he probably wouldn't have ended up selling drugs. He observed the only remaining person he loved cling on to the last of his strength and breath.

Gorilla Leek collapsed to his knees, just in time to grab hold on the banister and prevent himself from falling completely.

"Go!" he demanded.

Shaheen lifted himself from the wall and put the gun to his friend's head.

Gorilla Leek gazed up at the barrel, then let out a deep breath, before lowering his eyes back down to his feet. "I shouldn't have never fucked with your woman, my dude. I'm sorry."

"Yeah, I'm sorry too."

"Sha . . . ," Gorilla Leek humbly and softly spoke.

"What man?" Shaheen said with a trace of sadness in his voice.

"I would never hurt your boy. That's on everything I love."

Shaheen eyed him curiously, then spoke. "Yeah, well, whether that's true or not, it's too late now." Realizing his friend was not going to make it, he added, "I'm not gonna let them take you in. I know you don't want that, bro." Shaheen attempted to fight back the tears that were beginning to fall by swallowing deeply. He shot a look of dismay up into the air, then brought his attention back upon his dying friend. "This shot is because I love you, my nigga."

Shaheen closed his eyes as a tear escaped his lid and squeezed the trigger. The bullet slammed Gorilla Leek's head to the pavement, causing blood to splash across the floor. His body collapsed to the ground, causing it to vibrate beneath Shaheen. He then ducked down, settled his weapon on the floor, and shoved his hand into his dead partner's pants pocket. Finding nothing, he rummaged through his jacket and discovered what he was probing for. He pulled out a key ring and tossed it into his pants.

Picking up his gun, he stood up and faced the entrance. He then fired four shots through the window and ran toward the basement right before the officers returned his fire. As he bolted to the back of the hallway and through the basement door, he could hear sirens going off in the background.

CHAPTER 19

"Nooooooo! Aah, shiiit! Mmm . . . eh . . . Pu-pu-please, Chinnah!" The horrific sounds of agony along with the high-pitched cries of mercy leaped off Killa Kash's tongue in chilling stutters. Most of his fearful pleads were muffled by the blood in his mouth. He attempted to either swallow or spit it out, but each time he did so, more blood would flood his cavity. He could feel the handcuffs that restrained him cutting into the flesh of his wrist. The instruments restricted the movement of his arms as they were held in place behind the backrest of the metal chair he was confined to.

There was an extremely sharp yet throbbing pain coming from the top of his feet. He had just awoken about an hour ago to the discomfort of this torturous situation. When he discovered he was bound in a dark basement by himself, his desire was to get up and flee. He attempted to do so with much regret as agony shot through both of his feet from the long nails that had been hammered through them and into the floor.

The coldness of the metal chair he was bound to absorbed the remaining warmth his blood distributed beneath his naked flesh. He instantly felt goose bumps rise once he realized he was without clothing. His vision was a bit blurred, and he longed to rub his eyes but was unable to do so. He figured it didn't matter because the room was so dark he could barley detect anything.

The last thing he remembered before his world went black was walking into his apartment, then feeling a hard object crashing down upon his head. He had awoken to punches and kicks and then fell into unconsciousness again once they began using razors and hammers. Now here he was, eyes open again, in the basement of one of Chinnah's many spots, butt-naked, and in pain.

His dark-colored flesh was completely bare except for the blood smeared across his face, legs, and chest. His feet resembled wet and mushy french fries that had been drenched in ketchup. Someone had taken the liberty of smashing his toes in with a hammer. The path his tears traveled down his cheeks was now lined by dried-up crimson trails. He hung his head low as his bottom lip shook, causing blood to drip from it like a leaky faucet. There were several razor scars stretching across his mouth, forehead, and even one across his right eye.

His naked left knee had been pulverized so treacherously that it corkscrewed his leg into a gruesome position, leaving his foot twisted outwardly and part of his shin protruding out of his flesh. He was in extreme affliction. With his chin to his chest, he struggled to open his mouth once more.

"Please, Chinnah."

Chinnah stood over him allowing a smile to escape his serious demeanor as the boy began to plea.

"Pleeze? Yuh expek mi fi pleeze yuh? Wha, affa yuh dun involve mi pickni in sim bizness dat leave im fi dead!"[74]

Killa raised his heavy head. "I . . . I . . . argh . . . didn't have any . . . thing to do with set . . . setting the . . . the meeting up. I knew nothing about it. He . . . he . . . told m-mmm-me about it f-f-for the firs-first time when we w-w-were going there."

Yellowman came from behind Chinnah, holding a hammer. He approached Killa and, without warning, swung the tool into his right knee. It made a sick crushing sound like potato chips being smashed but louder and more violent. His knee

---

[74] "Please? You expect me to please you? What, after you have involved my son in some business that got him killed!"

shot inwardly, launching his foot upward, causing the nail in it to viciously rip the flesh. He howled out in agony.

"Aaarrgghh!"

Crying and whimpering replaced the scream as Yellowman rested the hammer in between the boy's legs.

"Nex gwan be yuh dickie. So chat bwoy!"[75]demanded Chinnah.

In between his sobbing, Killa tried to communicate without stuttering. "He was doing a deal with a pig, O'Reilly, to cop some girl from him that po po was taking off the streets. He was gonna get White Mike to hand over his store to Gorilla Leek and Shaheen to run the work out of. We was suppose to be going there that night to discuss everything to get it moving."

"Den ooh ah murda mi son?"[76]

"Dunno. I wasn't in the store when it happened. I swear to you." Killa began crying once more.

"Mon, cease yuh blood clot bawlin! Mi nuh deal wit nuh sopsy ma'ama man ere. All mi wan know is yuh vershun of whappen! Dat all, so ansah mi!"[77] ordered Chinnah.

Killa cleared his throat, then ejected spit from between his teeth. He regained his composure and spoke, "I think it was Gorilla Leek. I didn't see it happen, but before we got to the store, Copper called White Mike, and he said Gorilla was on his way there. After I heard the gunshots, I ran into the store but didn't see no one."

Chinnah paced back and forth like a lion in a cage. Suddenly, he stopped his movement and turned back toward Killa.

"So whey de coac?"[78]

---

[75] "Next it is going to be your penis. So talk boy!"

[76] "Then who murdered my son?"

[77] "Man, cease your fucking crying! I am not dealing with any weak sissy here. All I want to know is your version of what happened! That is all, so answer me!!"

[78] "So where is the coac?"

A display of ignorance covered Killa's face. "The coac?"

Chinnah was visibly disgusted. "Lissin mon, dunt chobble mi wit some ear-sey 'bout wha yuh tink appen ta mi pickni an mi coac. Dunt skank mi. Mi wan de trute. Mi wan de wuk mi son was sellin tru mi ouse pon fitty fust street. As well as mi product im ad da bwoy dem tief from deyso. Whey it tis?"[79]

Killa wondered how Chinnah knew so much. He started trembling because he knew he wouldn't be able to provide the exact location of all the drugs that were missing.

"I . . . I . . . know where he kept the work he had Blue Jay take from the spot before Leek and them hit it up, but I don't know where the rest of it . . . you know, the work them blood niggas snatched up . . . is."

"Well, whey de wuk yuh know 'bout den?"[80]

"Copper stashed it back at the cop's house . . . you know . . . till everything went down."

Chinnah flashed a peculiar grin. "Til e'reeting gwan down? Wha, like mi downfall? Yuh tink im wood ave dun so successfully?"[81]Chinnah raised his arms in the air, then held them up before waving the captive off. "Yuh ah fool!"[82]

Killa flinched from the unexpected gesture, then retorted, "Look, I was loyal to your son. I rolled with him without asking questions 'cause he was my loc. I didn't know what was going on."

Chinnah held out his hand to Yellowman, who passed him the hammer. Killa started shaking nervously in the chair. "Fi

---

[79] "Listen man, don't bother me with some hearsay about what you think happened to my coac. Don't trick me. I want the truth. I want the work my son was selling through my house on Fifty First Street. As well as my product he had those boys steal from there. Where is it?"

[80] "Well, where is the work you know about then?"

[81] "Until everything went down? What, like my downfall? You think he would have done so successfully?"

[82] "You are a fool!"

tell mi de trute, now . . . before mi bruck up yuh legs! Did mi son ave plan fi murda mi?"[83]

Killa seemed shocked. "Huh?"

"Yuh eard mi. Why wood mi own flesh an blood tief from mi, knowin ow mi andle men ooh take from I an I?"[84]

"Chinnah, I never heard him speak of harming you. I swear!"

Chinnah began swinging the tool back and forth in front of Killa but hitting nothing. Killa jumped each time it passed his face.

"Alms ouse!"[85]screamed Chinnah. "Yellow, bring de oddah fool owt."[86]

Yellow quickly disappeared into the shadows. Killa didn't take notice of which direction the man went in. He wondered to himself who the other fool might be and why he needed to be brought out now. He silently prayed it would not be anyone who would contradict his story. Within no time, Yellow returned pushing a wheelchair with a human figure reclined in it. Killa's vision was too blurry to discern who the person was or if he was even alive.

Yellowman brought the chair to a halt directly in front of Killa. *Oh shit!* Killa instantly recognized the disfigured face. It was Blue Jay. He didn't seem to be moving. Chinnah stepped closer to Killa and the motionless Blue Jay.

While assessing Killa's reaction, Chinnah stated, "Kuh de. Yuh see de mon dehso? Im fi told us ereting. Yuh know wha im seh?"[87]

---

0   "Tell me the truth now . . . before I break your legs! Did my son have plans to murder me?"

[84]   "You heard me. Why would my own flesh and blood steal from me, knowing how I handle men who take from me?"

[85]   "Nonsense!"

[86]   "Yellow, bring the other fool out."

[87]   "Look there. Do you see the man there? He told us everything. Do you know what he said?"

Killa remained silent. He felt his heart thumping as if it was about to explode through his chest.

Chinnah continued, "Ascordin ta im, unuh ad plans ta murda mi. Dat de two ah yuh ave bin wukin wit Babylon sellin dem coac tru mi spot. Im seh unuh made sim deal wit da bwoys dem, Gorilla Leek an Sha-Boogie. Dat mi gravelicious pickni de wan ooh fi ad Trevor kilt."[88] The volume in Chinnah's voice began rising with each word. "Dat Copper de wan ooh ah plan de jux at mi ouse!"[89] He paused to catch his breath. "Nuh true?"[90]

Again Killa said nothing. He was far from dumb. He knew that his death would come at any moment regardless of what lies he could conjure up to tell Chinnah. Chinnah could care less. Someone would have to pay. Killa did not want to beg for his life any longer nor was he about to show anymore signs of weakness. From here on out, he reconciled, he will go out like a true-blue soldier.

"Fuck it," he said with his head hung low.

"Wha yuh mean?"[91] asked Chinnah.

"Do what you gonna do."

Chinnah smiled once more. "Wha mi gwan duh?"[92]

Displaying no emotions, Killa defiantly replied, "Don't toy with me, yo. Just do it!"

Chinnah's smile disappeared. "Soon nuff, nuh need ta rail up . . . . mi ave wan mo kweshun."[93]

---

[0] "According to him, Y'all had plans to murder me. That the two of you have been working with police selling their coac through my spot. He said y'all made some deal with those boys, Gorilla Leek and Sha-Boogie. That my greedy son is the one who had Trevor killed."

[89] "That Copper is the one who planned the robbery at my house!"

[90] "Is it not true?"

[91] "What do you mean?"

[92] "What am I going to do?"

[93] "Soon enough, no need to get excited . . . . I have one more question."

With his head still hanging, he asked, "What?"

"If yuh so loyal ta mi son, den tell mi whey ta fine dis Gorilla Leek. Pauley areddi on im way fi andle im brethren. We jus cyan fine de pussy-ole Gorilla."[94]

"Chinnah!" The scream came from above as the sound of the door to the upstairs room could be heard opening. A ray of light escaped the crack in the entrance and shot through the darkness, causing a thin streak of luminance to stretch across the face of the man confined to the wheelchair. Killa shot a glance at him noticing that one of Blue Jay's eyes were opened. The other had been closed shut from swelling. It appeared he was trying to mutter something. Killa could see the word help forming on his lips but heard no sound. He returned his chin to his chest. He refused to cast his eyes upon him. It was because of his big mouth that they were in this predicament.

"Simiya!"[95]Chinnah hollered back.

Kam came running down the stairs, huffing and puffing. He brushed past Yellowman and stopped in front of Chinnah. Chinnah shot a look of confusion at the soldier who was following Shaheen.

"Whappen?"[96]

Kam began to slow down his breathing in order to get the words out of his mouth. "Mi fi try reachin yuh x-amount ta times yestaday."[97]

"Fi what? Pauley seh im nuh hear from yuh, so im sin Jimbo fi andle im."[98]

---

[94] "If you are so loyal to my son, then tell me where to find this Gorilla Leek. Pauley is already on his way to handle his friend. We just can't find the pussy-hole Gorilla."

[95] "I'm here!"

[96] "What happened?"

[97] "I tried reaching you several times yesterday."

[98] "For what? Pauley said he didn't hear anything from you, so he sent Jimbo to handle him."

"Mi know baas . . . mi know . . . de battaree pon mi phone fi dead. Mi travel ta Sha-Boogie's ouse but Babylon was ereweh."[99]

Chinnah grew visibly worrisome. "Huh? Yuh see Pauley?"[100]

"Nuhwhey. Afta mi try callin yuh an mi receive nuh ansah, I—"[101]

Chinnah cut Kam short. "Ya nuh get nuh ansah cuz mi jus informed dat mi pickni was murdad."[102]

Kam's head jerked backward, and his eyes grew wide. "Ah ooh? Ya dawta?"[103]

Chinnah appeared baffled by the question. "Mi dawta. Why yuh ask 'bout mi dawta? Mi tawk 'bout mi son."[104]

"Copper?" Kam wondered as he observed his environment taking notice of the two basement prisoners. "Wha ah gwan ere?"[105]

"Nevamine dat. Wha yuh wan an . . . wa mek yuh axe 'bout mi dawta?"[106]

Kam glanced at Killa. He did not know him personally but was familiar with him. He knew he was Copper's friend and pondered whether he had anything to do with the news Chinnah just laid on him. Fear started to seep into Kam's thoughts. He did not want to end up like the men before him.

---

[99] "I know boss . . . I know . . . the battery for my phone went dead. I went to Sha-Boogie's house, but police were everywhere."

[100] "Huh? Did you see Pauley?"

[101] "No where. After I tried to call you and I received no answer, I—"

[102] "You didn't get an answer because I was just informed that my son was murdered."

[103] "Who? Your daughter?"

[104] "My daughter. Why are you asking about my daughter? I am talking about my son."

[105] "What is going on here?"

[106] "Never mind that. What do you want and what made you ask about my daughter?"

He wondered how Chinnah would respond to the information he was about to give him. He opened his mouth.

"Chinnah . . . yuh mite wan sidung fi dis . . . an . . . uh . . . can yuh . . . uh . . . pleez place de hamma pon de groung?"[107]

*   *   *

The four train roared through the winding dark tunnel that had been burrowed beneath the noisy and overcrowded Manhattan streets. The passengers on board the speeding and shaking iron worm were too occupied reading their newspapers, conversing with other riders, brooding in deep thought over their unfulfilled life, or nodding off into la-la land to take notice of the man sitting alone profusely bleeding from his arm.

Shaheen had settled his tiresome frame upon the seat closest to the conductor's booth, watching the many sulky faces, hoping no one was cognizant of his physical predicament. The last thing he needed was for someone to see his arm, then alert the police. He contemplated getting off at the Borough Hall station, the next and first stop in Brooklyn, and hailing a cab instead of riding the subway. He decided it would prove to be a safer route than staying where he was and running the risk of an officer coming onto the subway car and seeing him.

As the train's movement howled out a warning of its approach to the next station, the lights on the inside of the car flickered, then went out completely, only to once again illuminate the interior. Each time they went out, Shaheen became nauseant. His arm was completely paralyzed. He began daydreaming about how life would have been if he had stayed in college. He prayed he would make out of this situation, so he could have a second chance at life.

---

[107] Chinnah . . . you might want to sit down for this . . . and . . . uh . . . can you . . . uh . . . please place the hammer on the ground?"

He observed the countless faces of the passengers, how dull and miserable they appeared. Shaheen was all too familiar with their expressions. It was the same hopeless demeanor his mother wore throughout most of his life. That sullen look which unceasingly displayed evidence of the afflictions brought about by poverty. The torturous thoughts of possibly getting evicted, not being able to pay the light or gas bill, securing a job, etc. He knew he did not want to be in the same predicament. He had no desire of incurring the same suffering that plagued their minds. To him, the worries and problems he possessed were bearable compared to the agony of being broke.

Shaheen secured the railing positioned to the side of his seat and struggled to lift himself up. The train began slowing down, causing him to almost lose his footing. He braced himself and prevented the fall. A couple of the passengers took notice of the blood oozing through the hole on the sleeve of his leather. The side of his jacket was shiny from being soaked with his blood.

They watched as he stood in front of the doors waiting for the train to come to a halt. Once the doors opened the many riders began conversing with each other about the suspicious wounded man. Shaheen stepped off the train and onto the platform, ignoring the comments that floated through the air. He limped toward the exit of the station and carried his heavy legs up the staircase leading to the street.

The cold air that dug into his wounded flesh felt like a hammer slamming against his arm. It surprised him that he was able to feel it. The icy wind that swept across his face burned his frigid and dry skin. As he walked out onto the sidewalk, he went into his jacket with his left hand and brought his cell phone out. Holding it in his palm, he used his thumb to dial a number. It did not ring long before someone answered.

"Peace and blessings," greeted Sheba.

Shaheen gave no response.

"Yes?" Sheba asked. "Is someone there?"

"Um . . . Yeah . . . whatchoo doin'?" He finally spoke.

Sheba instantly became excited at the sound of his voice. She had been thinking about him all day. She had never fallen for a guy so quickly, but there was something mysterious about him that made her highly attracted to him. She wanted to rush the process of getting to know him, so she could know for certain if he was the last stop on her path to finding love.

"Hey! I'm not doing anything but sitting here wrapping my locks. I was just thinking about you."

"Really?" The discomfort and exhaustion he was feeling caused him to slowly drag the words from his mouth. He sounded depressed, and Sheba took notice of his tone.

"Something wrong?"

While on the train, he thought about where he would go. He realized he could no longer return to his apartment because the police were searching for him. He was relieved he was able to escape the officers chasing him by running through the subway tunnel to the next station, but he was worried he would get caught soon enough if he could not find a place to lie low.

The problem with lying low was he was injured and in desperate need of medical attention. He was alone with nowhere to turn. Lola was with the cops, probably squealing her heart out; Gorilla Leek was dead, and he couldn't even go to Carla's apartment because he murdered her. He contemplated contacting Blades, but Blades stayed with his mother still, and he didn't want anyone relatives involved especially if they had a propensity to run their mouth to the police. The only person he figured he could turn to with safety was Sheba.

Though he barely knew her, there was something about her demeanor and spirituality that made him feel safe around her. The conversation they had last night warmed his heart and made him curious as to how a life with her would have been if he didn't have all the problems he faced on his plate. He needed to confide in her, so she could make sense of it for him. He was uncertain as to why he felt he needed to confess to her. It just felt like the right thing to do. So far, her advice had been on point. He decided he would go to her house and explain everything to her, from his son to the past moments.

He wondered if he was making a mistake doing so; however, he knew he had nothing to lose. His life was currently in shambles. He was injured and possibly on his way to prison for the rest of his life. If he would have known it wasn't his gun that killed his son, his reactions would have been different.

Now he was unsure if he would ever get out of the hole he dug for himself. His actions made his situation worse, and he was aware of that. Guilt began to overtake him. The guilt of hiding his son's body, murdering Lola's friend, and taking his best friend's life became too much to bear. He reconciled he would be able to live with killing Gorilla Leek because he was responsible for the death of his son; however, he needed someone to talk to. He had a lot to get off his chest.

"Kind of. I need someone to talk to. Do you mind if I come over?"

Sheba was curious as to what might have been bothering him. She could hear the tone of defeat in his voice. He was too good of a person to be going through whatever he was going through alone. *Yes, I will be there for him,* she thought to herself.

"That's fine. How soon before you get here? I was about to step out and get some food for the house."

Relieved she said yes, the pace of his voice began to pick up.

"I am downtown Brooklyn right now. About to catch a cab over there. Should take like twenty minutes or so."

"Okay, well, I'll leave the door open, in case I am not here. I shouldn't be long at all. Do you remember how to get here?"

"Kind of. What's the cross streets again?" His tone sounded more vibrant.

"Avenue D and Forty-second Street."

"A'ight, I'll be there soon. Peace, ma."

"Blessings king."

Shaheen closed his cell phone and tossed it back into his jacket. He observed a cab approaching him from the east and decided to hail it down.

Sheba hung up her phone, then sat in front of her vanity mirror. She began tying her locks back into a pony tail and fastidiously arranging her green-knitted headpiece in such a way on top of her head as to allow room to tuck her hair in. Lifting herself from the chair, she walked over to the closet. Retrieving a black leather jacket, she threw it on and zipped it up.

While preparing to walk outside and do some grocery shopping, a loud and startling knock at the front door froze her dead in her tracks. She cautiously strolled over to it and, without bothering to look into the peephole, opened it up. The person on the other side of the door was so closely upon it, he almost fell past her once she allowed him entrance.

Chinnah regained his balance and pushed his way past Sheba with Yellowman following behind. She jumped back as the men entered. Her mouth opened upon noticing the guns they were brandishing. She wanted to yell but couldn't find the voice to do so. She just watched in wonderment as the two men paid her no attention and began searching every room. Sheba was uncertain of how to react.

CHAPTER 20

Chinnah exited the kitchen area, which he searched diligently, and strolled over to Sheba while Yellowman ventured upstairs to conduct a more thorough investigation. Sheba tensed up as the tall man neared her. She started to speak, but he held his finger up to his lips and silenced her. He then placed both of his hands on her shoulders and scowled down at her, revealing his anger and disappointment.

"Whey im is?"[108] he solemnly inquired.

Sheba dropped her gaze to the ground. "Who?"

Chinnah pulled her into his arms, then stared down into her fleeing eyes.

"De mon ooh fi ad Copper kilt."[109]

Sheba's eyes met his as she asked with authority, "What! My brother's dead?"

Chinnah tightened his hold on her while he gazed around the room.

"Eeh,"[110] he calmly replied, sounding more depressed than upset, "im get murdad las nite an smaddy inform mi dat oonu was wit de wan ooh fi ad simtin ta duh wit it."[111]

---

[108] "Where is he?"

[109] "The man who had Copper killed."

[110] "Yeah"

[111] "He was murdered last night and somebody informed me that you were with the one who was involved with it."

Sheba's eyes became distraught with worry. "No . . . na . . . This is a joke, right? Copper's not dead, right?"

Chinnah could see she was going to be deeply affected by the news. Though she didn't spend much time around her father, her little brother was her whole world. The two grew inseparable. While Copper held a small degree of jealousy for his sister, she loved him unconditionally. In the back of her head, she always felt as if her father had forced Copper into his lifestyle while going out of his way to shelter her from it.

Chinnah decided to explain. "Noy, mi nuh joke. Im shot pon da face las nite. Dat why mi neeta know whey de mon yuh met yestadeh."[112]

Tears started falling from her eyes as Yellowman came down the stairs.

"It clear, sire. She ave nuh wan ere,"[113] Yellowman reported.

She wiped away her falling drops of despair and hugged her father. With a degree of authority, she spoke softly and without emotions. "His death . . . or murder . . . You know . . . is your fault."

Chinnah's head jerked back. "Wha yuh chat 'bout?"[114]

"Your lifestyle, your bad deeds, your crimes . . . they have all come back to visit your son . . . my brother. I know he wasn't innocent, but this was your karma. A son is an extension of life . . . your way into the hereafter . . . . The hereafter means here after your death . . . which can only happen if you reproduce yourself. Well, you did . . . You gave the new you life, and then you took it away with your unrighteous actions. Now you have no one to continue on your name or lineage. You have been

---

[0]   "No, I am not joking. He was shot in the face last night. That is why I need to know where the man is you met yesterday."

[113]   "It is clear, king. She has no one here."

[114]   "What are you talking about?"

cut off from the future. You have taken a brother from me with your selfishness," she chastised.

With his lip cocked up and eyebrow raised, Chinnah staunchly countered, "Mi . . . selfish? Wha mi do mi a do fi yuh an yuh brudda. Mi nuh wan dis lifestyle. I an I wood luv ta live a rye'juss life, but mi cyan! Mi came pon dis lan a foreigna wit nuh education, nuh money, jus mi yush tawk. Mi barely cud feed mi self, so mi sell cocaine ta live. When unuh was bawn, mi knew mi ad ta tek mi ahpreyshun ta de next level. Yuh tink mi wan do dis forevah? Ney! Mi cyan stop, cuz mi wan de bes fi unuh."[115]

Sheba sucked her teeth. "The best for us? What like Copper getting shot? Is that your idea of the best for us? Your avaricious nature murdered your son, not Shaheen!"

Chinnah raised his eyebrow. "So yuh know ooh mi chat 'bout, eh? Wha? Yuh im boopsie now?"[116]

Silence overtook the room as Sheba broke free of his embrace and walked over to the door. "If you came here to tell me about my brother . . . you did . . . Now you can leave. I don't need your shoulder to cry on. I'm happy. He is no longer in this life to suffer. He is at peace, so I am at peace. You can leave." She opened the door. "I was on my way out anyway."

"Whey de gun mi give yuh when yuh fust move ere?"[117]Chinnah asked, oblivious to her demand.

---

[115] "Me . . . selfish? What I do, I do for you and your brother. I never wanted this lifestyle. I would love to live a righteous life, but I can't! I came to this land a foreigner with no education, no money, just my Jamaican slang. I barely could feed myself, so I sold cocaine to live. When you were born I, knew I had to take my operation to the next level. Do you think I want to do this forever? Never! I can't stop, because I want the best for you."

[116] "So you know who I am talking about, yeah? What? Are you the woman he is spending his money on now?"

[117] "Where is the gun I gave you when you first moved here?"

She ignored his question. He approached her, placed his hand on the door, then forced it closed. He stared deeply into his daughter's eyes. "Whey yuh wan go, cuz mi nuh gwey."[118]

*   *   *

"Mr. Crooks, we don't have time to play games with you. You need to tell us what happened now. We have the gun that killed Mike Alvarez and Copper Lee-Chin with your fingerprints on it. You can either cooperate or we can let the judge know how difficult you made this investigation." Detective Torturro paused to allow his words to register with the young boy seated behind the iron folding table. "Look man, what the hell you think the judge is gonna do when he finds out you showed no remorse for killing that innocent little boy?"

Anthony Crooks, better known as Ant, couldn't believe what the detective just said. *A kid?* he thought, *now they gonna start pinning charges on me?*

"I ain't kill no kid," Anthony declared, not able to conceal the confusion in his voice. "Whatch'all talking 'bout? I don't kill kids. Nigga, I'm a gangsta! You wanna hit me with the other charges, then go ahead, but I ain't kill no kid."

Anthony rubbernecked around the room only to bring his attention back to the detective. An exaggerated smile covered his face. "I know what y'all trying to do. They did this to my uncle. Y'all got me on a couple of charges that's gonna send me up for a long time, so y'all like fuck it, let's put some cases we can't solve on him. Won't matter 'cause he gonna spend the rest of his life in the bing."

Torturro let out a sigh of frustration. "Look, Ant. That's what they call you, right? You can run all the game you want on the inmates you'll be cooped up with, but please save it when you're in here. I mean . . . man . . . don't you feel bad about ending a little boy's life like that. I mean, don't you have any

---

[118] "Where were you going? Because I am not going away?"

remorse? You are going to get life regardless, so why not fess up. Give his parents some peace."

Ant became angry with the detective's acting. "Give his parents some peace? I don't even know his parents, let alone him, 'cause I ain't kill no little kid!"

Torturro shook his head in disappointment. "You don't know him? Well, his name was Shane Mcfadden. His mother's name is Lola. She's in the next room. And his father's name is Shaheen."

Ant's eyes widened as his mouth shot open. He leaned back into his chair, gripping the table with his hand just in time to prevent himself from falling. "Shaheen? You not talking 'bout Sha-Boogie, right?"

Torturro regarded the display of surprise on the boy's face. He began considering that maybe the boy didn't have anything to do with the murder. *Plus,* he figured, *guns in this neighborhood changes hands so frequently that we could have the wrong person.*

Ant continued, "You not talking about Shaheen from Rutland Road, right?"

Torturro was too engrossed in trying to figure out whether the boy's recent reaction of shock was an indication of his innocence.

"Ay man . . . you talking 'bout Sha-Boogie, Shaheen?"

Torturro snapped out of his deep thought. "Yes . . . that's him. He lives in the building on Rutland and Ninety-third Street, right above Pioneer Supermarket. So you do know who I am referring to? You do know something about his son's death?"

Ant pulled his chair closer to the table and sat straight up. "Look, dude, I ain't kill that nigga's son. I didn't even know his son was dead."

"Yeah, well, how good do you really know Sha-Boogie? Because the bullets that killed your friend back at the store belongs to a gun that was used during a murder we suspect Shaheen was involved in."

Ant's expression of bafflement was detected by Torturro. Ant spoke again, "Na, that can't be. He wasn't there."

"Did you see your friend's killer?"

"No, I didn't see anyone. I just heard the shot and saw him fall."

Realizing he accidently admitted to being inside the store at the time of his friend and White Mike's murder, Ant cursed under his breath. He ceased his conversation to swallow, then shot his eyes up to the corner of his eyelids, and began silently consulting with himself. After about thirty seconds of doing so, he cast his eyes upon the ground and continued his discourse.

"Look man . . . Okay, okay . . ." He swallowed once more, then threw his face into his palms. "Yeah . . . I . . . I . . . I shot the Puerto Rican dude. B-b-bu-but I din't mean to shoot the other dude. He just walked into it. But I swear to you . . . You gotta believe me . . . I didn't kill Sha-Boogie's kid."

Torturro was a bit relieved he was able to get a sort of confession out of the boy for the two murders committed at the store. Now he just needed to find out how all this was connected and whether the seventeen-year-old boy in front of him was telling the truth concerning the death of Lil Shane.

"Then how did the boy end up getting shot with the same pistol you used the night after?"

Ant was uncertain of how to respond. He jogged his memories attempting to remember all that occurred that day. He thought about it for a moment, then it hit him like lightning. His head shot up into the air, and his mouth quickly opened.

"Shit! I think I know what happened. Where was the boy killed at?"

"In the parents' apartment," Toturro responded.

"In the apartment? Around what time?"

"About midday or so. Why?"

Ant once again dropped his gaze as he gritted his teeth. His jaw made slight movements before opening to say, "I think I know what might've happened."

Excitement and impatience leaped off of Torturro's face. He knew if he could solve this case before Thomas came back, he would earn the respect he has been craving the old man to give him. So he asked, "Well then, tell me. What happened?"

Ant frowned at the detective's eagerness then opened his mouth, "First, what kind of deal can you offer me?"

CHAPTER 21

The cab came to a complete stop at 677 Forty-second Street, between Avenue D and Foster Avenue. The door crept open as Shaheen struggle to remove his body from the backseat of the vehicle. His strength was beginning to fade rapidly. He could hear his heartbeat through his vibrating chest. As he exited the taxi, he lifted his chin up into the air and inhaled deeply. He held his breath in as long as he could, then slowly released it while relaxing his shoulders. Dizziness overtook him as he made his way toward the stairs leading up to Sheba's front door.

Before struggling up the staircase, Shaheen glanced around to take in the environment. Shifting his eyes up and down the block, he discovered something all too familiar situated directly in front of Sheba' house. It was an all-black Range Rover. He limped his way over to the back of the ride in order to view the license plate. Upon seeing it, he instantly became startled. His instincts went on alert. His head went from left to right in search of the owner of the vehicle. He knew that license plate all too well. It read SOL-JAH, which he knew did not belong to anyone else but Chinnah.

Not seeing him anywhere in sight, he deduced that Chinnah and his henchmen must have found out about Sheba and decided to pay her a visit in her home. He prayed he was wrong, but he realized he was unaware of how long Pauley had been following him, so it was definitely a possibility he could have found out about Sheba. He then deduced that maybe he was overreacting and that Chinnah's car was parked there for some other reason. *Maybe it's a coincidence,* he thought.

He quickly discarded the idea as he wondered what were the odds his nemesis would be parked right in front of the house he was on his way to a couple of hours after he had just murdered his number 1 enforcer. Then suddenly, discomforting thoughts began racing through his head. He contemplated what could possibly be going on inside the house if Chinnah was in there right now. He never intended to bring any harm to the nice young lady he met over the weekend, so he knew if she was in danger, he would have to help her, regardless of his condition.

He studied the first-floor window attempting to discern if there was anyone in the house. The dark green curtains that concealed the interior of the edifice made it impossible to detect any movement or bodies. He decided to not hesitate any longer. He pulled himself up the staircase and stopped in front of the entrance.

The main door behind the screen was cracked open a little. He slowly pulled the screen toward him as he carefully and quietly pushed open the door to the house. He peeped into the living room but saw nothing. Then, slipping his right foot into the entrance, he used it to open the door further as he retrieved his weapon. Holding the gun pointed to the ground, he crept into the room. His eyes searched the staircase in front of him as well as the rest of the rooms in view. Seeing no one, he made his way toward the back of the first floor to where the kitchen area was.

As he neared the back of the house, he heard two voices coming from the kitchen. He could not comprehend what was being said; however, as he closed the distance between himself and the source of the dialogue, he recognized the person doing most of the talking. It was Chinnah. Shaheen raised his pistol to his chest level and aimed toward the kitchen. With his gun pointed forward, he silently crept toward his target.

Chinnah had his back toward the entrance when Shaheen entered. Yellowman was facing his boss, when he realized the danger befalling them. At first, his vision detected the pistol closing in on Chinnah's neck, then he noticed the arm it was connected to. Yellowman instantly recognized the hunter. His right eyebrow went up as he moved his neck to look around Chinnah's body. Chinnah took notice and glanced over his shoulder to find himself at gunpoint.

He abruptly spun around bringing himself face-to-face with the barrel of Shaheen's weapon. Shaheen edged back one step, then allowed a nervous smile to escape his lips. Chinnah instantly heeded his wounds while Yellowman fumbled around his waist for his gun. Shaheen observed his efforts.

"Move and I will throw a slug right in this muthafaucka's face," Shaheen ordered as spit flew out of his mouth and onto Chinnah's chin.

Yellowman ceased his searching and stood motionless. Chinnah displayed a wicked grin as he sucked his teeth and said, "Mon, mi ope yuh shoot mi 'cuz if yuh nuh duh it . . . mi promise yuh . . ."[119]

He withheld his words as Shaheen placed the pistol directly on his lips.

"Say another word, muthafucka!"

Chinnah said nothing; instead, he waited patiently for his captor to make a mistake.

"Where is she?" Shaheen could feel his senses slipping away from him as his breathing became heavier. He knew, because of his condition, he needed to quickly find Sheba and leave the house before he lost consciousness.

"Ah ooh yuh chat 'bout?"[120] asked Chinnah.

---

[119] "Man, I hope you shoot me, because if you don't . . . I promise you . . ."

[120] "Who are you talking about?"

"Please don't play stupid with me. I don't have the luxury of time," angrily answered Shaheen. "Where's the person that live here?"

Chinnah sucked his teeth. "Psst . . . oonu tink mi gwan elp yuh. Oonu fi murda mi bwoy an yuh wan mi fi assis yuh?"[121]

Shaheen appeared baffled by Chinnah's comment. "Your son? I had nothing to do with that. I wasn't even around. As far as I'm concerned, I think your son was doing business with my peoples. But I was left in the dark about it, so I don't know. While I feel for your loss 'cause I just lost my son too, know that I'm not here to sympathize with you. I didn't do shit to your son, so that doesn't concern me. The only concern I have right now is where Sheba is."

Chinnah laughed. "Wha? Yuh tink mi dehya ta brang arm pon she?"[122] He continued cracking up. "Yuh nuh know. Duh yuh?"[123]

Shaheen became visibly impatient with the words of his enemy. "Man, I'm not going to ask you again. Where is she?" His hand began slightly shaking, which Yellowman took notice of. While the two spoke, Yellow had an ample amount of time to pull out his weapon, but he couldn't fire it because his boss was in the way. He held it behind his back, out of the sight of the person holding them hostage and waited for the opportune time to make his move.

"Is she in the house?" Shaheen impatiently inquired.

Still smiling, Chinnah answered the young man. "Yah mon, she eena de ouse. Mattas fack, er behine yuh."[124]

---

[121] "Psst . . . Do you think I am going to help you?" You murdered my boy and you want me to assist you?"
[122] "What? Do you think I am here to bring her harm?"
[123] "You don't know . . . do you?"
[124] "Yeah man, she is in the house. As a matter of fact, she is behind you."

Shaheen quickly spun his head to see behind him. What stood before his face wasn't expected. Sheba had a loaded .38 revolver aimed at him.

"Huh? What the fuck is this?" he nervously asked while still holding the gun on Chinnah and allowing his wounded arm to dangle alongside his body.

Her hand shook as she fought to control it and keep a tight grip on the gun. Tears were running down her cheeks as her chest repeatedly jumped with each sob she let out. Shaheen was uncertain as to how he should react. He couldn't comprehend what was taking place. He entered the house with the thought to save her, and now, he was the one in danger.

"Remove your gun from my father!" she shouted while crying. "Now!"

A sudden expression of surprise leaped from his eyes as he searched her face for signs of betrayal. When he heard her say father, he thought for a moment he had been set up by her.

"Your father? You shittin' me, right?"

Her hand continued shaking. "I'm not playing. Get your gun off my father!"

"What are you doing? I came here for you," he pleaded.

"You came here to do me harm like you did to my brother."

Shaheen glanced back at his two hostages to make certain they did not move. Turning sideways so as to keep his focus on everyone, and with the pistol still pointed at Chinnah, he aimed his pleading eyes toward Sheba.

"I didn't touch your brother. I had nothing to do with that. I wasn't even around when it happened. I am telling—"

"So what, you here to kill me too 'cause of my father?"

Shaheen began shaking his head. "No, no, no, I came here to talk to you, but when I saw his ca—"

She intervened once more. "So were you following me like daddy said? That whole meeting between us was planned? Just to get at daddy?"

"No . . . Look, I swear, it's not what you think or what you've been told." He brought his attention upon Chinnah and gave him a malicious look. "I don't want any problems with you, Chinnah. I came here to see her. I have no problems with you. I just thought you were in here to do her harm."

Chinnah, unemotionally demanded, "Den release yuh weppin an maybe we chat."[125]

Shaheen directed his attention toward Sheba, and then back at Chinnah. "Na, I won't be able to do that. I know you, Chinnah. Whether I have problems with you or not, you're not gonna let this slide. You know? Me holding you at gunpoint."

"I'm not playing! Put your gun down! Let my father go!" screamed Sheba.

"Sweetheart, if I do that, he will kill me. So for now, that is out of the question."

Sheba moved in closer to Shaheen. "If you don't put it down, I will put *you* down."

Shaheen quickly glanced over his shoulder again, then brought his eyes back to Chinnah who appeared to have closed the distance between them. He could feel the weight of Chinnah's head leaning against the barrel of the pistol.

"If yuh gwan shoot, den shoot!"[126] Chinnah shouted as he pressed his face against the weapon in Shaheen's hand.

"No, daddy. Don't say that!" Sheba screamed.

Shaheen's head shifted back and forth between each of his hostages, wondering if he was going to make it out of the situation. What he did not notice though was Yellowman slowly raising his weapon toward him.

"Sheba, if you want me to lower my joint, you have to lower yours. I mean, I really don't know what's going on here, but I promise you, us running into each other was not planned. I didn't know you were related to Chinnah, and I had nothing to do with your brother's death."

---

[125] "Then release your weapon and maybe we can talk."
[126] "If you are going to shoot, then shoot!"

"Im fi lie! Mi warn yuh dat im ave evilous intentions,"[127] Chinnah demanded with no sign of fear in his eyes. "Shot him!"[128]

Sheba braced her arm and attempted to slow down her shaking. Shaheen took notice and slightly lowered his weapon.

"Don't, Sheba. You are not a murderer. Let him do his own dirty work. Don't let him corrupt you."

Chinnah cocked his head back. "Mi corrup er? Or yuh? Dis mi dawta. An she fi know mi luv er! So mine ow oonu chat. Sheba . . ."[129] Chinnah stared deeply into his daughter's eyes. "Dweet!"[130]

Sheba's tears began pouring down again with no warning. She was unsure of how to react. She could not take losing her father so soon after the loss of her brother. However, she sort of believed the young man she just met the other day. Shaheen could see she was struggling to maintain control over the hand holding the weapon. He motioned his head completely toward her while keeping his pistol aimed at Chinnah.

"Sheba, don't. You're not built like that."

She composed herself just enough to say, "This is your last chance to put your gun down."

Shaheen's face displayed the expression of a four-year-old child in search of his lost mother in a crowded marketplace. His eyes pleaded with her but not his mouth. He removed his focus from her and turned to face Chinnah.

"Tell her to put it down. I didn't come here to hurt anyone," he asked, lifting his weapon up to Chinnah's head.

Upon seeing Shaheen aim his gun to the forehead of his boss, Yellowman quickly raised his arm pointing his barrel in the men's direction. Shaheen's instincts went on alert as

---

[127] "He is lying. I warn you, he has very bad intentions."
[128] "Shoot him!"
[129] "I will corrupt her? Or you? This is my daughter and she knows I love her! So mind how you speak. Sheba . . ."
[130] "Do it!"

he caught a glimpse of Yellowman's pistol targeting him. He quickly removed his gun from Chinnah and fired his weapon past his head.

Thinking he was shooting at her father, his sudden movement startled Sheba causing her to prematurely pull her trigger. As the first two slugs that left his gun tore into Yellowman's throat and chest, Shaheen felt the impact from the bullets that exploded from Sheba's revolver. They burned holes through his back. It caused him to step forward as he struggled to keep from losing his balance.

"Arrgh!" He gritted his teeth and swung around toward her.

Fearful for her life, she squeezed thrice more sending blood spurting from his chest, causing him to lose the grip on his weapon as two of the bullets ripped into him. His mouth shot open. He struggled to raise his arm toward her as if he was trying to shoot, but he held no gun. He stumbled forward with his arm stretched out as if trying to lay hold of her. She thought he was attempting to choke her until he collapsed to the floor, pleading.

"I . . . I . . . just wanted . . . to . . . to get to . . ."—he let out a deep breath—"know you."

Sheba watched as he lay on the floor, breathing heavily. He gasped for every inch of air he could inhale. She held her weapon on him, not knowing if he was still dangerous. Shaheen began crawling toward her when she heard the struggling voice of her father calling her name.

"Shee . . . baa . . . fagiv mi, baby. Mi ongle w-w-wan wha was b-b-bes fi yuh an Copper."[131]

Sheba gazed past Shaheen to see her father on the floor holding the place where his heart was located. Blood was rapidly soaking through his denim jacket. He began coughing after his murmurs, which appeared to cause him much discomfort.

---

[131] "Shee . . . baa . . . forgive me, baby. I only w-w-wanted what was best for you and Copper."

She could not believe her eyes. She had accidently shot her father with one of the bullets meant for Shaheen. She scanned the room, hoping Yellowman could help her, only to find him sprawled out on the kitchen floor, lifeless. She ran to her father and kneeled by his side.

"Oh my god. I'm . . . I'm sorry. I didn't mean to . . ."

Bringing his finger up to his lips, Chinnah struggled to console her. "Shshssh! Nuh wurri yuhself. It nuh yuh fault baby gal. Dis meant fi mi. I . . . I . . ."[132]—Chinnah inhaled deeply, then exhaled his last breath—"Ahhh." His eyes rolled to the back of his head, and he went silent.

Sheba was too busy grieving to notice Shaheen attempting to crawl out of the house. He pulled himself along the carpet, each movement shooting pain through his chest. He thought about his son, Lola, and Gorilla Leek as he moved across the floor. He thought how ironic it was that his life would end this way. He tried to look back at Sheba to make sure she was all right. His aching muscles and injured body wouldn't allow him to.

Suddenly, darkness began growing out of thin air, and it became immensely difficult to raise his eyelids. The little bit of light that found its way in between them afforded him a momentary glimpse of the blood puddle forming on the ground beneath him. He inhaled deeply. Pain stuck his chest as he struggled to exhale. It felt like his breath was stuck between his throat and mouth. He fought to force it out, but it wouldn't budge.

It felt as if his oxygen was growing heavier and more solid. It began slipping back down to his lungs. He gagged in an attempt to cough it out. His chest rose. There were explosions going off inside of it. He imagined it bursting; then suddenly, blackness was everywhere. The only image he could see was

---

[132] "Shshssh! Don't worry yourself. It is not your fault baby girl. This was meant for me. I . . . I . . ."

an outstretched hand directly in front of his face. His sight followed the vision of the arm beyond the darkness all the way up to its owner's face. It was his son inviting him to take a journey. Shane opened his mouth but uttered nothing before disappearing into the blackness. Sheba's pleas for her father to wake up was the last thing Shaheen heard before fading into oblivion.

CHAPTER 22

Lola sat in the interrogation room, fiddling with her fingers, contemplating her predicament, when Detective Torturro burst into the room, slamming the heavy door against the wall. With one large stride, he brought himself directly in front of her and stood on the opposite side of the table that kept them separated. She languidly lifted her head from her chest and allowed her eyes to meet his.

The detective was the first to break the silence. "Do you know a Malik Moore?"

Lowering her eyelids, she cocked her head back, then tilted it to the side before replying, "Hmm . . . Mmm. That's my baby daddy's peoples . . . Why?"

Torturro glanced back at the door to make sure it was closed. "We received a call from a station in Manhattan that an eyewitness gave a description of your boyfriend as being the shooter in a murder that took place in Harlem earlier today at a gas station. They then found his truck outside a brownstone on 128th Street, where two other murders occurred. One of the deceased inside of the house was a police officer, and the other was Mr. Moore."

Lola just stared into oblivion while her jaw slowly crept open. Her glossy eyes waivered as she began shaking her head from side to side.

"No . . . na . . . You're not talking about Gorilla Leek, right? Not him, right?"

Torturo cleared his throat before continuing his dialogue.

"I don't know his street name, just the one that's on his birth certificate."

Torturro could tell she was surprised by the news.

"How did he die?" she asked.

"NYPD tried to put him down during a shootout. However, the fatal bullet came from the same gun used at the gas station killing." Torturro paused as if his next words were difficult to get out. "Also the gun we found buried in the park, where your son's body was found was used in the murders that occurred a couple of days ago, one of which was at a restaurant where Shaheen and Mr. Moore were identified by witnesses as the shooters."

Her expression became distorted as she continued shaking her head and replied, "Are you saying he had something to do with those murders?"

Torturro sucked his lips into his mouth and deliberately nodded his head. "Hmmm. Pretty much. I mean, we have eyewitnesses, and the murder weapon buried next to his son. He is now wanted for murder."

Sheba felt as if she was in the twilight zone. She never fathomed herself being in this situation. While she understood that Shaheen broke the law every day, she never considered him getting caught for it. She was certain now she had to leave the state as soon as possible.

Hoping she wouldn't get charged with anything, she declared, "Well, if he is the one you guys want . . . why am I here? This will only waste your time as well as mine. So . . . may I leave?"

The detective's shoulders rose as he sighed. "Yes, you may leave. I was just hoping you would be willing to help us."

A knock at the door caused him to jump, then turn on his heels toward the source of the sound. He grasped the door handle and pulled it open. Detective Cannon stepped into the room and greeted Torturro.

"We got an ID on a suspect in the Carla Johnson murder."

Lola's jumped out of her chair.

"Who did you say?"

Cannon, taking notice of her, looked at the other detective and said, "Sorry, brother. I didn't know you performing an interrogation. They just told me you were in here. I—"

Lola barged in on their conversation. "Did you say Carla Johnson?"

Cannon shot a curious glance at his peer, then brought his sight upon the young lady.

"Yeah, the lady that was with you the other day," answered Cannon.

"My homegirl?" Lola could not contain the emotions that were beginning to multiply inside of her. Her voice betrayed the composure she was attempting to display.

Torturro could see that the news disturbed her. Out of curiosity, he asked Cannon, "Where did she live?"

Cannon decided to continue the conversation in hopes of Lola revealing pertinent information that could aid the detectives assigned to the case.

"She lived on Rutland Road, right next to the Sutter Avenue train station. Unfortunately, that's the same place where she was found."

Lola began crying. The two detectives locked eyes. Cannon spoke. "Well, here's the kicker. The suspect was identified from DNA found on a marijuana cigarette left on the floor at the location. It was still lit when we arrived."

"Shit! So you just missed him?" A frustrated Torturro blurted out.

"Yeah. The DNA on the cigarette matched the DNA we found at her"—Cannon pointed to Lola—"apartment."

Torturro wanted Cannon to cease the dramatics and get to the point. He threw his finger in the direction of Lola. "Her DNA?"

Once again Cannon glanced at Lola, who was eyeing him intently, hanging on to every word that came out of his mouth.

"No. It didn't match the sample she gave us or the deceased child. It's the father's. We found the same DNA on the buds in the ashtray at their apartment."

Lola's head dropped into her lap as she started crying uncontrollably.

"Why? Why would he do that? I can't believe this!" she exclaimed in between her bawling.

Cannon, wanting to change the subject, decided to inquire as to what the status of the murdered child's case currently was.

"So what's going on with the boy in the next room?"

"Who?" asked Torturro.

"The suspect in her son's case," he said, nodding toward Lola.

"Oh, we're about to send him to Rikers. They are getting ready for transport now."

"Did you get a confession out of him?"

"Kind of. He agreed to—"

"He confessed?" inquired Lola.

Torturro was unwilling to discuss the case any further while in the presence of the victim's mother. So ignoring her question, he walked over to the door, then turned back to her.

"I am going to go outside and speak to Detective Cannon for a couple of minutes. Is there anything you would like for me to bring you back?"

She nodded her head. "Na, but you can tell me when I am getting out of here."

"Soon, just have a few questions left for you. If you need to use the phone or anything, you are welcome to do so."

Cannon's phone roared to life, startling the three. He quickly opened it up and spoke into the receiver. Torturro opened the door and allowed Cannon to exit.

As he was preparing to leave, Lola spoke. "Well, I do need to use the bathroom."

Torturro attempted to throw his warmest smile at her to comfort her. "Yeah, sure. It's right out here." He pointed beyond the door.

Lola rose from her chair and followed the detective out of the room. Upon exiting, she detected the sound of the locks turning on the inside of the room adjacent to hers. The door flew open, and two plainclothes officers walked out escorting a teenage boy. She watched as the detectives guided him down a short corridor, past a threshold, and into a larger area containing several officers sitting at their desks.

They sat him in a dark blue plastic seat that was connected by an iron bar to a row of five other chairs situated to the left of the entrance. She recognized his face immediately. It was the older boy who was hanging out in their hallway with Lil John John the day she and Shaheen got into their domestic altercation.

"Is that him?" she inquired.

Torturro didn't know who she was referring to until his eyes followed the direction of her pointed finger. Suddenly, remembering Thomas's order to find out if the mother knew him, he decided to entertain her inquiry.

In a very nonchalant tone, he answered, "Well . . . the weapon that murdered your son was in his possession. He used it in another murder. That's how we caught him." He began walking toward the direction in which she pointed. Cannon followed while whispering into his cell phone.

"You sure it's him?"

Lola tried to keep up with the detectives pace as they ventured toward Anthony.

"So far, we don't have any concrete evidence to contradict our suspicions."

As they passed the seated teenager, he glanced up and immediately recognized Lola. He tried to get her attention.

"Ay . . . Psst . . . Ay."

She started to ignore him; however, her curiosity got the best of her. She wanted to know what the person who murdered her only son had to say to her. She snapped her neck in his direction.

"What?" Her eyes shot daggers of ice at him.

His expression revealed one of helplessness. "I didn't do it. I didn't. You have to tell Sha-Boogie that. I didn't do it!"

"Shut the fuck up!" one of his escorts demanded.

Lola hissed her teeth at him, then warned, "You tell him. 'Cause when you do, it will be the last thing you ever say. Shaheen is going to get your ass!"

"Maybe not," replied an officer, who had just made his way over to their area. He approached Torturro. "The Flatbush homicide desk just a got a call to go out to Forty-second Street. Said it came in from a young lady, claiming three men were murdered in her home. The lady claims to be the daughter of one of the victims. She identified that victim as Orville Linton Lee-Chin. The other person was Shaheen Mcfadden."

The officer eyed both of the detectives. "That's the suspect in your case, right?"

Expressions of shock covered everyone's face, including Anthony. Torturro spoke first while studying Lola from the corner of his eye.

"Uh . . . yeah . . . Are you sure those were the names?"

"Yeah," replied the cop.

"And both are dead?" asked Torturro.

"Mmm . . . Hmm. There are three dead at the scene. They've already dispatched a couple of cars to that location. They confirmed the names by the identification found in their pockets. I came looking for you and Thomas because I remember hearing you guys speaking about them."

No one took notice of Lola, whose silent tears were now forming puddles on top of her Donna Karan boots. She did not want to accept what she just heard. No matter what went on between her and Shaheen, she never wished death on him. She was still in love with him.

Her first instinct was to jump into a cab and rush over to Forty-second Street to attempt to revive him. She began daydreaming about the life they were supposed to have. She remembered the first time they found out she was pregnant. She remembered how they both struggled every night to get up when baby Shane started crying. She could still see the smile on Shaheen's face when their son said daddy for the first time. She thought about how unfair life was. While deep in her own thoughts, a voice traveled across the room and into her ears.

"I told him he would be dead soon."

She ceased her contemplation and motioned her head in the direction from which the words came. Anthony was staring at her and smiling.

"I told him. And that nigga said I had something to worry about." He glanced over his entire body. "Shiiiiittt . . . I'm still living." He started laughing out loud.

Lola looked about curiously, and then fixing her eyes upon an empty desk, she found what she needed. The officers kept conversing as she languidly dragged her feet past Anthony and over to the area where the desk was. With her back turned and without anyone noticing, she procured a silver pen. Torturro's attention was drawn to her as he scrutinized her curiously, unaware of what she was holding in her hand. She walked toward Anthony like a zombie lost in a trance. Remembering her desire to use the bathroom, Torturro spoke out.

"Miss, you do still have to use the bathroom, right?"

Lola kept walking and saying nothing. She didn't even hear the detective's comment as she neared the teenager, tightly gripping the pen.

"You murdered my baby." She came closer to him. "Shaheen is dead." She continued moving toward him. "My newborn will be born without a father."

Torturro, feeling something wasn't right, called out once more. "Uh . . . Lola . . . the bathroom is this way."

Anthony kept smiling at her as she closed the distance between them. He opened his mouth to address her. The words never had a chance to come out as Lola brought her hand up to his neck and thrust the pen into it, perforating his flesh, causing blood to spray out and onto her face. As her face became masked in crimson, she continued puncturing his skin with the instrument.

His hands shot up toward his neck fumbling between deflecting the blows and trying to prevent his vital fluid from spurting out. Each stab made a sickening sound that resembled a watermelon being cut open. Anthony's helpless eyes screamed out for the detectives as he strained to look their way. Cannon ran over to Lola and tried to grab her. She was too fast for him. She was able to get off five more pokes before he was able to seize her arms and disarm her. By then, it was too late. Anthony's ghost had left him as he sat lifeless and still in the chair. His eyes were bursting from his sockets as the blood poured out his wounds.

Torturro was in shock. He never saw it coming. By this time, more police had come to the aid of Cannon who was struggling to restrain a fighting and screaming Lola.

"'Cause of him, I lost everything! My baby is gone! Please let me go! I have to find my baby! I have to find my baby!"

Lola's eyes were wide as can be as she continued screaming hysterically. She was foaming at the mouth with spit caked up on the side of her lips. Her mind was gone. She had now crossed over from sanity to insanity.

"What the hell is going on?"

Everyone turned to find Detective Thomas standing in the doorway of the precinct accompanied by a very young boy in handcuffs. His attention was drawn to the bloody scene and the hysterical Lola.

"Jesus Christ!" were the words that exploded from his mouth.

Torturro was still in shock from what happened while Cannon was handing over his detainee to the female officers who arrived to assist him.

"Torturro, what happened?" Thomas sternly inquired.

Torturro snapped out of his mind-wandering to answer his partner. "She flipped out. All I remember is hearing her say 'You murdered my baby,' and the next thing you know she was on top of him stabbing him."

Thomas eyed her, then the bloody mess. Her face was drenched in blood. He just shook his head.

Noticing the boy who was with Thomas, Torturro questioned, "And who is that . . . John John?"

Thomas scowled at the boy. "See what you caused." Then bringing his attention back to his partner, he said, "Yeah, this is little Shane's killer. How did you know his name?"

"Anthony told me he gave John John his gun to stash."

Lola stopped struggling with the officers upon hearing the detective's words. Cannon's expression went blank. Then suddenly Lola realized who the boy was. It was Old Lady Wellington's grandson from next door. The fourteen-year-old who Shaheen had scolded three days ago and who also hung out with the boy she just stabbed to death.

Torturro, wanting to be sure, decided to ask, "So we are certain he is not the murderer?" He pointed at Anthony's spiritless body sprawled out in the chair.

"Unfortunately, he's not. From what I was told, our Anthony Johnson over there was stashing the gun at this young man's grandmother's apartment. He said Anthony asked him to hold it for him because he couldn't take it home. Well, according to him, he became curious as to how it felt to hold a weapon, so he took it from beneath his bed and began playing with it. You know, posing in the mirror, acting tough and so forth. He said while he was handling it, it went off by mistake. He didn't even know it was loaded. As a matter of fact, he didn't even know Shane was struck by the bullet."

"Okay, but how did it hit the little boy. Was he in the apartment with him?" asked Cannon.

"No," answered Thomas. "He lived next door. The bullet exited the chamber and went through the wall, hitting the little boy in the head. You know how the walls in the ghetto are . . . thin as hell."

Lola couldn't believe what she heard. She screamed out, "Nooooo!" She frantically searched the officers' face for sympathy. "I didn't mean to kill him. I thought he did it. I'm sorry . . . I . . . I can't go to prison . . . I'm pregnant!"

The young boy watched as the officers handcuffed and carried Lola off into the back area where the cells were located. Her cries for mercy echoed off the walls of the precinct only to fade away down the hall she traveled. He stood emotionless. He wanted to cry but deemed it would not help.

He thought about trying to escape, but he knew it would prove futile. Besides, Detective Thomas had told him he recognized he was a good boy who just so happened to be around the wrong people as most shining stars in the ghetto. He assured him his punishment would not be severe because of the nature of the incident and because he was also an honor roll student.

As officers came over to take the youth to the holding cell, a tear fell from Thomas's left eye. He wanted to go to the bathroom and break down. The past few days brought back memories of his own son, who lost his life to the streets. He was tired of seeing countless of black youth dying or going through the system for mistakes that could have been avoided. It pained him to see this young boy's life thrown away over foolishness, in the name of acting tough. He felt as if the young men of his race were cursed, destined to be incarcerated because of the blackness of their skin. *Or*, he thought, *was it just because of their ignorance?* Thomas made a 180 degree turn and ventured toward his desk where files containing more cases involving the youth of his race awaited him.